| AF. | BAE. | 08/19. |
| 2 n | | |

# SKIN

Also by E. M. Reapy

*Red Dirt*

# SKIN

## E. M. REAPY

HEAD
ZEUS

First published in the UK in 2019 by Head of Zeus Ltd

A catalogue record for this book is available from
the British library.

ISBN (HB): 9781789540949
ISBN (XTPB): 9781789540956
ISBN (E): 9781789540932

Typeset by Divaddict Publishing Solutions Ltd

Printed and bound in Great Britain by
CPI Group (UK) Ltd, Croydon CRO 4YY

MIX
Paper from
responsible sources
FSC® C020471

Head of Zeus Ltd
First Floor East
5–8 Hardwick Street
London EC1R 4RG

WWW.HEADOFZEUS.COM

*For my grandmothers*

# SKIN

# Sunset Kid

The humid air coats my skin. Stalled traffic has snarly wolf-like energy. Motorbike drivers rev, petrol fumes smog behind them and the noise from their unsilenced exhaust pipes makes my whole body vibrate, makes my ears want to bleed. I keep going.

'Hey Miss, Miss Miss Miss. Massage? Dancing? Taxi? Restaurant?'

'No. No. No.'

Sometimes I smile at the people but mostly I try to ignore them.

Bony dogs rove in packs, looting overflowing bin bags and cardboard boxes discarded on the sidestreets. I breathe through my mouth to avoid the open sewer stench. The sun is merciless.

'Yes?' A broad-smiling waiter wearing a red batik bandana stretches his menu out as I advance. His eyes roam my body and he wiggles his eyebrows. 'Yes, Miss, you will like?'

'No.'

The footpath is uneven. Going soft through the markets. The people yell. Joke. I see open mouths and cracked white teeth. Goosebumps prick my arms.

Unwashed fruit is piled on tables, rotting in the sun. Mangoes. Pineapples. Oranges. Lychees. Bananas. Snakefruit. The pungent durian. Flies hover.

I pass trays of eggs. Mountains of eggs. Caged cocks and hens. On melting ice, undead fish gulp air. Crabs and crayfish clack their claws. Little sarcastic one-handed claps at my attempts to stay calm. I trip over a blue bucket on the ground. It's filled with bloody water and beheaded eels snake around each other.

'Sorry,' I say.

I have just apologized to a bucket.

At another stall, black and yellow coinlike shapes float at awkward angles in a plastic bowl of water. They are mesmerizing. I squint, trying to figure out what they are.

The stall owner rises from his wooden chair to wave a hand over them. 'Fish eyes. Good for you, Miss. Eat and see.'

'Oh god, no. No thanks. No.'

'Come on. What do you want, Miss? Anything you want?'

If I knew that, I probably wouldn't be here.

They sell rice grains by the bag. Volcano magnets. Hand fans illustrated with temple dancers. Inflatable water toys. Paintings of Ganesha, the elephant-headed multi-armed deity. I push the hanging beach towels out of my way. Their colours bolder in the light. Electrifying blue. Raging fuchsia. Blinding yellow.

The beats, music, from somewhere, from everywhere. Gamelan gongs. 'Gangnam Style'.

I am shrinking.

Something burns. Sizzles. A slaughtered chicken. Its limp yellow foot dangles from a grill. Black meatsmoke.

I put my hand on my throat. I slow down to wipe my face but I'm shoved forward. Move, the crowd implores. Move. Sweat trickles on my skin. My sweat. Their sweat.

I can't take anymore. The stinking, deafening, teeming life of it. I duck into the restaurant on the corner, a vegetarian place with air con and teakwood tables, and take the nearest free seat. I place my hands on my ribs, try to compose myself.

There is one way to make the panic stop, if only for a while.


In the guesthouse courtyard, a woman with white-blonde hair sits on a deck chair, her head turned to the sun like a daisy. I recognize her as the one staying in the room directly across from me, the one who comes home at breakfast time with oversized shades, blearily bypassing the guests and banana pancakes to stumble to her room.

'Hey,' she says without moving her head as I pass. Her tanned skin glistens.

I mouth a hello and rush to my door. I search through my handbag for my key but can't find it. Shit. I move the stuff about, spilling gum sticks and receipts.

I glance up to see my neighbour watching.

'Damn it,' I hiss and tip the contents of the bag on the plastic white chair outside my door. I rifle through everything. It's not there. I pat myself down, sadly lingering on my stomach and sides, at the new kilos, at the bloat from earlier, but I don't have time to start on myself. I shake my head and check the bag with the food I brought home from the restaurant.

No key.

'Locked out?' the neighbour shouts.

I nod.

'Stop stressing. It's no big deal. They have spares. I've lost mine twice already. They'll give you another. Ask the grandmother.' She points to the guesthouse owner's mother who's further up the courtyard, making offerings to the statues. 'You'll have to wait till she's done.'

The old lady chants and burns incense, gifting little sweets and colourful flower heads to her cement gods.

I put everything back into my handbag and hold it in front of my stomach.

The grandmother keeps doing the rounds, devout, her hand waving with the smoke. Frangipani scents the air.

'Don't stand there. Grab your chair, come over here,' the neighbour says. 'What's your name?'

'Natalie.'

'You're travelling alone, aren't you, Natalie? Me too. I'm Maria.' She beckons me again.

I hesitate, doing a tiny to and fro in my head. Look at her. Totally perfect. I don't want to be seen beside that. But I can't not go. If I said no, what would I do? Sit in front of the door and look at her from here?

That would be even more awkward.

I drag the chair across the yard and plant it beside Maria's. The sun swelters.

She passes a bottle of factor 10. I squirt some of the coconut-smelling cream onto my palm, dab it on my face and the parts of my arms exposed to the sun.

Maria is taut and confident in her green bandeau bikini and black high-waisted shorts. The buttons of her shorts are open and the material is folded out to show the top of her matching green bikini bottoms. Her stomach has muscle definition, lines and dips, even as she sits.

In my grey V-neck T-shirt and long cheesecloth skirt, I am drab and overdressed.

'You not too hot?' Maria asks, mindreading.

'I don't like to attract attention on the streets,' I reply and instantly regret it.

'You think you blend in like this? We don't blend in, I'm afraid. We are never going to look like anything here other than rich white bitches.'

My cheeks blaze under the sun cream.

'You here for a while?' she asks.

'A stopover. On my way to Darwin, staying with an aunt for a bit and then going on a working holiday in New Zealand.'

'You liking it here?'

My shrug is barely perceptible.

Maria raises her eyebrows. 'What's wrong with you? This is heaven.'

I clear my throat before I speak and scratch the back of my neck. 'I never really travelled before. I was so excited about it. Told everyone. I didn't expect the place to be like this. It's so…'

'I'm here on a visa run from India. If you think this is…' she copies my pause, 'you should see India. You have to accept things here.'

'What do you mean?'

'You probably had all these expectations and now nothing looks like it did in the brochure and you don't feel like you thought you'd feel. Wah wah usual Westerner first time in the Third World story.'

'But I've been getting these panic attacks. And the mosquitoes. It's horrible.'

'I can see you've been annihilated.'

'The spray isn't working. They're biting me anyway.'

She nods sympathetically.

On my first night, I fell asleep without closing the net. Too exhausted from the trip, cold Dublin rain forgotten as I disembarked in soupy Denpasar. I stayed in a hostel near the airport and passed out. I came to, remembering the whine of one mosquito. Dreamily, I swatted at it but fell back to unconsciousness.

One fucking mosquito.

It devoured me. I have eighteen bites on my face alone.

The old lady gets closer, softly humming to the gods.

Maria taps her bottom lip with her index finger. Then she puts her hand down and asks, 'Do you have a husband at home, a boyfriend, that type thing?'

'Not for a long time, no.'

'Okay, this evening, you join your new friend Maria. We'll go and watch the sunset and get some beers. It's really fun. Loosen up. All this,' she says and sweeps the view, 'is yours.'

The old woman is confused at my request. She smiles though, showing her missing teeth.

'For the door,' I say. 'The door.'

She continues smiling but shows no sign of understanding.

'No English at all?'

I wonder what I'd do. Sit outside forever? I had enough food inside me to do me this evening, maybe enough reserves to last a few days, a month maybe. Then seasons, years would pass, me leathering and fading in the sun, skeletonizing and eventually dying there, a long hot drawn-out starvation. Vultures would swoop in and peck at my crispy skin.

I take a deep breath and mime putting an imaginary key into an imaginary door, unlocking it and stepping over the imaginary threshold.

The old woman mirrors my hand and wrist movement.

'Yes. A key. I need a key.'

'Ah,' the grandmother says and speaks in Indonesian before laughing. She gestures for me to follow her down a path, past wind chimes, past lush orchids and hanging baskets of pink and white hibiscus, past banana trees with limegreen stalks.

In their small thatched hut at the back of the compound, the guesthouse owner's wife is plaiting palm leaves and breastfeeding her baby. A loud chat show with people arguing plays on the TV in front of her. The grandmother disappears into a room further on. The woman mechanically trims a piece of leaf, braids it and pins it together to make a tiny tray. She hoists the baby back to her breast and begins again.

I am mesmerized as her hands deftly move – she's already made four of them while I stand there, neatly stacking them on top of each other. The woman keeps doing a flickering rotational glance, an owl-eye on her baby, the TV, her stitching and the big white tourist not sure of how to hold herself while waiting.

The grandmother returns. I try to display my admiration for the work of the woman by opening my eyes wider and smiling, putting my thumbs up. The grandmother picks a bit of the leaf and shows me, in slow motion, how to pin it. I attempt it but my fingers fumble. She is patient. I try again, pinning it. It is oversized but comes out okay.

She holds the key in the air with one hand and with the other she makes a gesture with her fingers splayed.

'Yes, yes, I know. Of course. Five dollars. Here,' I say, before returning into the vivid light of the day.


In my room, I switch on both fans and aim them at myself. I sit on the single bed I've been sleeping in across from the double bed that I've been using as a wardrobe. My rucksack is unpacked onto it. I look into the plastic bag with the takeaway food, the duty-free size dark chocolate bar and the garlic bread roll, but shut it again. Tonight there's something to do.

In the freestanding full length mirror, I inspect my reflection. The bites are like pox. My sunburn is a deep pink and patchy. The rest of my skin that hasn't seen the sun is bluey-white.

I shower under the tap on the wall in the bathroom. The water is cold and refreshing. I stay under it for a long time, but within moments of stepping out of it, my skin is damp with sweat again in the humid air.

The black tiled bathroom floor is flooded; the drain gasps as it chokes with the onslaught of water.

I try on different clothes and finally concede to a pastel blue sun dress. Using my tiny hand mirror, I pencil my eyes black and lips coral, evaluate myself in the big mirror. For a second, I think I might look good, then remember it doesn't even matter, the sun will melt it off within minutes. If anyone could even see me, they'd find it hard to see past the bites and fat.

I spray a cloud of peach perfume overhead and wait for it to settle.

After I lock the door, I deliberately place the key in the front pouch of my handbag. I zip it up and immediately unzip to check if it is still there. My stomach drums slightly as I cross the courtyard to Maria's.

Music leaks from her room. Joni Mitchell. I knock and wait. I knock again and wait. Maybe I should turn around. The sun is lying low in the sky, tempting sunset.

The music is switched off inside and Maria comes out, looking surprised. Her room is a tip with clothes strewn everywhere and a drink-stale tang.

'I totally forgot about you,' she says and leans over to grab a beach bag. She's wearing a long black dress; her bright hair is startling against it. 'You're joining me?'

I nod weakly. 'If that's okay with you?'

'Ready to get lucky lucky?'

'What?'

Maria laughs and links my arm, she smells like vinegar. 'No two sunsets are the same here. Such a magical place. I live in a concrete jungle in middle England, you see a tree and you're elated. What's your home like?'

'I don't really have a home.'

'You don't strike me as homeless. Homeless people are street smart.'

I upturn my palms and explain. 'I lived in Dublin this past while but I'm from the countryside. I gave up my house and job to travel. My housemate Kim and her boyfriend moved into an apartment together, so it all worked out in the end. For them anyway. I don't know where I'd call home.'

'What was the job?'

'I was a teacher but then did some other stuff.'

Maria raises her hand to her forehead. 'I can't bloody stand kids. They're so needy and annoying. Wet all the time too. Snot or piss or spit or spillage. How do they always get themselves into those states? They're always leaking. Ugh.'

'The children were fine. I quit because...' I pause and release a long sigh. 'I thought I was doing the right thing. What I was supposed to do. Got good exam results, went to uni, got qualified, got a job, did the job for six years and then, I dunno,

I felt like an alien. Like I was living an out of body experience daily. Did you ever feel disconnected?'

'Teachers aren't much better than kids either,' Maria says, looking into the distance. 'Power tripping bastards.'

She leaves the gate at the front of the guesthouse open behind her. I hesitate but jog back to shut it properly.

A merchant sells street food at a table as we walk towards the main strip. Deep fried battered something. Maria waves at him, gives him a warm smile. He offers a skewer with some peppers and white meat. I consider it. She'd be well able to do the bartering for me.

'No, no,' Maria says, 'we go party. Eating is cheating.'

He laughs and shakes his head.

I continue, 'I packed it in and moved to the city and did these silly jobs to have some money. Temping and events. Tried to figure out my goal in life. Couldn't. I seemed to be alone in this too.'

The words stream out of my mouth; it's the first time since I landed that I've spoken more than two or three polite sentences to someone. I can't seem to stem myself, even though I know I'm talking too much.

'Everyone has their shit together. Well, except those who visibly don't but at least those guys, they have something to aim for, to get clean or get off the streets or get work or whatever. I haven't a clue. Everyone started getting married and having kids. I felt no pressure to do that.'

Maria sniffs. 'I don't care about those things.'

As we walk the high street, Maria effortlessly rejects the salespeople's offers with a flick of her wrist or a look.

'Do you think it means I don't want to be a mum? A wife? I've been told it does. I could have done the whole get a house thing, have a lovely big wedding, live in the suburbs, get a new car every year. A B C D. I started feeling trapped, suffocating. My old housemate Kim, the one with the boyfriend, she said travelling had cleared her head. Made her see life differently. That's what I decided to do. That's why I'm here. I don't even want to be here. I'm so uncomfortable all the time.'

'Stop.' Maria turns and puts her hand up. 'You have to stop this. I'm not Oprah Winfrey, am I? I might be visiting Asian temples but I can't solve your problems. I can only offer you some fun, something which you seem to know little about.'

I open my mouth to reply but nothing comes, like a fish on ice on a market stall waiting to die. I scowl instead and Maria laughs, nudges me playfully. We walk the rest of the way without speaking.

The sky is crimson tinged when we arrive at the beach.

'Where to tonight?' Maria scans the area. 'There looks promising.' She points to a spot near a bunch of young local men playing volleyball.

I follow her. Maria pulls a royal blue sarong out of her bag, unfurls it and lays it on the white sand.

'Now, let's relax and enjoy the view.'

The guys are lean and muscular. Their brown skin is smooth. Some have their long black hair in high top buns, others have theirs loose and flowing down their backs. They wear board shorts with colourful print designs.

I look around and notice that we aren't the only young women there. Or white women. Some drink, some sun themselves, some read. Some are solo, and others are in pairs.

A whistle is blown, there's jeering from the game, commotion. The men high five and then check the beach. Get deployed.

One approaches. 'Maria, *indah*, how are you this night?' he says and kisses her cheek.

'I'm good, Zander. This is Natalie, she's in my guesthouse.'

He appraises me. 'Natalie, beautiful lady. You are loving Bali?'

I give him a half-hearted smile.

'You gotta meet my pal Jacob. Jacob,' he calls behind him.

Jacob comes over; sweat shimmers on his chest. He pants. 'Hey bro,' he says and shakes Zander's hand.

'Meet the friend of Maria. She is good, no,' Zander says and his lip curls. 'Big girl. Big love.'

I follow the interaction unsure of what's going on. It's happening pretty quickly. 'Hi.' I let Jacob kiss my cheek. I get a hint of sweat and something cherry flavoured off his hair.

'Beers?' Maria asks.

'This lady. Clever,' Zander says. 'She has everything.'

'And this man,' Maria says and smiles at him, 'could charm fish out of the trees. Come on, Nat, let's get some drinks in.'

I walk dazed behind Maria. The sky's azure blue is now tracked with deep orange shades and red flares. The moon wanes, looming overhead like someone exiled and sulking.

At the bar, I recognize Western pop music.

Maria shouts, 'Isn't this fun?'

I don't answer.

'Do you want something harder?' Maria asks.

'No, a beer is fine.'

Maria downs a shot of arak and buys four bottles of beer, passing two to me. Icy tears of condensation run off them.

We trundle across the beach in the evening heat. I kick sand out of my sandals. The sunset casts the sky a fiery orange and scarlet and the wisps of clouds are ominous shadows. I try to shake away some mosquitoes but my hands are full.

Zander strums on a ukulele. Jacob takes it from him and tunes it. A different woman sits on a small hotel-room towel beside our spot. She is maybe in her late fifties or early sixties and has soft fleshy arms, a kind smile. Her hair is a brassy ginger colour.

'Hey you guys, I'm Bev,' she says enthusiastically as we approach.

'We've met already,' Maria says. She gives me a look.

I smile at Bev but Maria glowers. Zander makes a little insect, a sort of grasshopper, from bamboo leaf for Bev. He slides it in her hair.

She grins at him.

I look at it and realize it's a flower, not an insect.

Jacob puts the uke down and takes a beer. He cheers and taps his bottle off mine. 'You are from England?'

'Ireland.'

'Where?' he says and smiles in his confusion, all his perfect white teeth showing.

'It's beside England,' I say and put my right hand out. 'England is here, Ireland is here.' I try to show in the empty space of my palm where Ireland would be on the map.

Jacob remains smiling. 'You are very beautiful.'

I blush hard.

'Shy? You are shy?'

I bow my head and take a big gulp of beer.

Bev asks Zander to sing a song. 'He has such a great voice, a Balinese Johnny Cash.'

Maria says, 'I know. He sang to me last night.'

Bev presses a smile so tight, her top lip disappears.

Zander picks up the uke and strums it gently. He mumbles a song that I vaguely recall the melody and words of but can't place.

Jacob traces my hand with his index finger. His touch makes me jump initially and he smiles at this. 'It's okay,' he says.

I relax and allow him to continue. The sun is a livid red now as it gets swallowed by the ocean.

I lie down on the sarong. Jacob gently touches my fingers and places his hand into mine. A bird flies above us cawing manically like it's calling out for a lost child. The beer is going to my head. Zander sings on gently. Women laugh in little groups nearby, with their own beach boys charming them.

I look at Jacob and think he could be almost ten years younger than me. He's maybe eighteen or nineteen. Or is he older? I can't judge the age of people here. His body is broad. He has little white scars all over his chest and arms, tiny. I wonder what happened to him. I wonder what kind of life he leads.

The sun finally surrenders.

Maria, Zander and Jacob go to get more beers for everyone. Bev and I sit and wait.

'I love it here,' Bev says. 'I feel young again.'

'Yeah, maybe I could learn to like the place,' I say. 'This evening has been nice.'

'You're going to hang out with Wayan for the night?'

'Who?'

'Wayan. No. Excuse me, I meant Jacob, that's the name he's taken lately.'

'I dunno,' I say and a warm sensation floods my stomach. 'Maybe. He seems sweet.'

'He's a good kid. His wife is carrying their second child so he needs the money. It's interesting how they set them free from their families to provide. Not bad work if you can get it for these boys though, eh?'

'Wait, what?' I say, feeling like I've just woken from a dream.

'You don't have to pay him anything but it probably would be a good gesture to give him a little something. He needs the money for his family.'

'I don't understand.'

Bev looks at me with pity. 'It's a big world, isn't it? You know, back home in Arizona, I'm a waitress. I save my tips for the whole year to come out here for a month. In the States, people look down on me. An old divorced childless woman, waiting tables, too old to find a new man, too old to learn new tricks. Over here, I'm rich. I'm attractive.' She puts her hands up to the darkening sky. 'This heavenly place.'

My skin flakes as I itch my mosquito bites, the fresh and the old ones. My vision blurs a bit so I pinch my eyelids.

I stand and wipe the sand from my legs.

'I have to go, Bev. These bites. I need to put lotion on them before they bleed.'

Maria and the boys are coming, all laughing, holding beers in their hands. I give a quick wave and trudge through the sand, get off the beach.

The merchants shout as I walk through the high street.

'Miss.' A waiter pushes a menu at me, obstructs my way with it. 'Yes?'

Don't do this, Natalie. There's dinner at the guesthouse.

'You want' he says and his eyebrows flash.

'I'm okay.'

'Yes, Miss, you will like?'

'Well, not—'

'I know you will like, Miss,' he says, slowly, assuredly.

'I'm not—'

'Miss, come on, you will like.'

I nod tentatively and follow him into the restaurant.


I snap awake at 5. I wipe my forehead and the back of my neck. My stomach is bloated. I feel blocked. Gassy. I want to stab myself with something thin and sharp to release the pressure in my belly. Instead I jab it harshly with my fingers.

Cockerels crow in the near distance. I wonder how far away they are from the strength of their cry. It's still dark outside. I try to distract myself from how sore I feel by trying to count them, I get to eleven and quit, unsure if I'm counting the same cock twice.

I massage my stomach and think about Bev, Maria, Zander, Jacob, the whole set-up on the beach. As I replay it, I wonder if there's something I misinterpreted.

A bout of nausea hits me when I remember how much I ate in the restaurant.

I groan.

I want to punish myself for overeating by eating more.

When it gets brighter, I open the flimsy curtains and check Maria's room, to see if she's back, if she has company. It looks the same as when I went over last night. I scan the courtyard; the grandmother wrings clothes near the family's room. I wave at her but the old lady doesn't notice.

I open the plastic bag with the garlic bread and chocolate and peck at them. I wonder how I can face Maria again. I'm embarrassed about leaving. I'm embarrassed about being there in the first place.

Absently, my fingers pick at air and I look down. Crumbs and flecks of melted chocolate remain.

I don't want to go to the breakfast area in case I bump into Maria coming home. There's supposed to be an English bookshop somewhere but I haven't been able to locate it yet, but I decide this morning, I'll find it, even if I have to ask the locals where it is.

The high street bustles. Dublin would be only warming up now with traffic and workers, but here it's already like lunchtime. I ignore all the cries for my attention, go down the street, armed with a map and the name of the bookshop. My thighs chafe against my denim shorts. I try my best to keep my breath even in the crowds of foreigners. I'm the foreign one here.

Stopping to take out the map, I stall at a doorway. I check whether anyone's watching. I'm carrying little cash if I'm to be mugged at gun or knifepoint. All I have is the equivalent of thirty dollars in local money.

I figure out where I must be on the map and turn it upside down to see if the street goes in the direction I'm going in. Right. Third turn on the left. It should be beside a surf shop. There's nothing that resembles a bookshop on the street. I go up and down it a few times. I stop suddenly. That's the problem. I'm expecting to see an Irish-style store when it probably is nothing like one. With a fresh perspective I turn back on the street and start over. The sun is risen, yawning and stretching white rays in the calm blue sky.

I concentrate and locate the building; it's lined with frangipani and succulents in cement balcony planters. Once I find it, the sign is obvious. 'Bookshop' written in a simple yellow font on a red background. How did I miss it? There are two bookshelves in one window but also loads of souvenirs, paintings and cards. In another window, colourful tapestries of Balinese art backdrop small wooden handcrafts. It looks like all the tourist shops I've seen here.

The front door is locked. A sign beside the shutters says in English that the place stocks new and used books in twelve different languages, and it says something else in a language I assume is Indonesian. The daily opening hours are written underneath. Fifteen minutes to wait. I lean against the wall, under some shade, and admire the town around me. The heat is bearable and the sun's hard light makes the colour and vibe seem fun. I notice how friendly the people are to each other, their laughter and smiles. Jesus, they never stop with the smiling.

An older Western man wearing a dazzling white shirt and black jeans walks down the street, stops at the bookshop.

'Is not open?' He turns to me. French, I guess, from his voice.

'Not for another five minutes at least,' I say and look at the time on my phone.

He whistles. 'Western time or Balinese time, I wonder.'

He has horn-rimmed glasses. His paunch bulges slightly under his shirt. A gold chain around his neck glimmers when it catches the sun. He smiles at me and I find myself smiling back.

'You,' he says, 'you enjoy to read?'

'I finished my book and have re-read it already. Need something new. Badly.' I show him the book.

He takes it from me; his nails are trim and clean. He inspects the book, opening the first page, reading the last page.

'This looks rather interesting,' he says.

'It's only okay,' I say.

'What genres do you like?' he asks and stands nearer. His cologne is freshly cut citrus.

'I don't really know. I haven't read much since school. I only picked this up in the airport because it was in the number one spot on bestsellers and I thought I'd heard of the writer before.'

'It's a romance, no?'

'Yep.'

'You do not like romance?' he asks.

I scan for sarcasm in his comment but can't find it. 'I do – well – I dunno. I thought the book was silly. Unrealistic. The characters in it, they didn't seem like real people.'

He chuckles. 'They are characters. They are not real people.'

'I know,' I say. 'But the storyline wasn't credible. What they did to each other, if they did that in everyday life, I think that the other one would steer clear or maybe call the police. It was a romantic book but not about real love. Real living love.'

'And what would that be? Real living love?' he asks, wrinkling his nose.

I relax a little. 'Isn't it what makes you whole? You can trust that it's safe to be yourself. That you're attractive being yourself. That you're okay.'

'Do you not feel these ways, little lady?' He edges forward; his chin is at an angle.

'What?' I move back.

'Do you not feel these ways within you already?'

I shake my head and turn my torso away, unsure of where he's going with this.

'Then how could somebody else give them to you?' he asks and puts his hand out. 'I am Jean-Luc.'

A young Balinese woman stops beside us and smiles. 'Moment,' she says, unbolting the door's shutters.

The bookshop feels airy with its high ceilings and natural light flooding in, but the aisles are cramped with piles of books and random musical instruments. Jean-Luc strolls around and returns with finds. 'You will enjoy these.'

I read their blurbs but in the end swap my book for another schmaltzy romance.

'Is about real living love this time?' Jean-Luc asks, his eyes twinkling.

I giggle and touch my hair. 'Don't make fun of me. Do you read in English or French?'

'Pffft.' He waves. 'French, but of course. My English is not to that standard.'

'It is,' I say.

'No, no, not so. But I accept the compliment.'

Though both of us are finished browsing, we linger at the doorway. I can't find a way to hang on to him so I ask him about the different writers of the books he showed me earlier.

'I do not want this to end either, little lady, but I am hungry. Have you eaten?' he asks.

I blush recalling the chocolate garlic gorging I did earlier.
'No.'

'Would you like to join me for brunch, I know this beautiful
place near to here? It's where I eat all my meals.'

'Yes,' I say and smile at him.


Down a winding side street, I steal glances at Jean-Luc from the
corner of my eye. I notice the black strands amongst his silver
hair, try to picture him twenty years younger.

The café is roomy. We walk by the kitchen where lemon-
grass crackles on a massive black pan. In the courtyard at the
back, Jean-Luc is greeted by the local waitresses who kiss him
on both cheeks.

One of them tosses me a look.

'My new friend, Natalie,' Jean-Luc introduces me.

The waitress covers her mouth with her hand and sniggers
for a second then she turns and smiles. She passes two menus
to him.

I pick imaginary threads from my skin.

He hands me a menu. It's handwritten in English, German
and Japanese and stuck on bamboo leaves. The place mats are
bamboo leaves. The plates are bamboo leaves. The dishes are
Balinese but with Western prices.

'My favourite spot,' he says and directs me to a small table in
the shade. We have a clear view of the soothing fountain with
floating lily pads and a concrete Buddha statue in the centre. The
offerings lying on the edge of the fountain are wilting in the sun.

\*

I correct my posture as I sit across from Jean-Luc. 'An actor in Paris? Really?'

The smile is fastened to his face. 'Yes, in theatre – why is that difficult to believe?'

'I never met an actor before. Are you in any films?'

'Come on, no. The movie industry is an industry. Theatre is art.'

I wish that I wore something else. Not this thin spaghetti top with my too deep cleavage showing, with all the swells of my body clinging to it. My denim shorts are too short. My toenails are jagged and dusty in my leather sandals. I'm totally inelegant to be opposite someone this cultured. I am a cave woman.

'And you? What is it you do? Why are you here?' he asks and I bite my lip before changing the subject.

On his suggestion, we eat avocado and eggs, which comes with a side of mushrooms, feta and lemon onion marmalade. He tells me stories of old Bali, how dramatically its landscape has changed with the demands of tourists.

'Have you been to the wild beach parties here in Kuta?' he asks and I wonder if his teeth are his own as he pokes at them with a toothpick. A crack runs dark down the front right one so I guess they are. False teeth are flawless.

I shake my head. 'Not quite. I think I want to get out of town and go to some temples, go further into the countryside.'

'Me too,' he says. 'My partying spirit is not dead, not yet, but it takes a special occasion. What do you say to dessert?' he asks. 'I know it is quite early but the vanilla cheesecake is…' He puts his fist to his mouth before kissing his forefingers and releasing his hand. 'We shall live a little.'

'I'm full,' I say and pat my belly. It might be more glamorous to turn it down.

'How about we share?'

Jean-Luc scans the menu. He beckons a different waitress over, the one who sniggered at me. He speaks Indonesian to her. I'm impressed but wonder why he didn't speak it to the bookshop assistant or when he ordered the breakfast from the older waitress.

The young waitress giggles and is jokey with him. He waves and laughs, says something else and she smiles, puts her pen away. I get the impression she's looking at my mosquito bites. I try, and fail, not to scratch the ugly red spots now her focus is on them.

'Tiger balm, Miss, you know?' the waitress asks. 'Help your skin.'

I blush, thank her in a mumbled sort of way.

Jean-Luc talks about theatre again, the differences between acting in London to New York to Montreal. He tells me about his son, Clément, who's my age.

'You're married?' I ask.

'No.' He shakes his head. 'No, my wife died fourteen years ago,' he says, touching the chain on his neck.

'Sorry,' I say.

He's quiet for a minute. I ask him to tell me more about his son.

He says Clément listens to music with sirens, thumps and klaxons. 'Noise,' Jean-Luc says with disbelief. 'But not even good noise. He listens to noise associated with trauma. I do not understand it. Maybe I am too old.'

'You're not old,' I say and brush my hair back off my face.

'I am in my middle years,' he says. 'Happily in my middle years.'

He leans across the table and pulls a strand of my hair down. 'It is very beautiful this way.'

A slight flutter runs through my chest.

We look at each other for a moment, neither dropping our gaze.

Jean-Luc takes a deep breath. 'What do you do for this evening?'

I pause. 'Read maybe? Count up the mosquito bites on my body?'

He laughs. 'Everyone white skinned gets eaten here.'

'I feel like an itch personified.'

'It is not obvious, Natalie, I promise. How about you join me for dinner, maybe we could catch a show afterwards?'

My heart speeds up. 'Yeah?'

'Oui. I will see you here for 19.30?'


At the guesthouse, I close the gate and hear, 'Oi.'

I look around.

'Oi, teacher girl.' Maria's sitting in the main courtyard at the breakfast table, her iPad in front of her. 'Why did you run off on us last night? Not cool to abandon friends without explanation.'

'I said it to Bev.' My head dips towards my chest.

'Bev was too busy trying to steal my man to let me know.'

'Oh.'

'She's what I'd consider underclass,' Maria says and wipes her hands.

'Did you and Zander have a nice time or did he go with Bev?'

'Well, because you fucked off on Jacob, and by the way, I thought you two looked super cute together, he and Bev ended up dancing and I don't know. Zander and I went to a club and then to a quieter part of the beach.' She grins.

'Bev said Jacob was married.'

'So?'

'That he has a wife who's pregnant.'

Maria looks away.

A silence lingers.

'Is that not a bit messed up?'

'Don't judge.' Maria blows air out her nose and shakes her head like a horse. 'It's how things work here. It's not like we're sex tourists. There's no shagging unless you wanted it. It's a bit of fun. Cuddles. Compliments. All those things bloody Western men are too scared to do.'

'I didn't know what was going on, so I left,' I say and absently scratch at my mosquito bites.

'Is this a common theme in your life?'

I force a smile. 'Actually, I met a Western man earlier, from France, he complimented me.'

'Yeah?'

'Yeah, he was an actor from Paris. Funny and interesting. He invited me for dinner this evening.'

'Well, ooh la fucking la to you. I wanted you to come for the sunset tonight,' Maria says and sighs. 'I couldn't bear to hang out with Bev if I choose Zander. Zander will be with Jacob. If Bev's with Jacob then I'll have to bloody be in her company again. She makes me sick when I look at her. Such a desperado. I would rather choose someone else for the night than be around her.'

My stomach churns all day. I keep glancing at my phone. Time is sluggishly passing. I shower and try to tie my hair in a fishwife's braid but give up and put it in a high ponytail.

From the window, I see Maria saunter off towards the beach.

I decide to go and find the restaurant early so that I can be calm when I meet Jean-Luc. I can loiter in the shops near it to pass the time until dinner.

It looks slightly different in the evening. I walk through the restaurant but a new waitress calls me before I can check the courtyard.

'Excuse me, Miss. Reservation?' the waitress asks.

I check the time. 'I think so?'

'Name please.'

I hesitate. 'Jean-Luc, the French man?' I say. My face feels taut and hot. 'I don't know his surname.'

'Jean-Luc?' the waitress asks and nearly laughs.

'Yes, he eats here every day?'

Her eyes are surprised and she gives me a once over. She giggles. 'Okay, Miss. Come. Jean-Luc's table.' She motions for me to follow her outside.

Big orange lanterns hang overhead from branches. There are well-dressed diners at a handful of the tables. The water in the fountain streams loud and constant, sounding like someone emptying a full bladder.

I rub my arms and check my phone again, 19.43. He did say 19.30, didn't he? Or was it 9.30? Did I get the time wrong? My eyes dart around the courtyard to see if there's any sign of him. I shift in my seat. It'd be too embarrassing to leave now. Or maybe I should eat solo and take my time and he'll be here in an hour and three quarters, if it was 9.30 not 19.30 he said.

I sit, play with the candle on the table, spilling some hot wax onto my fingers, and seriously consider leaving but then I hear his voice.

'There you are,' he says, his arms wide.

He's wearing a long-sleeved bright white shirt and has a brown and yellow cravat tied around his neck.

'My little lost lady.'

I nearly slump to the ground with relief but manage to stand. He kisses my cheeks.

'How are you?'

'Gosh, sorry, I thought I had the time wrong.' I let him hold me.

He glances at his watch. 'No, it was around this time we decided. Sit, sit,' he says. 'How was your day?'

'Yes, nice. You?'

'It was so so. It could not live up to your charming presence this morning. I am quite glad to see you again now.'

The waitress still has that smirk on as she passes us menus. Am I paranoid?

Jean-Luc says, 'What would you like to eat? Something with lots of spice, yes?'

I scan the list. 'Not sure what any of these dishes are.'

'You should try the tongseng kambing. Delicious.'

'This one?' I point at the menu. 'It says it's lamb. I don't really like lamb. Tastes too meaty.'

'Natalie, try it. The Indonesian spices will collaborate with the lamb in a way that they will lead the taste sensation. It is spectacular.'

The vegetables stewed in coconut milk and rice with it sounds okay.

He closes his menu and the waitress comes over. He orders for us both, including a white wine which she returns with almost instantly.

'A dry white. From Belgia grapes. The vineyard is in the north of the island. Obviously it is not French but this one is of a sufficient standard,' he says as he pours my glass.

I take a sip and the sharpness of it makes the right side of my face lift and my right eyelid shut automatically.

Jean-Luc laughs. 'It has a fresh finish, indeed.'

When our food comes, I see the meat in my bowl is still attached to the bone. My stomach coils a bit at this. I know there's something ironic about how much food I'm capable of eating except for red meat, which can make me feel weak just looking at it.

I take a swig of wine and try the dish. It tastes of lamb and the lamb flavours the stew that it's in. I'll have to force myself to eat it. I swallow another big gulp of wine.

'It's very good, yes?'

I nod and suck back the saliva that's thickening in my mouth.

'I knew you would approve.'

I struggle through the dinner, leave a third of it uneaten. Jean-Luc orders an ice cream dessert for us to share. He speaks of the different temple shows we can visit. 'I would like us to see some magic. The costumes shall be astounding and the illusions will make us scratch our heads.'

I smile. 'Sounds interesting.' I tighten my hair in the hair-tie.

Jean-Luc leans across. 'Did I not say it is very beautiful this way,' he says and tugs out a strand that's tucked in.

My fingers touch the roots of the hair he's pulled and my eyes narrow.

'Sorry,' I say and leave the hair on my face.

He excuses himself and goes to the bathroom but stops at a table near the entrance to the building where another Western man sits alone. He jokes with him, the other man laughs hard, then Jean-Luc disappears.

The waitress approaches. She holds a giant bowl in front of her; two orange plastic spoons jut out of it like antennae.

Mindlessly, I scroll through social media on my phone.

I take a selfie with the ice cream, tag the picture.

#delicious #paradise #flavour

I stare at the screen and try to imagine what someone back at my old job would see when they look at it. My exotic adventure. My wonderful life. Is it better than, equal to, or less than theirs? I delete the photo, put my phone away.

Jean-Luc returns from the bathroom and stops at that table again, another comment that I can't hear and another bout of laughter. A young local woman has joined and greets Jean-Luc with a hug before sitting down.

How popular he must be in this place. Everybody seems to like him.

He makes his way back to the table; the ice cream is melting. He claps and rubs his hands together fast. 'I had an idea just now, Natalie. What do you say, it's only me and the motor. I have rented a car for my two weeks here. Would you like to join? I could certainly do with some companionship? You could too, I see.'

The space around us changes like it has become night-time all of a sudden, or maybe it's the first time I notice the darkness.

'We would visit many fantastic temples, enjoy the gastro-nomy, watch the setting sun together.'

My thoughts rise as if caught by a wind. They whirl around my head. Incense. Huge golden statues. Him cleaning his glasses. Taking medicine. Shame. The sunshine through the car window. Paddy fields. Orgasms. My covering myself up after sex. His dimpled skin, loosened from his muscles by gravity. People wondering if he's my father. Falling in love. Falling out of love. Death.

I shake myself out of it and take a deep breath.

'Come on, we shall live a little,' he says.

I rub my sternum. 'I don't think we know each other enough to—'

'Don't think, exactly. Thinking is the problem. Say yes, little lady. Maybe you don't see, you are too young, but we get these instinctive signs, we trust them. These plans from the ether.' He grasps at the air in front of his face as if something has dropped down. 'These gifts.'

I am silent.

He runs a hand through his hair. 'Natalie, you must remember, you are a foreign woman. It's not safe for you to be alone.'

I tick my tongue against my teeth.

'We could share our loneliness.'

My voice wavers. 'Jean-Luc, I don't know if it's a good idea.'

'You are a young woman. Live a little.'

'It's not because you're old,' I say quickly, to placate.

'Yes,' he says, in a harder tone. 'I now see. The age difference.'

'No, it's not that at all. I feel we don't know each other enough to—'

'Our Western world's bullshit conditioning.'

'I'm not saying that.'

'But it is what you are thinking.'

I shake my head, my hands are up in a surrender pose. My throat feels tight. I say, 'Sorry, Jean-Luc.'

I spoon the ice cream greedily. It's yellow and chunky with pieces of mango. It's repulsively sweet.


When the young Balinese waitress comes to clear the dish, he speaks to her as if I'm not there. I offer to pay for my meal but he makes a swiping gesture with his hand and ignores me after that.

'I must discuss something with my associates. It is a long time since we met,' Jean-Luc says eventually, pointing with his elbow to the table across the way.

'Okay,' I say. I up and leave. There are no goodbyes.

On the street, I'm confused.

How did that get so fucked up so quickly? I wander and get lost but recognize a road that leads to the beach.

Maria might still be around. I follow the road because I don't want to go back to the guesthouse with this loneliness pounding at me.

The beach is full with people hanging out, drinking, chatting. I check but it's hard to pinpoint her. Lots of white and Japanese women sit on towels with local men beside them. I look for the volleyball nets instead. They're further down. I spot Maria on her blue sarong.

Zander sings and plays guitar. Jacob massages Bev's back. He stops when he sees me.

Maria squeals. 'Look who it is.'

She jumps up to hug me and invites me to sit with them.

Jacob says hi and I say hello. Bev says hello but in a stiff voice.

'Hi, Bev.'

She nudges her head and looks at Jacob's face. He's looking at me. He scoots onto the sarong beside me.

Bev announces she's going to the bar, and stands up from her hotel towel, brushing sand off her legs. 'Jacob, help me bring the beers down.'

He looks at her and then me and back to her. She double taps her handbag in some sort of code way that he understands.

'I will return to you, Natalie,' he says in a low voice, and rises.

'How was the date with Monsieur Silver Fox?' Maria does a Pepé Le Pew accent.

'I'm not sure,' I say. I tell her what happened at the beginning with his being late and the food. 'Then he invited me around the island with him in his rented car.'

'Woohoo,' she says and wiggles her shoulders.

'No, it wasn't like that. Or maybe it was.'

'Tell me all the sordid details.'

I sigh. 'He asked me to go with him for two weeks. I was tempted. But like, isn't it a bit risky asking a stranger to join you on something like this? What kind of person is he? What kind of person would I be if I agreed?'

'Would you go round the island with me?' Maria asks.

'Yeah,' I say without hesitation. 'Of course.'

'Well, you don't know me or what I'm capable of.'

'I wasn't sure if it was some sort of romantic offer, to put it delicately.'

'You would be his kept woman, mais oui?' Maria smirks and says, 'I'd have fucking done it. No questions asked. He was rich?'

'Aren't we all rich over here?'

'Not Bali rich, Europe rich?'

'Maybe, by the looks of him. Though he's an actor so it's hard to tell. He was graceful and he paid for all the food.'

'Are you going with him?'

'No, I said I couldn't.'

'Why?'

'I couldn't. Like I told you already, I didn't know what he'd expect from me for it.'

'You're fucking stupid to miss out on that one.'

I rub my eyebrow. 'Am I?'

'Most definitely. That wouldn't be something I'd turn down. Especially if he's cute.'

'He's handsome. Dashing, even,' I say. 'And he's interested in me.'

Maria sucks in some air. 'Fucking stupid.'

My toes and fingers curl. 'Am I?'

She looks out towards the immense sea. 'Nat, can I tell you the truth here? I am literally going to vomit if I have to look at Bev for the night. When they come back, let's you and me, Zander and Jacob totter off to a different place. There's a karaoke hut near the lifeguard tower that can be pretty funny.'

'Aw, I dunno. I can't sing well and wouldn't it be nasty to leave Bev?'

'Nasty?' She laughs. 'Bev is nasty. She's all over Jacob and he's not interested in her. He likes you.'

'Jacob is married, I'm not going there.'

'We'll drink the beers, send her to the bar and skedaddle when she's gone.'

'Maria, that sounds like bullying.'

'Bullying? Bev is a grown-ass old woman, how could it be bullying?' She laughs again. 'You're such a teacher girl, Natalie.'

'Look, this evening's already been too much.' I shake my head. 'I really don't get this place. And the lamb keeps repeating on me.'

'Well, what are you going to do? Because I'm not hanging around that hag for much longer.' She looks at her nails.

'I'll go back to the guesthouse. I have my new book. I'll read or something.'

Maria fakes a yawn. 'Come to the karaoke hut if you change your mind.'

'I probably won't. See you, Maria.' I get up off the ground.

'Hey, Natalie,' Maria shouts after me. 'Try to live a little.'

*

Back at the guesthouse, I read but can't focus; instead I stare at the black patterns on the wall formed from damp, notice a tiny spotted gecko, motionless in the corner. I fold the page and put the book down.

I switch the bare bulb off and try to sleep but I keep mulling everything over in my mind. I do overthink things. Jean-Luc was right about that. Maybe there isn't a problem in going with him? Maybe this is the opportunity of a lifetime?

'I know how to live a little,' I say eventually and decide what I'll do.

I manage to drift off then.

In the morning, I put on my pedal pushers and a purple V-neck top. I still look like a tourist but maybe like I haven't been trying too hard.

Will he be back again for brunch? Will the offer still stand? Maybe he'll think I am too changeable, too silly for him. No, this is living. I will cast off old Natalie and be this brave, cool new person. One who goes on adventures with French actors, so breezy, so chic.

I head out, off the main street, retrace my steps back to the bookshop, and from there I get lost but eventually find the place. The light is bright but the heat isn't too intense. I step into the restaurant and wonder what time he'll be in. I hope I haven't missed him. I take his seat in the corner and order a Coke. When I finish that, I slowly sip a green tea.

I'm inspecting the bamboo menu when someone comes into the courtyard and is greeted affectionately by the waitress. I hear his accent, the tone of his rich voice and I tremble a bit with excitement. I look up to the doorway, about to call and wave when I see his shirt is open, revealing his plump belly, his hairy breasts. He is turned around talking to someone who I can't see from my table. Then he leans in and pulls the person into view by giving them a great hug. The local girl is petite with straight black hair that goes down to her ass. She wears a black vest and a short pink skirt which clings to her slight body. He kisses her on the head and cheek and then clamps her face with his hands as he kisses her mouth. I duck behind the menu. Jean-Luc and the local girl are guided to a table at the opposite side of the courtyard. They're jovial and boisterous with the waitress; all are speaking Indonesian.

My heart pummels my chest. I drop the menu and get up, trying to leave the restaurant before I'm seen, but I can't go out the way I came in without passing by them. Is there another way? I walk to the far end of the courtyard, take a tiny pathway between the side of the building and a roughly cemented wall, follow it, jumping over loose cables and a swampy sewage pit. I keep going until I get to a large steel bin at the end of the path. I sigh with frustration, realizing it's a dead-end. Then I grow hot and feel trapped and hyperventilate. I can't go back now because they'll think I'm a thief too, having left without paying. There's no way I can go back and get out without being obvious.

Fuck. Fuck. Fuck.

Maybe I could scale the bin and then the wall? My arms
are weak as I try to hoist myself up; the bin stinks. My hand
lands on top of some indeterminable brownish fatty material.
I wipe the grease off my hand, and pray the bin will bear my
weight as I stand on it. I grip the top of the wall. With much
exertion, and swearing, I haul myself up onto it, grazing my
elbows and the back of my arms.

It's more than an eight foot drop the other side, onto an
empty backstreet, and I try to slide down but my weight
is too much for my arms and I have to let go, landing
hard on my feet sending a wave of white pain up through
my body.

I'm disoriented, not sure which side I came out from and
afraid to go by the front of the restaurant again, so I stray left,
to get far away.

I walk around stung. I am fucking stupid, like Maria said.
And now I'm lost again, typical. This maze of a place.

I turn onto another random side street, straight into the
sun's glare. It's too hot. I sweat profusely and my pedal pushers
are damp and scratchy.

My breathing quickens when I recognize that this street
must adjoin the strip, from the hum of the out of sight
traffic. I charge down it, hoping I've heard the far-off bustle
correctly.

I walk like I'm losing my balance.

Calm down, Natalie. Just get food.

A voice comes from out of the brightness. 'Hey Miss, Miss
Miss Miss.'

I'm about to get more hassle. Someone trying to sell something. Everyone's on the sell here.

I squint into the sunlight and see a kid. I anticipate the usual, 'Taxi, massage, restaurant, painting?'

He's outside a dusty one-storey detached house.

I can barely see him with the sun in my eyes.

He calls again. 'Miss Miss Miss.'

I keep ambling. Notice he's moving. Something's moving. I'm puzzled. Something's wrong. But the sun blinds me. I shield my eyes with my hands and look again.

He has a big broad smile. His arm is moving. I look down. His hand. Up down. The brown shaft of it. Steady rhythm. Up down.

'Hey Miss, Miss Miss Miss.'

I gasp. Punch in the gut feeling. My legs and arms go limp. His kid's head. His man's body. He's older than I guessed. Has to be older. A young man.

'Yes, Miss, you will like?'

The sun thunders. I sprint to the main street and don't look back. Go around the corner. Lean against a wall. Try to catch my breath. A stitch compresses my side.

I gag.

His penis. His childish face. His hand. Why did he call me? Did I do something? Did I do something to make him call me?

Puke sensation. I can barely hold myself upright. I spit sticky saliva. Elegant Japanese women with fancy umbrellas and pasty skin pass. I can't translate the fragments of their comments but guess 'pig' or 'scum'. The black clouds from the traffic fumes are suffocating. My head tightens and spins. A mangy dog comes over and sniffs my leg with his wet nose.

I focus on the menu and the goosebumps on my arms dissolve.

The waitress takes my order. Citrus juice to drink. Gazpacho and spring rolls starter. Nasi goreng for mains, and a coconut cream pie for dessert.

It's not enough. I call her back and order large fries and a chickpea curry with brown rice.

She looks at the empty seat across from me. 'For your friend?'

'That's my order. With the mains. For me.'

'All for you?'

I bow my head and nod.

She smiles sadly. 'Okay, Miss.'

I eat rapidly as soon as she drops the food down. I don't even care that she can see me or that anyone else can. I taste nothing as I shovel everything into me.

My stomach is full and guilt gnaws my whole body when I order a second dessert – a cashew ice cream and a local coffee. I repeatedly think about what happened with Jean-Luc, of the teenager wanking.

My attention returns to the room when the waitress places the coffee in front of me. I wince at its bitterness and heat as I swallow, burning my tongue and the roof of my mouth.

I finish the coffee, the ice cream, and at last, I feel numb.

I sit there for a while in a stupor.

On the way out, I stop into the shop part of the restaurant, buy a bag of dry roasted peanuts and a long baguette with soft cheese and spices.

I point at the tiramisu cake that's on display.

'You would like a slice of this?' the boy behind the counter asks.

'No. The full cake.'

Outside in the sunshine, the food feels like it's clogged my windpipe.

I keep rambling on towards the guesthouse. I stub my toe off a crack in the pavement and hear laughter behind me on the streets. My stomach balloons. I want to devour the tiramisu with my hands. I barely resist.


Maria is locking her door when I walk dazed through the courtyard.

'Hey, you okay?' she shouts over. 'You look more highly strung than usual.'

'I'm fine,' I say weakly.

'Nat, are you sure? Your face is green.'

'I'm fine.'

'You going to join me at the beach, I'm leaving shortly?'

'No.'

'Come on. It's only a bit of fun.'

'I don't want to go.'

'Natalie, chill out, you're gonna have to—'

'I don't want to fucking go,' I say through my teeth and make a gesture like I've broken something in half. 'How many times do I have to tell you?'

Maria's eyes go big. 'Your circus, your animals.'


In my room, the heat is trapped. I lie down and try to sleep. I can't. I shuffle to the other side of the bed. The cool side. I strip the sheet from me and point the fan at the bed. I switch back to the other side of the bed. Put the sheet back over myself. Point the fan at the ceiling. I fling the sheet on the ground and get up to look out the window. I open the curtain, the daylight fades.

The sky glows red on the horizon. Maria would probably be there on the beach by now.

I wolf down the peanuts and bread with such intensity that I can barely breathe. I grab the bakery bag with the tiramisu. I open it to see some flies have got at the dessert. I recoil and bat them off but they hover over it and land again.

And the teenager, what he might have done after – maybe cleaning himself up with a tissue, going inside for an orange, flicking on the TV in the dining area, sitting on the cushions in front of it. His grandmother bickering with him about being lazy, about getting a real job. Him rolling his eyes and turning up the volume. Lighting a cigarette.

I could still eat the cake. Even if the flies have laid eggs in it.

He'd shower, put on his nicest jeans, his cleanest linen shirt. Splash some fake CK One onto his cheeks, his neck, his underarms. Kick a stone down the busy streets glowing in the dusk and neon. Abandon it when he reached the sand.

He'd scan the women, stay aloof, mysterious, wait for them to choose him.

The mascarpone cream is turning a crusty yellow at the edges where it has melted and re-set. The flies rub their forelegs together.

Maria, in trying to get away from Bev, trying to make Zander jealous, would signal the teenager over with the curl of her finger. She would slow-dance and dirty laugh and drink Bintang with him in a beach hut. The sun would eventually engulf the night.

I cram the cake into me as quickly as I can, try to make myself feel less empty, or feel sick, feel anything other than afraid.

When I'm done, I'm breathless, lying on the ground, sweating, weighted down, knowing hellishly, miraculously, I have never felt worse.

I double over.

And in the next moment, I split.

I float up and I'm above myself. From the roof, I neutrally look at my bloated body, my panicked guilty expression. I watch myself being helpless. There I am lying on the floor in a ball, full of self-loathing and sugary food.

There I am wishing I didn't exist.

I'm brought back down and return into myself, gasping and looking at the ceiling. What the absolute fuck. Was that real? I wiggle my toes. I clench my stomach, which grumbles and creaks and is overfull.

For the first time in a long, long time, I let myself weep.


Night descends and I sit in the white plastic chair outside my room. Hold myself. It's serene. After being utterly disconnected, so out of it, I now feel like I'm in my body again. I can't remember the last time I felt this way.

The grandmother walks by. She stalls suddenly. Looks at me.

I nod and she gives a warm, open smile then she continues on.

I sit there in a trance but notice everything; frog song, the whir of flying insects, far-off children's laughter. The balmy air is perfumed by night blooming flowers – jasmine, honeysuckle. The leaves in the courtyard sway slightly, rhythmically, making soft hushed oceanlike noises. I eventually go inside, fall into a deep unbroken sleep.

In the morning, I stretch noisily and feel my blood flow. The day is being rinsed with clear sunlight.

I get up to open the door and let some fresh air into the room. On my doorstep, a misshaped palm leaf basket with a few grains of rice, some frangipani petals, a cracker and a single smouldering stick of incense.

# Eyes Down

Sunlight guzzles the walls as I step out of the shower. The A/C is broken in the bathroom. It's like a sauna. The mirror is fogged up and I'm grateful for that as I towel-dry my hair. I slap shea butter on my stretch marks, bumps, humps. Lady fucking lumps.

Dolores' surprise sixtieth is on in the evening. It was already arranged by the time I got to Darwin from Bali. When Bruce told me about it, he warned me that Dolores was not to find out.

'I understand the concept of surprise parties,' I assured him.

I walk around my dormer bedroom in a towel, gathering what I'll wear to the party. A floral print dress with a lot of give at the stomach, pink open-toe heels. I hang the dress on the back of my door and drag a brush through my hair. It gets stuck. With extreme force, I wrestle it out, and lose a small clump of hair.

I massage my head and add some argan oil to detangle the knots before I attempt combing it again. My hands are slick.

The doorbell rings downstairs. I wipe my hands but my fingers are still too oily to go rooting through my wardrobe touching clothes. I ignore the bell and look around for a T-shirt or something to put on over the towel.

It rings again.

I sigh.

A third time. Fourth. The buzzer is pressed without release now.

'Okay, I hear you,' I say.

I tamp downstairs on the lush cream carpet; my footprints leave wet dents. Through the peephole I see Bruce's thick silver hair. He mutters to himself as if practising in advance what he's going to say. I tighten the towel around myself and clock in the code. I hope oil doesn't drip into Dolores' high tech alarm equipment and blow it up. The door opens automatically and I stand behind it as I greet him.

'Is she here?' he asks. The morning air outside enters the house.

'Nope, she's at yoga.'

'I knew she would be. Great,' he says and claps. 'Is everything alright on your side? For the party?'

'Yep,' I say.

He tries to step in but I keep the door firmly where it is. The sky is a sharp blue with hefty white clouds lingering. Monsoon season is coming soon, or the 'green season', as Dolores calls it.

'I've all the pieces from home rounded up, will put them on a USB stick now. Or when I get dressed,' I say.

Bruce glances at the towel around me.

I grow uneasy in the silence.

'Dolores knows nothing. She still thinks it's going to be a meal for two. Niece – auntie bonding birthday meal.'

He claps again. 'And Keano's people? He was organizing the Irish contingent.'

'I'm yet to meet the mysterious Keano. I haven't heard from him, have you?'

Bruce tuts and tightens his hands. 'That pipsqueak, all guns blazing about organizing this party then being messy about it. He raises my blood pressure.'

'It'll be fine, Bruce,' I say, in defence of Keano. The praise I've heard Dolores heap on him has given me a confidence in the lad. 'He won't let us down. How many people are going to be at this thing?'

'I reckon thirty, at least.'

'Thirty?'

'What? Why have you that face on?'

'Most of them will be strangers to me. I'm not so good at these big crowds.'

I'm worried, and excited, about the food. Bruce has organized a buffet. What if I eat myself stupid with the unlimited servings?

Bruce blinks slowly. 'It's just as well tonight ain't about you, Natalie.'

His comment catches me off guard. I step back. The door opens fully.

He flicks a look up and down me. 'I better let you get dressed.' Then his eyes move slower over my towelled body. I feel red creeping.

He shakes his head suddenly as if remembering himself. 'See you in The Gardens at 7 p.m. I'll bring the cake.'

He walks in a sprightly way towards his house across the road.

'It's just as bloody well, mate,' I say imitating his accent and shut the door.

I sit on the couch with my laptop open and watch the clips of my Irish aunts; they seem old-fashioned with their mullet perms and comfortable clothes. All their complaining about aches and pains make them seem even older.

Dolores is different. She's lived in Australia for over half her life. She works as a corporate consultant for sustainability, speaks fluent French and is now learning Chinese.

I pick up one of her copybooks from the coffee table. I enjoy looking at the symbols, trying to decipher what the characters might mean. She showed me a few before, how they were drawn from six strokes inside an invisible square. The scratch with his arms out meant sky, day and heaven amongst others. These are the closest thing to our English letters. She says it's complicated, but like anything, you try it, make mistakes, learn from them and repeat. Keep practising until it's automatic. At some point, your brain understands and it becomes a natural process.

I save the clips to a USB and go online to look up how to prevent buffet bingeing.

1. Sit far away.

*Would the bus stop outside be a sufficient distance?*

2. Use smaller plates and glasses.

*Making your hands look fatter.*

3. Chew food twenty times.

*Lockjaw will render it impossible to eat more.*

4. Put your knife and fork down between mouthfuls.

*Sure why not go for a jog in the meantime too while you're at it?*

I shut the laptop and switch on the TV to the celebrity entertainment channel. They discuss who wore what and how they wore it to a glitzy event.

The beep of the door's code being entered from outside makes me sit up in the chair and straighten myself out. I put the USB stick into my pocket. The door opens and Dolores' bright energy enters the room before her. I should probably go with her to yoga sometime, to try it out. I'd love to know what it feels like to have that afterglow, but I'll have to drop a couple of kilos first.

Armed with her navy yoga mat and a tote bag with leafed groceries bulging out of it, Dolores turns to smile at me.

'G'day, kiddo. Everything okay?' she asks. Her usually sleek black bob curls outwards at the bottom and her fringe sticks to her forehead.

I nod.

She tidies her mat away in the closet under the stairs and hums as she presses playback on her answering machine. In the kitchen area, she empties the bag, placing green vegetables and glass jars of honey, jam, pickles and other colourful textures onto the kitchen island's black marble top.

'There's this fab farmers' market by the studio Thursday mornings,' she says, opening a jar. She walks over and offers me black olives floating in a green garlicky oil.

I decline and return to the TV.

'Jesus, that outfit is septic,' I say. A movie star wears a mermaid-style silver dress. 'She looks like a bit of salmon wrapped in tin foil about to go in the oven.'

'Why you watching this junk?'

I can't think of an appropriate answer so I say, 'The show's only on for ten more minutes.'

'You gotta be more discerning about what you consume.' Dolores' jaw tightens as she looks at the screen.

The presenters discuss another celebrity, donning a red skin-tight playsuit and giant strappy heels. Her hair is in a high bun.

'God, she's fabulous. Imagine looking like that,' I say.

'You don't know what her life is like.'

'It wouldn't matter what anything is like if everyone thought you were that thin and beautiful.'

Dolores puts her hand on my shoulder. 'Beauty's not about what anyone else thinks. Do you want a coffee?'

I follow her and stand behind the kitchen island. She grinds coffee beans and thumbs a different switch on the machine, laying a cup under it. Then she opens the fridge door and bends over, disappearing except for her backside rounded out in her black yoga leggings. She's not skinny, nowhere near it, but still, I feel a hot twang of envy flush through me.

'You seem so comfortable, Dolores.'

She stands and turns around, holding a carton of coconut water. 'What do you mean?'

'In yourself. You seem to be fully yourself.'

'Well, kiddo, I've been myself for sixty years now. There comes a moment in life where you have to give in and be like, okay, I suppose this is it. This is me. I might as well start bloody enjoying it.'

She leaves the carton on the counter and stacks some of the veg into the fridge.

'But are you not scared of getting older?' I tap my fingernail against the marble. Steaming water and coffee blend into the cup.

'No. I'm slower, for sure, but I prefer how I am now to when I was younger.'

She doesn't seem slow to me, always prancing around light-footed, learning new things; even when she meditates on her patio she seems energetic and she'd only be sitting there, looking ahead, with her hands resting on her knees.

'The body breaks down. But Nat, getting older is a privilege.'

'What?' I scrunch my face up at her crazy talk. The way people bitch and moan about it. Afraid of it. Disgusted by it. 'Is it not a burden?'

'No, it's a gift. Think about it. What's the alternative?'

I want to probe more and make her say something negative, to dim some of her lightness.

'Would you be tempted to get surgery?'

Dolores raises an eyebrow. 'That's a blunt question, Natalie.'

'I'm not saying that you'd need it. I swear.' I fill with a familiar awful sensation, already regretting my stupid words.

'For my breasts, is it?'

On mention of them, I look at her chest. 'No, I meant for your wrinkles, Botox or a facelift or something. What's wrong with your breasts?'

Dolores smirks. 'Natalie, I don't have breasts.'

I feel a thunk inside, like my heart has dropped.

'You know this already? No?' She stares at me.

'No.'

'Removed eleven years ago. All clear since.'

'No, I didn't know.' I look at my aunt's face and down to her chest again. 'But you do have breasts?' I point at the curved mounds under her white T-shirt.

'No, I have double mastectomy bras.'

I check again and then scan her face to see if she's joking. She remains neutral. I'm the Coyote, falling off a cliff. Nowhere to backtrack or scramble to. I cover my eyes with my hands. 'Sorry, Dolores, I didn't know. I'm such an asshole.'

She says nothing but plucks a glass from the cupboard and pours the coconut water into it. Then she takes her cup, and puts an empty one under the machine. Pushes the button to fill it.

The coffee trickles.

Finally, after what feels like half a century, she says, 'Look, it's okay. If you didn't know, you didn't know. Your coffee's there; I'm gonna sit out front for a while. Get some vitamin D. The Build-up is upon us, the air's getting heavy.'

She gives me a thin-lipped smile as she walks by and goes out the sliding door to her deck.

I've fucking ruined everything. And now something comes back, all those years ago, when I was in first semester of teaching college and my mother was worried – Dolores in Darwin was having a big operation, doctors were hopeful, my mother's joy at the news that it was a success. One of my classmates was my boyfriend, a young man who loved teaching kids and loved taking speed at the weekends.

How the hell did I forget?

I grab a big pack of lentil crisps from the cupboard, stuff handfuls into my mouth. When I'm finished I look for something else but sigh at Dolores' healthy food. I pull a strip off a head of lettuce and wrap it around a tomato. I squirt mayonnaise on it, add a couple of olives and take a huge bite but it's not the same. I toss it in the bin and take my coffee from under the machine. Dollop honey into it. Burn myself with a mouthful.

Maybe I'll pack my stuff and go. Let her know about the party, leave them all to it.

I sit in front of the TV. The presenters snigger at a male musician's orange and red checked waistcoat and tie for the event.

'Did he not get the memo that waistcoats went out of style three decades ago?'

I think he looks cute and awkward as he picks at his guitar on stage. He sings sincerely in the clip.

'And our final fail of the evening is Kara Perlance, wearing a tent? Is it a green tent?' She turns to her co-presenter. 'Maybe it's a dress, and a home for when she camps with bears.'

Her co-presenter chortles. She of the lollipop head and stick-like body. 'Camps with her family, you mean?'

The first presenter catches her breath and says, 'You are too much.'

The camera zooms in on Kara Perlance, a famous actor in a popular crime drama, standing with her partner, on the red carpet. She's gloomy-looking as the cameras flash and people call her name. She squirms and rests an arm across her belly.

'Kara, is it true you're pregnant?' a voice shouts from the crowd.

Kara swings a sad glance to her partner. He puts his arm around her. The presenters laugh at the journalist's comments.

I switch the TV off and look out to Dolores, where she sits, motionless, hands on her knees, watching the sky gather clouds.

★

In my room, I lie on the bed and decide to tell Dolores about the surprise, and that I'm going to slip away later. Won't be in her home scoffing all her sunflower seeds and mushroom ravioli anymore. Then I'll call to Bruce, give him the USB stick and the new plan. They can go to the event together and I can pack up and move on.

They'd still have a great night. A better night, without me being in the big fat way of their tidy lives and their surviving cancer and divorce and growing old gracefully. It's too hot for me here anyway.

I slink downstairs and out to the decking. The daylight is greyish. Dolores smiles. It's so oppressively humid, it's as though some invisible animal is breathing all over me. I'm reminded why I stay indoors and downstairs most of the time, cocooned by cold air.

'Dolores, I forgot to tell you earlier, the A/C is broken in my bathroom.'

'Bruce will have a look at it. It disconnects every so often in the upstairs rooms. It's happened before. No big deal. Can you smell the rain? I reckon it's on its way.'

I pick at my skin.

'Are you okay, Natalie?'

'I'm sorry, I should think before I speak. I don't know how to apologize, everything I say is wrong. I didn't know you had your breasts removed.'

'Natalie, relax.'

'And I didn't mean to be pushing at you. I'm like an elephant who stamps around on good things and it makes me—'

'Kiddo, I've let it go.'

'What do you mean?'

'Relax. It's gone. I'm not holding it. Cancer taught me that much.'

I wipe sweat off my forearms. 'Did it hurt?'

'Did what hurt? What you said or the cancer?'

I wince. 'The cancer. The surgery. Were you in a lot of pain?'

'Sit down, you'll make me nervous too if you keep standing there like that.'

I sit on the bench beside her.

'Yes. I was. Afterwards I was bruised and swollen. I had drains to gather fluid around the wounds. But I was very dizzy. The dizziness was more a confusion, there were parts of me gone. I'd never get them back.' Her eyes darken. 'It was the end of my body in the way I'd known it for my adult life. And I couldn't get my mind around that at the beginning. No amount of research prepared me for that. I had to learn my body again.'

I cross my arms and hold my shoulders, resting my chin on my right wrist. My legs are weak as I imagine the experience.

'I became numb for a while. I don't know if that was from the operation or if it was me blocking it out. Then I started to wake up at night with these horrible tickles. My chest would be numb and tickling at the same time in a really horrid way. This went on for months.'

'Does it still happen?'

'No. I began to see a woman, a New Age-type therapist, and she told me to speak to the tickles, find out what they wanted.'

'Are you joking?'

'No.'

I suppress a nervous laugh. 'Did it work?'

She looks me dead in the eye. 'Of course it did.'

'What did they want?'

'They wanted me to make peace.'

'With what?'

'With lots of things. With my ex-husband, mostly.'

'I never met him.'

'Lucky for you.' She chuckles. 'We were a good couple initially but we were young hippies and didn't know how to be honest with each other.'

I don't want to ask a stupid question so I say nothing.

'We didn't know how to fight.'

'Was that not a good thing?'

'I'm not saying we didn't fight, we did. But we didn't know how to do it respectfully. We'd get annoyed with each other but never spoke about it. We'd force being nice and peaceful but we grew bitter and things would eventually erupt into drama for us. One of us always thought they knew what was right. One of us would always have to win.'

'Is that why you got divorced?'

'It was probably the underlying issue, yes. We were unconscious to what we were doing to each other, and drifted. I made friends with a colleague. One who I felt safe to speak to. It was never sexual. My ex-husband used to go crazy because of this. Also because he considered my colleague to be a square. I got some sort of sick thrill from that. My fury would be satiated by it. Of course my husband met someone else. He said I drove him to her.'

'That's sad, Dolores,' I say.

'That's life, Natalie. In many ways, he was right. I wasn't sleeping with my colleague but I was giving him the respect and emotional intimacy that I should have been giving my husband. I didn't acknowledge that until much later, until I'd forgiven things.'

'Are you friends now?'

'Friends?' She laughs in a high pitch. 'No. No. I have no idea where or who he is anymore. But look, I've forgiven the whole lot. Him, myself, the lot. I wish him joy. Forgive everyone everything is what I believe now. I still struggle to express anger and I have to be careful about that. I've to check that I'm being nice for genuine reasons.'

She nods then gazes into the middle distance. 'Because sometimes you can hold a grudge for so fucking long it goes underground. You've forgotten all about it, but it's there, rotting.'

The air crackles. I glance around. 'Is a storm coming?'

'Possibly,' Dolores says.

We sit for a while, saying nothing, and then she leaves, silently. I hope I haven't stirred uncomfortable stuff in her for later. I try to picture her bottling up the thick dark liquid of her anger in an actual bottle to smash. Wielding a big shard of its glass at the party, tearing and kicking, screaming profanities and insults, pinkfaced with rage, but my mind's eye won't allow it – Dolores keeps turning into me in my daydream.

I check my watch and go back upstairs to change into my evening wear, promising that I won't slash at myself in my head with nasty comments about my appearance.

We stroll into The Gardens and I wink at the waiter when I give our name. He nods conspiratorially. Dolores is glamorous in a black high-necked dress with a pearl collar. It has long lacy sleeves and falls a little past her knees. She wears sensibly heeled beige shoes.

The waiter writes in a large white book and asks us to follow him outside. 'We'll seat you in the function room tonight, ladies, as the restaurant is full with an event.'

'Do you mind?' Dolores asks, shifting her stance.

'No, it's fine. I don't mind at all,' I say.

'You think they'd put the event in the function room and let the diners be in the restaurant? This is bizarre.'

'It's quite a hip place. Maybe they do things differently here,' I say.

Dolores reluctantly agrees. We follow the waiter out through double doors to a terrace lit with fairy lights, onto a dark, cooler area. He pushes open a door.

The lights are off.

'What's happening?' Dolores asks.

The waiter switches on the lights. 'SURPRISE!' roars the crowd. Stevie Wonder's 'Happy Birthday' comes on over the speakers.

Dolores takes at least twenty seconds to figure out what's going on. Her eyes are glazed and her hand rests on her chest.

'Surprise, Auntie D.' I kiss her soft cheek. 'Happy birthday.'

Different acquaintances and friends swamp her. Bruce and his teenage sons sit by the bar. I'll hang with them but a lot of people are here. My skin feels tight. I'll probably have to talk to them all. I don't have many conversational ideas. What if things fall into awkward silences? I scan around the room for the food.

There's a table with canapés in the corner; I try to guess what they are. Salmon, maybe, roast beef, avocado and corn, prawns with lemon mayonnaise, some sort of spiced meat which I learn is crocodile from a passing waiter.

Beside that is a table with less fancy party food, pizza, wings and fries. Some crustless egg and cheese sandwiches. Vegetarian nibbles.

I stand by the food table and check to see if I'm being watched as I fill my plate, placing a second pizza slice on top of the first one. I scoop a handful of canapés and move away to the opposite corner of the room.

Bruce jumps up and goes to the bar when Dolores does, to get her a drink, even though he's put a tab down. He wants to hand the glass to her.

They laugh and cuddle. I eat on.

Bruce hasn't let himself go completely, like many men of his vintage. His skin is olive so the harsh Australian sun hasn't ravaged it, even though he works in construction. His hands are gentle-looking too, lithe fingers that are delicate but still masculine. Years of hard work have given his body definition instead of plundering it.

When I finish eating, on Bruce's cue, I set up the video messages on the projection screen and feel warm hearing all the familiar accents from home. My mother cheerfully wishes her sister a great sixtieth and makes a joke about how they used to be squashed in the car, five of them in the back, to go to Enniscrone beach on holidays. Best seat was the middle and they'd puck each other for it. Dolores would usually be granted it, being the youngest. How the sun shone all the time in 1960s Ireland, which probably gave Dolores the taste she had for sunny weather.

For a moment I wish I was home at my parents'. The familiar rooms of where I grew up. But as soon as the longing hits, it vanishes again.


There's a lot of commotion and then silence. I've snuck back to the food table and see someone cough and clear his throat. A big redhead takes centre stage in the middle of the room. He holds a microphone and sings The Wolfe Tones' 'Streets of New York' adapted with his own lyrics about his emigration to Australia.

This must be the famous Keano. He has the crowd enrapt, singing with an intensity and theatricality that seems too staged to me.

I grimace as he rolls into the third verse. He's self-indulgent. I chomp on another mini-burger.

Keano finishes and gets great applause. The DJ immediately puts on a cheesy party record and I sigh with relief. There's far too many Irish expats here. The night could easily turn into a session of singing after Keano's performance.

Dolores hugs Keano and he looks at her in a way that confuses me. Is he trying it on with her? His chest is up and he has a cocky smile on his face. Dolores is being maternal with him but he's trying to flirt, to impress her. His comments fall flat.

I drink enough prosecco to go along when one of Dolores' colleagues pulls me onto the dancefloor. I notice the brightness of Keano's red hair.

One of the Australians calls him a ranga, after orang-utan, and Keano does an imitation of a monkey, scratching under his arms and going 'oooh oooh oooh', then turns into a gorilla and bangs on his chest.

Dolores blows out the six and zero candles on her cake. People are so fond of her. Would my colleagues back home ever put something like this together for me? Maybe at my old school but only while I was there. After I quit, I attempted to stay in touch with four of the teachers I was closest to but that dwindled to one and even with him it was usually a stray comment on social media that kept us together. Can that even be considered a bond?

If I hosted something, who'd come? No one, probably. Paper plates with slices of birthday cake are passed around. I take one, then another, and decide to never throw a party.

Dolores goes on the microphone, making a speech in her wacky Irish-Australian accent. I think she sounds more Australian than Irish but the Aussies think it's the other way round. She thanks the venue and everyone who put the event together. She's honestly been surprised.

'This scallywag niece of mine let nothing out,' she says and points over, the spotlight of attention falling on me and my mouth stuffed with cake.

I swallow it down. Lick and wipe my lips with my forearm, give a quick wave and a smile to the crowd. My neck burns.

Dolores raises a glass. 'To life.'

People clink bottles and glasses.

She turns to the DJ and gestures for more music.

The men in the room smile as Dolores talks and moves. Why doesn't she have a man? All these bucks are clearly interested.

The DJ plays Abba. Everyone goes wild on the dancefloor. I grab another slice of cake and turn to see bright orange coming towards me, it's like a fire blazing on his head. His skin is paper white up close, translucent nearly. He's in a GAA jersey and light blue denims. A trail of laughter follows as he walks through the party. I clean my front teeth with my tongue, pull at some food lodged in my back teeth. I hoist the V of my cleavage up so it's not too revealing but the weight of my breasts drags the dress down again.

'You're the niece?'

I nod.

'I'm Keano. I meant to reply to your texts but, I don't know, one of the times my phone was dead and the other time, I was training or somewhere.'

'That's okay.'

'Howaya anyway?' He puts his hand out and I shake it. It's cool, dry. He gives me a once up-and-down. 'You don't look like Dolly at all.'

'Who?'

He appraises my body again. 'You and the Doll, ye don't look alike.'

'I don't know what you're talking about.'

'Dolly? Dolores? She is your aunt, isn't she?'

'Oh, yeah. I never heard her called that before.'

'Ye aren't similar.' His voice has an edge – disappointment or frustration?

'I'm probably more like my father's people. Did you just get back from the mines?'

His eyes have a glint that's not friendly or comforting. It's a hungry sort of look, a wild sort of look. As he drops his gaze to my chest, I feel like a huge piece of prime steak and that this lad hasn't eaten in years.

'Just out of hell, yes,' he says, ravaging me again with a stare.

'Why do you call it hell?'

66

'Three weeks in. Cock fest. Clouds of flies in the air. Searing sun. Zero craic.'

'Why do you do it?' I eye up the buffet, which is being restocked by a waiter.

'Money, Natalie girlshine. Money. Hard cold dollars. Thousands upon thousands of them. I've forty-six grand saved this year already. Do you want to see my bank account? I've online banking. I can show you it on the app. My balance. It's fucking beautiful.'

He clicks some buttons on his phone.

'I don't want to see it. I believe you.'

Keano seems disappointed. 'It'd only take a second to bring it up on screen.'

'No, don't bother.' I wave it off.

Keano puts his phone in his pocket, gives me a hard look. 'I heard something's off in your room, Dolly told me, the air con isn't working in the toilet, is that right?'

'Yeah, but she said Bruce will call over and fix it. With organizing the party, he didn't have the time yet.'

'Bruce doesn't know shit about shit,' Keano says.

'He works in construction.'

'Believe me, girlshine, I'll have it done more efficiently, with more zest and skill than old Brucey could do with all his wrinkly equipment.'

'Are we talking about the same thing here?' I lean back.

'I'll be around tomorrow when me hangover dissipates. 3:30 p.m. I have the code, will let myself in.'

'Okay. Well. Thanks.'

'Right, I better get to work on the aforementioned hangover. Do you want a drink?'

'No, I'm grand. I might have a sausage.'

Keano strokes his cheek with the back of his fingers. He's undeterred with his eyes. I fold my arms across my stomach, covering all the new layers. He winks and goes to the bar.

The party is in full swing but I'm drained and decide to book a taxi. I offer Dolores, Bruce and even Keano a lift, but everyone's too busy in their merriment to join.

I receive a text that the taxi's outside. I skull the rest of my prosecco and grab my handbag and scarf.

The car is a big white people carrier. I open the front door, tipsy from the alcohol. It's spacious and calm inside.

'Hello, Madam, Natalie Dillon, you go to Greenwoods?'

'Can I sit in the front or do I have to sit in the back?'

'You can sit wherever you like. What number in Greenwoods?'

The roomy leather seat squelches as it takes my weight. 'It's 72 or 74. Can't remember. I'll know when we're there.'

The driver raises his eyebrows. His face is lit by the GPS navigation device mounted on the dashboard. 'You don't know where you live, Madam?'

'I do. I always get mixed up on 72 or 74. I've been drinking too. Never helps.'

'You drink?' He checks all the mirrors as he pulls onto the main road.

My teeth chatter. He turns the air conditioning down a fraction.

'It was my aunt's birthday party. Do you not drink, Mr—' I search for his registration badge. 'Mr Ahmed Khalil, born 1.6.1986. You and me have the same year of birth, Ahmed, what's your star sign?'

Ahmed laughs and looks at me; his dimples are even more prominent with the smile he holds after. 'Do you believe in the stars?'

'Why not? We're all made of stardust. Have you heard that one before, Ahmed? After the Big Bang explosion and expansion, we were all born of the stuff of stars. Are you a Muslim? Am I allowed to ask?'

He nods. 'Yes, I am.'

'Where are you from?'

'Here,' he says and takes a slip road to the highway, turning on his full headlights in the darkness.

'You're as much from here as I am.'

'I'm an Australian citizen, Natalie Dillon. My mother is British Iranian. But I was born in Tunisia if that's what you're fishing for.'

'I suppose it is. Do you miss your homeland?'

'Here is my home,' he says without a beat.

'Do you not miss where you're from, the weather and food and people? The understanding? I miss those things sometimes.'

'I only live in the moment. I cannot be nostalgic for what was, when I appreciate what is.'

'That's beautiful, Ahmed,' I say, wanting to touch his arm. 'That statement was made of stardust. Definitely.'

He laughs. A big gorgeous laugh.

I smile but then feel an edge of nausea. Maybe it's the new car clean leather smell or motion sickness from the alcohol in my system.

'Can I tell you something private? Between us, taxi fare to driver.'

He nods.

'I'm jealous of my aunt.'

'Why?'

I inhale deeply through my nose and let it out. 'Because she's kind and beautiful and totally okay with the fact she's imperfect. She has a lovely house and friends and she has overcome life or death stuff. She's overcome actual problems. And she's smart and can do yoga.'

'Envious,' he mutters.

'Excuse me?'

'That's envious, not jealous. Jealous is when you think something you have may be taken from you.'

'Okay, I'm envious so. Doesn't make it much better? I love her but I feel crap about myself around her. She's so good to me that it makes me feel even worse. Then I wonder if I like feeling bad about myself. That I'm addicted to it somehow and need a fix of it if things are going well. Need to mess things up. That's destructive, isn't it? I wish I could be more like her. Have her outlook. Her lifestyle.' I raise my voice for effect. 'And she's sixty. She's over twice my age.'

'You're in the business of counting other people's blessings instead of your own.'

'Excuse me?'

'It's something my mother says.'

He looks at me, his brown eyes sparkling. I feel a shockwave, somewhere deep inside, somewhere lower body I haven't felt for a long time. The black sky is awash with stars, pinpoints of light twinkling, smiling down.

'When did you come to Australia?' he asks.

'A few weeks ago but I go to New Zealand soon.'

'And you're from?'

'Ireland.'

He whistles. 'This Irish and alcohol.'

'Yes, what a cliché I am tonight.'

'Would you stay in Australia?' His hand goes to the gear stick and I restrain myself from touching it. His fingernails are pale pink.

'It's a good country but I don't know. I don't know what I'm doing with my life, you see, Ahmed. Years ago, generations ago, I'd be a mother of eight by now, probably. I wouldn't have time to be solipsistic.'

He eyes me, looks at my head, neck, chest, lingering there, and then goes back to my face, eyes. He locks eyes with me.

I fold my arms.

'You're pretty, star lady.'

I blush again but this time blood hums and tumbles down my body, making it warmer. 'Thanks. I don't see it at all,' I say, bowing my head.

'You might be a bit crazy too. It's the alcohol. That isn't good for the mind.'

'It's apparently called fun, Ahmed.'

'I like you.'

I perk up in my seat. 'But you don't even know me. You know nothing about me.'

'I know there's electricity here.' He waves at the space between us.

I can't deny it. I desperately want to touch him. To touch his face. To strip his shirt off and hold myself against him. To stroke the skin on his back with the tips of my fingers. More.

We're almost at Greenwoods. Ahmed dips his full lights as we pass some cars, and streetlamps begin to line the footpaths.

Bruce's truck is parked outside his house.

'Would you like to see me again?' Ahmed asks.

I hesitate. 'Are you married?'

'What?' He scratches his scalp.

'Don't Muslims marry young? And only marry other Muslims?'

'No, Natalie. Not everything is set in stone. Muslims can marry Christians. People can live how they choose. I have citizenship. We could marry. You could live with me. I have this nice place, by the lagoon. Even for children it is a good place.'

'Why are you proposing to me, Ahmed?'

'Because I would like to sleep with you.'

He parks in front of 73.

I'm moved by his chivalry, or, at least, his honesty. 'I have to go inside.'

'Are you home alone?'

'No. No,' I say quickly. 'I live with my aunt. And uncle. And three cousins. Irish builders. My brother, too, Keano. He's home from the mines. He's inside as well. The party will continue all night. We will keep drinking. Us Irish.'

Why have I lied? He hasn't made me feel unsafe.

'Will you take my card, give me a call, if you'd like to meet me?'

I take it from him without touching him.

'My offer is authentic,' he says as I pay the fare. 'We could make it work.'


Dolores stews a pot of milk thistle tea and we watch wildlife documentaries until midday. She decides to go for a swim down in the communal area of the estate, to sort her head out.

'Come on,' she says. 'It'll be good for you.'

I groan.

'Come on,' she says. 'You spend too much time indoors. Darwin's brilliance is outdoors.'

'I know but I get too sweaty, Dolores, I'm gross.'

'Sweat is natural.'

I sigh. 'Give me a minute to change.' I tramp up the stairs.


Palm trees surround the kidney-shaped pool. I sit at the edge of a beach lounger. It's muggy out, my T-shirt and sarong are damp. Dolores strips off, revealing a strapless vintage-style blue one-piece bathing suit with little white anchors printed on it. I look at her breasts, or lack thereof, and still can't tell.

She dives a perfect arc into the pool.

'You coming in? It'll make you feel better for sure,' Dolores shouts.

'Yeah, I will, soon.'

Can I risk it? Most people would be at work. I can't.

I realize I missed a patch when I shaved my legs. I grumble looking at it. I try plucking the hairs out with my nails but only end up breaking the nail on my middle finger.

'Come on, Natalie,' Dolores says. 'It's too hot to be out there.'

'What if someone sees me?' I look around again.

'Why are you so afraid of being seen?'

I eventually undress, inspired by how much renewed energy Dolores has. I'm flubbery and uneven in my turquoise halter top and bikini shorts. I'm like something about to burst from the seams.

She cheers.

I pull my knees up tight, dive-bomb into the pool, hitting the water with my ass, and make a massive splash.

Dolores is laughing and splashes me back when I come up for air.

We float about for a while.

'I'm sorry about yesterday,' I say, bobbing in the water.

'Kiddo, an apology is unnecessary. Why bring it up again, it's not an issue?'

'But I—'

'Why are you still carrying this, Nat?'

Why am I? I don't know.

'I loved last night. It was so much fun. Thank you for organizing it,' Dolores says, changing the tone.

'Bruce did most of the heavy lifting. Do you think he's in love with you?'

Dolores flips some water at me. 'What does it mean to be in love?'

'He fancies you and he does nice stuff for you.'

'Can't a man and a woman be friends?'

'I don't know, can they? I've never really had male friends.'

'Short answer is, yes, they can. And because Bruce is divorced and I'm divorced doesn't mean we should get together. You know people can be perfectly fine on their own. There's all this bloody pressure put on relationships. People always hoping that others will complete them, be their other half. It's dangerous. We're already whole. Don't halve yourself for someone.'

She averts her gaze to something behind me.

'Well, speak of the flaming devil,' Dolores says and in an instant hops out of the pool. She wraps her towel around herself and kisses Bruce's cheek.

'My favourite sexagenarian,' Bruce says. 'I've been looking for you, ladies.'

He's wearing his sandal – sock combo.

I say, 'Oh fuck,' in a low voice. How can I get out of the pool without Bruce seeing me? I can't. I'm trapped. I plunge underwater and swim to the edge. Hide by the wall.

Bruce waves at me and tells Dolores about calling around yesterday to see if everything was in order for the party.

'You pair of snakes,' Dolores says, jokily. 'I knew nothing. I couldn't have even expected it. Not on a weekday.'

'We're a good team.' Bruce winks at me. I duck closer to the wall. 'I wanted to invite you for lunch with me and my boys. No surprises. You two glorious women and us cowboys.'

'Sure.' Dolores looks expectantly at me. 'You coming, kiddo?'

'No, I – I'm going to Skype my friends at home. So I won't join.' I can't bear the thought of getting out of the pool in front of Bruce. Even sacrificing a meal would be a lesser hell than that.

Dolores stares at me for a moment. 'Maybe get a taxi later and follow us in?'

I half-nod. Ahmed's handsome face comes to mind.

'You'll be okay on your own, Natalie,' she says. I'm not sure if it's a statement or a question.

She smiles and walks away with Bruce. I hear her laugh at his jokes.

I swim for a while and get out when I think enough time has passed for them to be gone. I like the idea of an empty house. I can chill out. Eat in peace.


I lounge around for the early afternoon, wonder whether to call Ahmed and get a taxi and meet Dolores and Bruce, but instead I watch a made-for-TV movie and mull over options of what to have for dinner.

It's still hot out and I enjoyed my swim earlier so I get a notion that if I have another swim, my head will be clear, I can order and eat a pizza without guilt and have a lovely evening solo.

I turn the coffee maker on and grind some beans, place a cup under it.

I go upstairs and change into my bikini again, which is still damp from earlier. I look in the mirror at myself. How do people become comfortable wearing these things? I step into my pink high heels, and being higher up makes me feel less roundy. I take them off; my feet are sore and blistered from wearing them last night.

Instead I put my sunglasses on and look in the mirror. The tinted view is more flattering, I have a bit of distance from the bright light harshness of my figure. I pretend to be someone else as I walk around the room.

I go downstairs to get my coffee, still wearing the sunglasses.

In the kitchen, I feel undercover with my eyes behind the darkened plastic. A different version of myself. I sip the coffee and lean against the counter.

The code is beeped in from outside. I put the cup down and dash towards the stairs but it's too late. The door has already opened, a shock of orange.

I look around for something, anything, to cover myself up and grab a cushion. I place it in front of my bikini shorts, then over my chest but move it to cover my belly.

'Natalie, is—' Keano seems lost, unable to find what he's going to say.

He stops talking and his eyes are down. He won't look up. I lift my shades for a moment, to see if it's because he can't find my eyes. It's not that. He's speaking to my breasts.

'I have to fix the – in your room. Where is—'

'Where is?'

He makes some muddled sound. Then he looks at himself, checking, and tilts himself away from me slowly.

'Do you—' he says and lets his voice trail off again. 'Is the woman? You know?'

I relax my grip on the cushion. Keano's more self-conscious than me. I gather some poise, stand straighter. Adrenaline courses through my body. I allow myself to smile at him.

'She's gone out with Bruce. She'll be back tonight, if that's what you're asking?'

'And you? Are you?' He clumsily moves his arm to block the side of his body.

'I'm going for a swim. I assume you'll let yourself out when you're done. See you later, Keano,' I say, walking by him with my head up, feeling his eyes still on me, following my soft white ass as I move.

At the pool, I dive in and realize I've never been this heavy before. I tread the water. My body has made me feel ugly.

No. I made myself feel ugly. My body is getting all this attention.

I look down at myself, wondering when Keano stared at me, what did he see? When Ahmed proposed? Bruce and his flickering gaze?

I undo the thick strings of the halter neck and lower them. I look around. There's nobody about. A nipple sneaks out from under the loose material. I check around again. I leave it out. No birds fall from the sky. No tumultuous roar. Life goes on. I leave it like that for a moment. The afternoon sun bakes behind thick ashy clouds. When will the rain come?

I click the clasp of the bikini top and take it off. Throw it poolside.

These breasts, bigger than I've ever known them to be. Too big to cup. An armful.

This softening body. I lie back, breathing saturated air and float weightless in the pool.

Something quivers in the shadows behind me and I turn my head quickly. But nobody's there. It's just palm leaves rustling languidly, the splut of the water, me and my body – maybe they aren't such separate things after all.

# Please

I hold the document with my left hand as the fingers of my right hand drift over the numerical side of the keyboard, rapidly pushing numbers to enter them onto the screen in front of me. I pause after every twenty or so, click File Save, and check if they're correct. Kelly approaches my colleague, the other side of my cubicle. I can't see him without craning my neck over the partition, but she's in clear view from her torso up, in an immaculate white blouse and pink crystal choker. She flips her glossy hair behind her shoulder.

'It's my birthday tonight. Food in Murray's at seven. Then we'll go to Courtenay Place for a bop after. Bring a friend,' she says and rotates to the next cubicle across from him, repeating her speech. It always seems like she's aware of her mouth, of how her lips are being viewed.

I haven't any plans for the evening other than swimming. Kelly preens herself and struts in an anti-clockwise direction. She invites the other staff who sit at their L-shaped desks in our workstation.

She gets to my cubicle and gives me a fake smile but says nothing. Her brown patent leather heels squeak on the linoleum as she moves to the workspace across the way.

The sheet is limp in my hand.

We're not friends, even though we're the only single women, and the only ones on holiday visas, in this office. The odd time, we small talk at the photocopier, or the vending machine. I open the bottom drawer of my desk and take out a pack of neon-coloured jellies shaped like wild animals. It's fine. I don't care. I'll swim after work and hang out in the hostel. I probably wouldn't have gone if she invited me anyway.

I wring the chlorine water out of my swim costume and rinse it under the taps in the changing-room. I wrap a towel around it and bundle it into my gear bag. I hover by the hairdryers and mirrors but it'll wolf into my evening too much to try and blow-dry my hair. I leave it wet, dripping softly and swirling into ringlets on my shoulders. I put my bag on the wooden bench in the middle of the room and walk barefoot to the corner of the duck-egg coloured lockers, to the scales. This is probably the only reason why I come to this place with such frequency, though on the days I don't swim I pine for it. I'd be itching to return to weigh myself.

The monotony of doing laps in breaststroke up and down the pool thirty times helps clear my head from the office talk too, I suppose.

There's no need for me to be upset about earlier; I wouldn't join anyway if she asked but it seems like she said it to everyone in the office except me. I shake my head as I realize I'm stood in front of the scales, holding my towel, vividly reliving the scene at work in my head.

Let it go, Natalie.

I dry my feet and step onto the metal plate of the scales, take a note of my weight in my phone. I'm down two hundred grammes since yesterday. Halle-fucking-lujah. But I'm up forty grammes since I went into the pool. I discount it for my clothes and my wet hair.

I figure out the calorific significance of this and look forward to stopping in the supermarket on my way home.

It was a warm evening when I left work and now it's a cool night with a blustery wind. Wellington's erratic weather reminds me of Ireland. The automatic doors beep, sensing me as I enter the supermarket. I yank a small green plastic basket from the stash and divert straight to the discounted section in the fridges. Poking through the knocked-down items, I stumble on a reduced-price noodle stir fry and Cajun potato wedges.

Next stop is the hot food section for a cooked chicken breast. I also buy a fizzy grapefruit drink and corn snacks for later on.

I zip my jacket up around my ears, and eat the chicken breast with my hands as I walk through the city. I pluck all the white meat from it and then peel the crispy skin off. I wipe my greasy hands on the foil packaging and wish I had a napkin.

A chicken breast would be about two hundred grammes.

It's drizzling outside. I walk under the city's awning and pass the superpub Darina works in on Courtenay Place. She's been my roommate since I got here. We share a four-bed but have had no one else in the room since the Chinese guy left two weeks ago.

I peer through the glass to see where she is. She smiles brightly as she hands a plate of food to a customer eating alone at the bar.

I put my weight against the brass push handle of the heavy front door. The pub is dark, and smells of cider and beef burgers. A golf competition is muted on the big projector screen, as well as on the smaller HD screens over the seating areas; green rye grass being thwacked, a tiny ball soaring in the sky, and spectators politely clapping. This is soundtracked with New Zealand reggae music, coming from the speakers.

Darina rushes from behind the bar.

'Hang on,' I say, as she tries to hug me. I put my shopping and swim gear bag down.

'How are you? How was work?' she asks, releasing me from her hold.

'Grand.' I think of Kelly, jab myself with that sinking humiliated feeling again. 'How are you?'

'All good,' she says and returns behind the bar. She leaves her hand on an ale tap. 'Are you sure you're okay, your face looks sad?'

'Yeah. Or maybe—' I start. 'No, never mind.'

'Fancy a drink? Take the edge off whatever's bothering you?'

I shake my head no.

'Go on, it's on the house.'

'Nah, thanks though. I've to put dinner on. Wanted to say hello.'

We chat for a few minutes while she rinses and stacks glasses into a tray.

I say bye and she winks. I see her sup from a pint of beer hidden under the bar.


I turn the hill to my hostel and spot a blue tour bus parked outside it. A New Zealand Quest coach. It's a notorious party bus. The receptionist usually sleeps 'blow-ins' on the first and second floors and those of us here on working holidays live on the third and fourth floors. It's a good dynamic. It's not too loud at night in our area, and if you want to party, all you've to do is go downstairs. Even then, you've to leave the common areas by curfew, at midnight. The Tongan security guard takes no shit from anyone. No one would be stupid enough to give him hassle about drinking or playing music and hanging around after that. He's six feet four and a hundred and twenty kilos.

I greet the receptionist. The randoms in the kitchen drink and jeer. I don't recognize anyone. I go down the hall to check the common room for the regular stoners and the other workers.

A handful of people watch a horror movie. Screams fill the room as the characters on TV flee through desolate fields.

'Hey Nat,' Lawrence says with a smile that lets me know he's high. 'Sit here.'

He shuffles his broad torso and strong legs to the left to make room for me on his yellow beanbag.

'Are they all Quest people in the hall?' I squish in beside him.

'Yup, a Big Blue Fuck Bus has landed and all the rich kids are gonna party.'

I hope we don't have to share with anyone.

'Have you been swimming?' he asks.

'Yes. When are you going to join me? I have free membership passes.' I always invite him to swim even though I'd probably die a bit if he saw me in my costume. I find it disturbing how he smokes himself slow when he finishes his cleaning shift in the hostel.

'Not ready yet but I like the way you smell of the pool. It gives me comfort.'

'Oh, thanks, Lawrence,' I say sarcastically.

'Pool and shampoo and girl products. I'd probably get the sweet whiff of chlorine from across the street.'

He looks away wistfully. Sometimes my heart tingles for other people and the pain they're in. I have that feeling looking at him now.

'Any plans tonight?' I ask.

'Chilling. Get some beers in shortly. Fancy a smoke?'

I shake my head. 'I don't need any assistance with the munchies.'

He laughs and rubs his belly. 'But tomorrow is your day off, isn't it?'

'Yep.'

'Well, get some beers at least.'

'We'll see.'

I enjoy the odd night out but more at the weekends than during the week. Sometimes I go with Darina to her bar on her nights off. I can't understand fully why Darina spends the nights she's off from the bar the other side of it. I would not hang out in my office on my days off.

The empty bunk has bags and cases on both beds. I put my swim gear away and watch some music videos on my phone. About half an hour later, two boys burst in. One waves and I take my earphones out.

'Hey there.' He wraps his warm hand over mine. 'I'm Aaron.'

I introduce myself. The other guy unsteadily climbs to the top bunk and gestures from there. 'Jake.'

'Natalie, will you have a drink with us?' Aaron asks.

'No thanks.'

'Wrong answer,' he replies as he pours vodka and lemonade into three red plastic cups. 'Natalie, you promised me a dance.'

'I did?'

'Put on some Prince, Jake.'

Jake plays 'Kiss'. Aaron mimes all the words in a melo-dramatic way and has a full dance routine for the chorus. It's hard to resist laughing.

'Okay, give me that drink,' I say.

Aaron cheers. He hands me a cup.

'Wellington party time,' he toasts, takes a long slurp.

We chat for a while. Aaron tops up our drinks any time he feels like it. He's an archivist from London, and Jake's from Wales. He worked as a roofer to save for the trip.

'You're on a holiday visa?' Jake asks.

'Yep. I'm in an admin role for the council here. The only point of my job seems to be that I make twenty bucks an hour. Even my supervisor told me when there's nothing else to do, tap around on my keyboard and make myself look busy.'

Aaron says, 'That sounds painful.'

'It's fine.' I don't tell them that I'm always busy, even when it's quiet, researching the calories of different foods and calories burned by particular sports. The drink loosens me up all the same and I feel confessional. I say, 'Yeah, it's fine. Except there's one of my colleagues, Kelly, who's kind of awful.'

'Work wankers. No escaping them.'

'She's super pretty until you get to know her then her looks sour.'

'Like Aaron,' Jake says and Aaron pouts.

'I'm fabulous inside and out.' Aaron blows his fingernails. 'Don't you forget it.'

I ask about the tour they're on. They began in Auckland, went all along the east coast and go to the South Island the day after tomorrow.

'Can't wait for the South,' Aaron says. 'Christchurch, Picton, Abel Tasman—'

'And Queenstown,' Jake interrupts. 'Bungee jumping in the place it all began.'

'You don't even want to do it,' Aaron says.

'Fuck off,' Jake replies.

'Well, do you want to do it?' Aaron asks accusatorily.

Jake sighs. 'Nope.'

'Why do it so?' I ask.

'I'm afraid of heights.'

Aaron explains, 'Jake has acrophobia so he's going to smash it. He's been warming up by sleeping on top bunks.'

Jake says, 'Shut up, gay boy.'

'Make me,' Aaron says and laughs.

'Why aren't you doing the jump?' Jake asks. 'Too chicken?'

'I don't need to prove anything to myself.'

Jake looks hurt.

Aaron backtracks. 'Kidding, Jakey. Not doing it 'cause it's too expensive. Fuck that.'

'How much is it?' I ask.

'Nevis is two hundred and seventy-five dollars.'

They ask me what I've seen in New Zealand.

'Not much,' I say and my ears get hot. 'I flew from Darwin to Sydney to here, and found a job almost straight away. Needed to earn money again. But I've fallen into a routine – work, swim, the odd night out. I haven't even seen much of Wellington, other than the harbour and Te Papa museum.'

'Seems like a quiet city,' Aaron says. 'A quiet country.'

'Our bus tour is rowdy as fuck,' Jake says and Aaron laughs, agreeing.

Jake speaks a lot about women he wants to 'pull'. Aaron responds to this chat by talking about various conquests on his travels and celebrity men he wants to back into him.

'Have you a partner, Natalie?' Aaron asks.

I shake my head.

'Anyone of interest?'

My mind draws blanks. 'Can't think of anyone,' I say.

'Lucky you and your drama free life.' Aaron fills us another vodka. 'Who sleeps there?' He points at Darina's bed above mine.

'She's from Scotland,' I say. 'Very sweet and maternal, but loves partying. Sometimes she gets in from a night out after her shift when I'm about to go start my day in the office. It's like we live in different timezones.'

'We should go to her pub,' Jake says. 'She sounds mint.'


It's student night and the place is mobbed with young women in short dresses and young men who look like they could be in One Direction. Darina is half-drunk behind the bar and ecstatic to see me. I introduce her to the lads and she gives us free liquorice shots. A list of drink promotions and a slideshow of attractive people having a good time at the pub replace the golf tournament on the screens.

We drink and laugh. Jake is bit standoffish and I wonder if he's annoyed with Aaron for talking to me or with me for talking to Aaron.

The DJ stops playing dubstep and switches to recent chart music. We dance for a while. Aaron quick steps with me and swirls me under his arm. I turn and abruptly sober up a bit. Kelly from work is at the edge of the dancefloor. She has so much make-up on I barely recognize her.

'She doesn't look like that in the office,' I say to Aaron.

'A face of lies.'

I go to the bathroom and, on my return, Kelly summons me. She introduces me to the two men with her. All three of them seem to be standing around, waiting to be noticed.

She points at the guys from my dorm room; they're singing Avicii's 'Hey Brother' to each other. 'You've got those friends who look like fun.'

'Yes, I do.'

'I didn't realize you went out or did anything. You're so quiet in work.'

'I do things,' I say.

'Yes. Maybe I pigeonholed you, Natalie.' She gives a pageant smile, showing all her square white teeth.

I don't want to ask her what she means. I'm afraid of the answer.

'It's your birthday?'

She sighs, 'Yes, it is. The big three-oh. It's my last one.'

'Your last birthday?'

'Yes. I'm staying this age until I get married.'

'Congrats,' I say. 'I didn't know you were engaged.'

'I'm not.'

Aaron fetches me for another dance, and I'm relieved. I let him lead. Kelly watches us curiously. Darina returns from behind the bar with more liquorice shots for us. We clink them together, toasting our room, knock them back. I lick the stickiness off my fingers after. My stomach is in flames.

Kelly and her friends slither out from the edge of the floor and eventually dance beside us. Her friend Sol sidles up to me. He says he'd love to talk to me somewhere more private.

Aaron and Jake egg me on.

Sol finds us a seat near the DJ box. He has a sculpted beard and light blue eyes. We try to chat for a while. It's mostly a misheard conversation, shouting over the music. A sliver of hair wax that he hasn't blended is like a snail trail on the crown of his head.

I slide it out and show him. He puts his hand over my fingers, and leans in to kiss me. I laugh but kiss him back. He buys us both cocktail specials, radioactive green drinks with ice and slices of orange floating in them.

He throws his striped straw on the ground and drinks the cocktail from the glass. He finishes it and belches.

'You know what, Natalie,' he says, earnestly, 'you're actually pretty funny and nice. It wouldn't even be that much of a sympathy shag if you came back to mine.'

There's a ringing sensation in my ears that resounds throughout my body. I try to recompose myself.

He leans in to kiss me again. I find it hard to match his rhythm. His mouth is cold from the drink. My face has gone numb. He keeps kissing me anyway.

Sol goes to the bathroom and I dash over to Aaron and Jake. They're moshing to Britney Spears's 'Work B**ch'. Alcohol and stupidity are a dangerous mix and I can feel tears coming.

'I'm going home,' I shout.

'What about your friend?' Aaron asks.

'Not for me. I'm off.'

'Wait,' he says. 'We'll walk you.'

They both escort me.

We talk loud on the street, our hearing slowly recovering from the banging music in the bar.

'Fancy the gay club?' Aaron asks. 'It'll stay open for hours yet.'

'I need to go to bed,' I say.

'Jakey?' Aaron says, and gives him a serious look.

Jake coughs. 'No. What?' He puffs his chest out. 'No fucking way. I'm going to Maccy-Ds.'

He ducks into the chipper.

'Later,' Aaron says in a catty way. He cuddles me as we walk.

'Been so good to meet you, Nat,' he says. 'You feel like a sister.'

He drops me to the door of the hostel.

'Are you not coming in?' I ask.

'No, going on the cruise, my darling. See you tomorrow.'

The Tongan security guy gives me a brief nod. I take the lift up to our floor and change into my fleece-lined pyjamas.

My hangover cuts. I rub my head and open the window to let some of the alcohol-breath air out of the room. The two boys and Darina are asleep. I haul myself off to the gym mainly to weigh myself after the drink but I also want to shake the overwhelming self-pity I feel.

I swim and cry underwater, accidentally swallowing some. I hope no kids pissed in the pool.

The sadness fades by the time I hit the showers. I structure the rest of my day off, which is mostly a plan of what to eat and prepare for dinner and tomorrow's lunch.

When I return to the hostel, lots of people are around for lunch so I go down to the common room. I half-watch a Kiwi soap opera about doctors enmeshed with each other and their patients.

Lawrence vacuums around us making a big deal about how serious he is about his job. He turns the hoover off and lands beside me on the pleather two-seater couch with the hard seats. The side of his bony ass digs into my hips. He wriggles and gets cosy.

'I should be paid for this job, I should be promoted even. Head hoover guy.'

I laugh.

'How was the night out? You were swimming again?' He sniffs at the air.

'The night was weird,' I say.

'Why?'

'I went out with two from the fuck-bus.'

'Were they okay?'

'Yep, they were sweethearts, well, one of them was. The other one is a bit, whatever. But I met this girl I work with, Kelly, and her friends, at the bar. One of her friends, Sol, approached me. He seemed grand and we were having a laugh. Ended up kissing.'

Lawrence nudges me gently. 'Get you, girlfriend.'

'No, wait. I'm not finished. He goes, "So this wouldn't even be much of a sympathy shag, you're pretty nice and funny."'

Lawrence closes his mouth tight. 'He said what?'

I repeat it.

'Jesus, Nat, I'm sorry.'

'Why are you sorry?'

'People can be shits.'

'Why do you think he said that?'

'I don't know him; my first reaction, though, is to punch him.' He balls his fist. 'Maybe he was immature. Insecure. Blind.' He pulls me in for a hug; his jumper smells of cigarettes. 'You know you're lovely, right? Don't let anyone talk to you like that.'

'It's true though – look at the size of me.'

'You talk about yourself like that, you give others permission to do it.'

'What?'

'The things you say to yourself get matched up externally. It's neuroscience. The brain doesn't like to be wrong. It'll scan the world for confirmation of this truth you're feeding it.'

'How do you know that?'

'I used to see a sports psychologist as part of my training. When I didn't make Beijing, I told myself repeatedly what a fucking loser I was. Now I get it affirmed from the outside world all the time.'

'Why not say something nicer to yourself so?'

'Exactly. I tell myself I'm an incredibly handsome loser now. Look, I'm still licking my wounds, catching up on that misspent youth I didn't get to have when I was training every fucking minute of the day. This lifestyle is only temporary for me right now.' He points at the ground as he speaks.

His supervisor, a Polynesian woman, comes into the common room and scolds him.

He gets up from the couch, grimacing. 'Only temporary,' he says, dragging the vacuum cleaner out to the corridor.

The boys are still in their underwear in the dorm at 4 p.m. I unpack my gym bag. Darina is at work. Aaron pours a vodka for himself and Jake. He offers me one. I mime barfing. He tells a debauched story of a man he met in an alleyway.

Jake exhales noisily and announces he's going out for beers and sandwiches. He comes back with a small bar of white chocolate for me.

I thank him profusely.

'Okay, calm down, it's hardly twelve red roses,' he says. He's quiet for a moment and then asks, 'Why does this town smell of burnt toast?'

'It's from all the coffee roasters,' I volunteer.

He rakes his hair. 'Thank fuck for that. I thought I was having a stroke.'

Aaron giggles. Jake watches him and smiles.

They offer me a drink again but I'm working in the morning. I've no interest in going out two nights in a row.

Some other fuck-bus people come knocking for them and the lads leave.

I prepare enough dinner that some can be leftover for lunch, then I go to the common room. Lawrence is baked, along with everyone else in there watching TV. It's another horror movie, this time about a couple who are stalked by masked people while on holiday in a remote plantation house.

'Are you not scared watching this shit?'

'Nope.'

'Do you want to swim with me tomorrow when I finish work?'

'Do you want to have a joint with me?'

'I'll have a joint with you when you swim with me. Deal?'

He smirks and goes for a cigarette.

I drift upstairs and get my work outfit ready for the morning. I cleanse and moisturize my face and go to bed early.

★

The boys crash into the room near 11. They startle me awake. Jake precariously clambers up the bunk's ladder. They whisper loudly, initially trying to keep it down, but then forget. Jake invites Aaron to his bed. Aaron declines so Jake gets off his bunk more awkwardly than he'd climbed it.

He bounds in beside Aaron in the bottom bunk.

'No. Stop. Get out.'

Aaron tells him again to go. But he doesn't. I try to drown out everything with my earphones but the energy shifts in the room and I feel uncomfortable. I take them out and catch more of the conversation. Jake is trying. Aaron begs him not to. They kiss briefly.

I cough loudly to remind them I'm there.

They ignore me.

'Lads,' I say, 'other people are in the room.'

'Please,' Jake says. 'Please.'

Oh Jesus.

Aaron sounds like he's crying. 'You don't want this. Really you don't.'

'I do. I'm in love with you.'

'Your girlfriend?'

'She's not my girlfriend, you know. It's a holiday thing. Me and you. We get on so well. You understand me like nobody I've ever met before.'

'But we're too drunk, we're both too drunk, please.'

'Lads,' I say loudly, 'please. I'm in here.'

'I love you,' Jake says.

'You don't, please stop this, I can't. You know I've feelings for you.'

'You're hard for me.'

'Don't. Don't touch me.'

'You want me too. I know you love me too.'

'Jake, you're not gay.'

'I love you. Do you not love me, Aaron? Do you not feel the same way?'

'I do,' Aaron says, sniffling. 'You know I do.'

There's a yearning silence. Then the sounds of furious, wet kissing. They maul each other, grappling flesh; their bunk shakes as they toss around in it.

'For fuck's sake,' I say and get out of bed. Take my trainers from under it.

They can't hear me. They are oblivious, blackout drunk. I put my coat over my pyjamas and sigh a lot. I open the door; the light from the corridor spills in and Aaron spits on his right hand.

The stoners seem like they're being sucked into the couch as they watch MMA on TV. I check my phone, hope that by the time the show ends, the lads will be done in the dorm. That it won't be a drunken hump, desensitized sex that goes on all night.

Lawrence's eyes are unfocused. 'What you doing down here this late on a school night?'

'I think the two lads from the fuck-bus are having a moment,' I say.

'What kind of moment?' Lawrence asks.

'An argument or something.' I suddenly feel protective. 'Could I have a drag of a joint?'

Lawrence slowly registers what I've said. A quarter-smile comes on his lips, his mouth is raised one side. He nods. 'Of course, my friend.'

On the gable wall in the smoking area, a stencil mural of a Maori Tiki has its head sideways and its tongue stuck out. Lawrence sparks up a joint and passes it. I take a drag and hold it in; the smoke pricks my lungs. I cough on exhaling.

I take another deep drag.

In the common room, the bloodied fighters on TV strike each other on the ground of the ring, one choke-holds the other and I feel an overwhelming paranoia that everybody is looking at me or talking about me, the way I talk about myself, like Lawrence said.

Fatfuckingbitch, stupidcunt, outofcontrol, uglymonsterfat, nobodylikesyou, beachedwhale, stupidfuck, nobodyfucking-likesyou, don'tevenlikeyourself.

'It's as if I'm not even real. I'm not even here,' I say.

Lawrence eventually replies, 'Why?'

'I could be anywhere. New Zealand. Home. Nowhere.'

'Nowhere's good.'

'I think and feel the same way and do the same thing in a different place. I'm the same person in a different place. Same hamster wheel. Rut. Going nowhere.'

'Everywhere you go, there you are, isn't that the phrase?'

'God, I wish this would fade,' I say to Lawrence. The words take an eternity to come out and to be in the air. 'I don't feel well.'

'Your pain?'

I inspect him, not sure if I heard right. Or if he even said it.

'Your pain?' I try as a response.

'I've never been better,' he says and lies back. 'Who needs the Olympics anyway?'

The shapes move on the TV and I struggle to follow what is going on; my sound and vision aren't in synch with each other or with my meaning-making capacities. Everything is disjointed.

The high finally passes and I go back to the dorm when the Tongan kicks us out.

Thankfully, the two boys are asleep, cuddling each other. They look peaceful.


I'm wrecked when my alarm goes off. I open and shut drawers and rustle bags as I get ready for work. I'd make more noise if Darina wasn't there.

Jake's eyes open; he snuggles closer into Aaron then looks around. I give him a knowing stare. Panic crosses his face. He jumps out of bed, naked, climbs up to his top bunk shakily and seems even more embarrassed as he covers himself with his blanket.

'It's not what it—' he starts.

'I'm too tired to care.'

I leave for work with dark circles under my eyes.


My stomach grumbles in the canteen and I fill a mug with steaming black coffee. Kelly leans against the counter beside me, her orchid perfume heavy. She asks if I enjoyed the time in the bar.

I smile as pleasantly as I can.

'Sol wondered where you got to? He asked me to get your details.' She flips her iPhone out.

'No,' I say.

'He's a good friend of mine.' She keeps her phone out, ready to take my number.

I blink a few times.

Her eyes narrow. 'Do you not want to meet someone? He's actually keen on you.'

I take a deep breath. 'I said no, Kelly.'

'Did you not have fun with us?'

The contours of her face are made by darker make-up, a line at the cheekbones, at the sides of her nose, the top of her forehead and bottom of her chin. It looks muddy.

'Isn't it funny we ended up hanging out together when you didn't even ask me to your party,' I say.

Kelly places her hand on her hip. 'Excuse me?'

'You invited everyone from the office except me.'

'I didn't invite anyone.'

'I heard you, Kelly. I heard you invite them.'

'Don't know what you're talking about. Are you giving me your number or not? I thought you were single?'

'I am.'

'You're playing hard to get?'

I touch my temple. 'I'm not playing at all.'

'You'd prefer to be a cat lady?'

'A cat lady?'

She purses her pink lips. 'Don't you understand, Natalie? Time's running out for people like us.'

'I don't want Sol to have my number,' I say and slam the mug down on the counter, much harder than I meant to, so coffee spills over the rim. 'And being single isn't a terminal illness, Kelly. Now, if you'll excuse me, there's somewhere I've to be.'

I rush past her, unsure of where that edge came from.

I don't have anywhere to be but I can't hang around for lunch now. I march to the hostel and practise my Queen Bitch on the walk back, ready to tackle the two boys in my room over their behaviour, rehearsing some things I might say about respecting other people's space.

I charge into the room all ablaze and stop immediately. Aaron is packing his things into a monochrome suitcase and seems morose. He's the only person in the room.

'Where's Jake?' I ask.

'He left.' The sharp triangle of his Adam's apple rises and lowers.

'On the tour bus?'

'I don't know. I don't know. He's gone though.'

'Darina?'

'Showering.'

I can feel his sadness. 'You okay?'

Aaron audibly breathes in through his nose. 'I'm alright, yeah.'

'Can I hug you?'

'Please do, Natalie.'

He opens his arms. His T-shirt has a hint of fabric softener. His chest trembles as he holds onto me.

'You two kept me up and I'm annoyed about that. But I'm sorry this happened to you. He might come back. He might not. You'll be okay.'

Aaron sucks a breath and rolls his shoulders. 'I didn't want to. I mean, I did, of course I did, but not like that. I knew this would happen. Bloody straight guys.'

'They're not all bad,' I say.

He stares at me; his eyes are a teal colour with brown specks. He swallows rapidly. 'Nat, sometimes I don't want to be me. I don't want to be this. I hate being me. Is there anything worse? To deny yourself?'


I fill a glass of water under the tap in the kitchen and sit beside Darina on the long bench. She smells of talcum powder and drinks Corona from the bottle.

'I know it's early but I can't help it. Woke with the shakes.'

I take a sip of water.

'Do you want one?' She raises the bottle at me.

'No.'

'Why are you back so early? Half-day?'

'No. Remember that girl, Kelly, whose birthday it was the last day? She was in your bar with the two guys.'

'Yes, the super stylish one you kissed.'

'I kind of had an argument with her so came home for lunch. Bit afraid to be around her now.'

'Why?'

'In case she comes at me again.'

'No, why did you fight?'

'Because she invited everyone in the office to her party except me. But now she's denying that. I heard her ask them to join. Ironically, I was the only one who was at it.'

'Do you work with those two men that were with her?'

'No.'

'And you were the only one from work at the bar for her party?'

'Well, I was out with the new boys from our room.'

'Nobody went, Natalie.'

'What?'

'She's obviously saving face by denying inviting people.' Darina drains her drink and gets a second.

Maybe nobody went to Kelly's party? That's why she said she didn't invite anyone? Jesus.

'I know what you're thinking,' Darina says.

I nod.

'I mean, I'll go to meetings if it gets out of hand. It looks bad but I have it under control, I swear.'

'What?' I blush. 'Wait, no, I was thinking about Kelly.'

'It's okay, Natalie, I know I've a drink problem but I'm not an alcoholic.'

'No, I was honest-to-god thinking about Kelly.'

'Do you want one?' Darina offers again.

'No, I better go back to the office. Then I'll probably go to the pool after work.'

'You're so healthy with the swimming, Nat. I wish I was healthy like you.'

'Healthy like me?'

I walk out of the hostel stunned.


I observe Kelly from my cubicle. She's at the photocopier, talking to one of the women from accounts.

I would probably have declined her invite, after all. I was coming up with ways to get out of it. Obviously, everyone else did too.

She threw a party and nobody really went.

Kelly gathers sheets from the side tray of the machine and smiles that condescending smile of hers to the woman.

Maybe it's not condescending, maybe it's desperate?

Maybe it's the shape her face makes?


After I finish work, I swim lengths and think of Lawrence, his childhood spent in the pool, how disappointed he must have felt missing the cut off for the Olympics by a fraction of a second.

I resist getting something to secretly munch on as I walk home but I stop in front of Darina's bar, peer through the glass. She grins and serves a tray of shots to a group of men in suits, downs one herself.

Everyone with their own secret pain, their own coping strategies.

The wind rises and whips the branches of the street's pohutukawa trees.

The fuck-bus is loading up as I turn the corner to the hill. Aaron queues, sombre, headphones on, head down. I see Jake cross the road, going over to him.

They look at each other and then Jake hugs him. They stay in that embrace, Aaron's face beaming. Jake's eyes are closed.

My heart tingles. Imagine being rejected and loved again.

# Clear

'Have you cabin fever in the west yet?' Kim asks and sips from her apple cocktail. We're in a newly opened Dublin bar. The staff are tattooed and have nose piercings and give out sticky sweets popular in the nineties with drink receipts.

'Not really.'

'Post-travelling blues?'

'Not really,' I say. 'Glad to be back.'

'And the job?'

'It's fine.'

'I think the fitness centre has gotten into you. It's a cult. Sporty people are in a cult,' Kim says. 'You're drinking vodka soda lime for Christ's sake.'

'They're not really, Kim. They just like moving.'

'It's bizarre that you're not on longnecks and ordering pizza.' She pokes at the ice in her drink with her straw. 'I'm worried.'

'It's the environment I'm in, it's rubbing off on me.'

'Should I be worried? I don't like the sound of this Andrea.'

'She's cool, Kim. You would like her if you met her. She's sound.'

'Do you want another one?' she asks, tilting her glass in my direction.

'I've got plenty left here.'

She flicks her gaze upwards and slinks out of the booth to the bar.

Fionn's the other side of me. He asks, 'What does she mean?'

'I found a job in my hometown's leisure centre. Doing admin and office work. It's pretty dull. But I've made friends with one of the instructors and Kim's jealous.'

'Must be a good place to work.'

'It's fine. I can swim for free when my shift ends. That's quite nice.'

'It must be fun to work.'

'What do you mean?'

'To see people daily, have stuff to do.'

I pause. 'It's grand, yeah. I'm living with my grandmother at the moment to save up. Very chilled between life with her and the job but I don't really know what to do with myself.'

'Me neither. I'm so fucking blue in this city. I feel like I'm choking.'

'Do you work?'

'Not in that traditional sense. Actually, not in my own non-traditional sense either. Since my collection came out, I can't write. I've seized up. The city is pulling me down. I'm straddling the deep.'

'The city is great but I'm not long back from New Zealand. I never realized what a lovely part of the world I came from until

I went out into the world. The pastel skies here, blanketing, comforting. I never appreciated it. All the fields and trees. All the plants and animals. Ireland is beautiful. I never even noticed before.'

'I've never been to the west. Hear it's nice.'

'You've never been?'

'Nope.'

'It's only two and a half hours away by car.'

'I think we went to Limerick once but no, I've only been across the water. All around the UK. Same price sure might as well go to a right country.'

'Ireland is a right country.'

'You know what I mean,' Fionn says. 'Tell me more about your place.'

'Well, it rains all the time. But it's pleasant rain. Or at least you can have a fire on and not feel guilty about doing nothing all day. Like, it's quiet. Boring if you want to look at it that way. But sometimes quiet and boring are underestimated, don't you think?'

'Yes. My life has been too turbulent. I crave serenity.'

'My gran, she's old enough now. Very sweet. A little old stereotypical grandmother. She's cute. You'd like her. Everyone likes her.'

'I am great with grandmothers.'

'Sometimes in the evenings, she'll be cooking up tea and I'll go outside to watch the sun setting over the fields of sheep and I feel so lucky to be able to breathe easily.'

'That sounds delightful.'

'It is.'

'When I look out the grimy window of my bedsit that I can barely pay for with me dole, at the fucking dismal day outside, I wonder am I suffocating with panic?'

'I used to panic a lot too. Annoyingly, I think the swimming helps it.'

'Why is it annoying?'

'Because it's what's recommended, isn't it, movement as a way to heal? With my anxiety, I know the unease is there lurking, like in a box that I feel curious to open but if I do it jumps out and catches me by the throat so I swim and leave the box closed.'

'Do you reckon I could come to the west sometime?' he asks.

'Yeah. Totally. It'd be cool to have you there. We've a spare room. My gran won't mind. She often tells me to invite friends to visit. I think she doesn't want me to leave so she gives me these incentives to stay.'

'Thanks, Nat,' he says and I smile.

Kim leaves a drink down in front of my half-filled glass and scooches back in beside us. 'You'll drink that when you're done. I'm not queuing at the bar again.'


I didn't think we were being serious, me and Fionn, thought it was only the drink talking, but he texts me to confirm it when I'm on the train home. I say he's welcome whenever. He messages me about getting there Friday.

A published poet coming to stay? It'd be like hosting a celebrity. He was a big deal in the Dublin literary scene when his debut collection came out. That's what Kim said. A big deal. I tried to read it but wasn't fully sure what was going on. The line breaks were weird and there was a glossary at the end of each poem.

But I could help him out of his funk. All the places I could bring him to release the clutches of his anxiety; the mountains, the sea, lakes, forts, fairy trees, old grottos, castle ruins, the holy well, the white strand, the waterfall.


I collect him at the train station and show him around my hometown from the car.

'I work there.' I point out the leisure centre. 'There's the library, it's lovely inside. Converted old town house. I'll show you around it tomorrow after the lake.'

'Cool.'

'I'd my first kiss behind it. A slobbering, dreadful affair but memorable too, I suppose. I spent most of it with my eyes open, looking at him. We weren't together, just set up to go and kiss, then come back to Supermac's for curry cheese chips or strawberry sundaes, and let the next pair go for their turn.'

'A rite of passage.'

'Yeah, was yours romantic?'

'My first kiss was with a girl, believe it or not. She was a neighbour and a friend. Our mothers worked in the same restaurant. We were in my room, watching *The Thing*, I remember it clearly. She was afraid so I put my arm around her and we ended up kissing. We laughed about it after. I was pretty certain, at age thirteen, that I liked boys. We're still good friends to this day.'

'That's kind of romantic.'

'I might write about it, actually.'

I smile. He's already inspired here.

'There's where I went to school. They say it's haunted by old nuns and boarders who died on the grounds. Before them, the Irish peasants hanged by the local Protestant landlord. Those spirits knocking around.'

'Did you ever see them?'

'Nah. It was eerie at dusk. When I'd be doing supervised study after school or whatever and there wasn't much activity, in some rooms you'd get chills but that was the central heating's fault more than ghosts.'

I park in the square and bring him to my local, a small two-roomed bar. The bartender greets me warmly. We sit on stools at a table beside the fireplace.

The trad band are setting up.

'Do you like trad?'

'It's cool, I guess,' he says.

'This band are decent. Otherwise I wouldn't torture you with it. The fiddle player was in that group that toured the States all the time. Big in America. The woman on accordion is also a world champion Irish dancer.'

'This is what I'd expect from the west of Ireland. This and mist rising from fields.'

'Wait till the morning for that.'

He has three pints to my one. I drive us back to my gran's place.

'Natalie,' he says, 'I'm buzzing here. It's been fun to see your town, to hear the stories. To taste what I'd have called the countryside. I'm excited, I think I'm going to go in and write. I can feel my words galloping home to me. Thank you.'

'That's great, Fionn. Tomorrow we can go to the lake and the library and then I was thinking we could climb some of the mountain. It's not too strenuous but the views are pretty sweet from it.'

'Sounds good, but if it's okay with you, I need the morning hours for studying, undisturbed. I have a routine.'

'Oh,' I say. 'Sorry. Yes, of course.'

'I'll be out of the room by lunchtime, hunger will get to me.'

'I can leave some breakfast outside on a tray so your creativity isn't disrupted.'

'Natalie, you're too good.'

I go to bed smiling.


On Saturday, when Fionn's writing routine finishes, I take him to the local sites. We walk around bogs and go to the waterfall.

He explains the pleasure it gives him to be writing.

'It's the only time I know that I'm doing what I'm supposed to be doing.'

I show him the white strand beach at sunset and then we return to Gran's. I offer to bring him for another night out in town after we've eaten but he says he'll go to his room and work for the night now he has his flow back.

Gran sits in her chair beside the fire, propped up by a cushioned back-support. 'Will we go to mass this evening?'

'No, Gran, mass is only on Sunday mornings anymore. Church is too empty otherwise.'

'Yes, I remember that now. Will you have something to eat?'

'Gran, we had our tea? You made us grilled cheese sandwiches.' I look at the clock. 'We had it fifteen minutes ago.'

'Of course, of course. My memory is getting worse. Can I ask a favour, will you drop me to mass this evening?'

I take a deep breath. 'No, Gran, mass is only on Sunday mornings. I'll bring you in the morning. Maybe Fionn will come too.'

'Who?'

'The poet. The one staying with us? You made him food? Tall thin fella with the curly black hair?'

'Yes, of course. A nice lad. He's like that fella out of the play. The Prince.'

'What play?'

'The Prince of Denmark. No, Hamlet. He's like Hamlet, all in the black and the moping. A nice lad though.'

\*

On Sunday, Fionn shows no sign of leaving all day. I wait to drop him back to the station but he never asks me for a lift into town.

At 10 p.m., I realize he's staying so I go to bed.

On Monday morning, I knock on his door and offer him a lift before I start work. He says he's grand.

Confused, I drive to town.

Andrea clocks in and asks how the weekend went.

'Good. It was lovely. I had a guest stay.' I tell her all about him. 'He's still here,' I say and scratch my forehead. 'He showed no sign of leaving and now he's stuck out in the countryside with my gran for the day. I'm a bit worried.'

'Give her a buzz sure and see if it's okay.'

I dial Gran from the office phone. 'Hi, it's me, Fionn is still there. That's okay with you, is it?'

Gran crunches on her cornflakes. 'Who?'

'Fionn, the poet fella. He's in the spare room.'

'Ah yes. Your little writer friend? He's working away. I gave him a cup of tea. Grand lad.'

'Okay, well, I may go for a swim at lunch instead of after work so you don't have to be entertaining him.'

'He doesn't take much effort, Natalie. He's like a wee ghost.'

'Okay, Gran, if you're sure?'

'He's grand.'

★

After work, Gran has dinner ready for us and Fionn thanks her.

He asks me how my day went.

'It was good. You?'

'Brilliant day. Wrote loads. I'm mad inspired here. I'm going for an amble after dinner if you'd like to join. Your gran gave me a torch for walking on the boreens.'

Gran's watching the telly and ignoring our conversation.

When Fionn leaves, I ask, 'Is it okay him still being here? I can tell him to go if he's inconveniencing you?'

'Who?'

'Fionn, Gran, the poet fella.'

'I don't mind him at all. We do have lovely conversations.'

My eyebrows lift. 'About what?'

'Patrick Kavanagh.'

Andrea gives me a tour of the gym floor as I've never used it. She explains different moves that can be done with free-weights and on the mats. Her body is super toned and muscular.

'Did you always enjoy all this?'

'All what?'

'This fitness craic.'

She rubs some red lip balm on her lips. 'I suppose I did. I love it even more now that I've the kids. Teaching classes here, I get to unwind. Go home in great form for them. It's a good life.'

'You're very positive.'

'It makes everything easier when I am. I'd have loved to have gone to a sports college, done strength and conditioning for teams, sports psychology, all that type of thing.'

'Why don't you do it?'

'That ship has sailed for me. My kids are too small. That sounds like an excuse, a children excuse, but it's not. I'd prefer to use my time while they're young by being with them.'

I go for my usual swim after work and it helps me leave my annoyances behind. I feel calm driving home.

I eat my fish and two veg dinner, with one veg being a mini-mountain of mash potato, and read a little, beside the fire. Gran potters around, doing her thing.

Fionn joins us while we watch the 9 o'clock news.

He's smiling.

'How are you?' he asks.

'Grand. You?'

'I'm mighty, Natalie, the words are pouring from me. This part of Ireland is magical.'

'Were you not bored all day?'

'No.'

'I have to work again tomorrow but we can do something in the evening if you'd like?'

He shrugs and says, 'Yeah, if you want.'

'We could go to the cinema?'

'Okay.'

I say goodnight and go to my room. I don't even want to go to the cinema but what will he do all day on his own here with Gran after being here all week doing nothing?

We watch a thriller about a woman in smalltown America who thinks she's losing her sanity.

Fionn enjoys it but doesn't say much in the car on the way, or afterwards. I get the feeling he's itching to go back to the house. I've torn him away from the place.

On the way home, I ask, 'What about your dole?'

'I've been on the dole so long that I've the one that goes straight into my bank. Super handy.'

I click my tongue and say, 'Lucky.'

He's not asking for anything and doesn't seem bored. He's pretty content. He goes to his room when we get in.

In the kitchen, I lower my voice and say, 'Is he bothering you?'

'Who?'

'Fionn,' I say and nudge my head at the door. 'The poet.'

'Who?'

I scan Gran's face for any sign of her joking. 'He's been here since last Friday, the writer lad.'

'Oh yes,' she says. 'Gosh I'm getting forgetful. Will I drop him down a cup of tea?'

'No, Gran. He's fine. Do you want him to go? Is he making you feel like a prisoner?'

'A prisoner?'

'Or a babysitter?'

'No, he's grand. It's nice to have a bit of company during the days. He's a quiet sort.'

'I can tell him to go if he's bothering you?'

'Natalie, he's fine. I don't mind him at all.'

I offer to bring him to the station the next morning, but he waves me off.

'You're very kind, Natalie, but there's no need,' he says, pouring some hot water in his flask.

I don't know what his answer means.

I chomp on my porridge as he occupies the kitchen space.

At work, I talk to Andrea. 'He's a bit strange. How come he doesn't know it's time to go?'

Andrea asks, 'Did you tell him to go?'

'No. How can I do that? I realized we never set a date. He said could he come to the west and I said yeah. Do you think he's going to move in?'

Andrea laughs. 'Natalie, instead of swimming tonight, come to my spin class. It might help you release some steam.'

'Spin class? Are you fucking with me? Look at me.' I do a dramatic wave over my body. 'I would die at a spin class.'

'No, you wouldn't. You can go at your own pace. It's a high intensity workout, it'll relieve some of your stress. Go swim after it then.'

'I want to kill him.'

'Smash the stress, seriously.'


After work, I find Fionn in Gran's good sitting room, poking around, looking at old family photos.

'So here you are,' I say, like I've busted him.

'Yep. Wasn't everyone beautiful in old pictures?' He points at one of my gran's wedding day.

I melt. 'Yeah, I suppose.'

'I'd love if we were all in black and white nowadays. The glamour of it.'

I tell him some things about my family. He tells me about his; his parents divorced when he was small. His mother brought him up until she died of a sudden brain haemorrhage when he was fifteen. He moved in with his father and stepmother then.

'They're cool but I always felt like an outsider. My two half-brothers are ten years younger than me. My stepmother adores them. She was nice and all to me but she didn't really want me there. My dad was gone, as usual, always working. Some people's dads hit the drink hard in my area. Mine hit the office. We never saw him much.'

I feel sorry for him again. I even forget that he shouldn't be in the room, he's invaded Gran's privacy by being there, with her treasured antiques and old photo books, with the couch that still has the plastic covering on it so it won't ever get dirty, or used. It has a film of dust over it. Everything in the good sitting room has. I itch my nose.

'The house is a bit of a mess.' I suddenly feel claustrophobic and rub my hair.

'Is it?'

Andrea's voice comes back to me. I check the time. 'Fionn, I'm off to a fitness class. I'll see you later or in the morning.'

'Sound.'

I need some 'me' time but I can't have it if he's lurking. I head to Andrea's class, reluctantly. I don't want to have to murder Fionn if I stay at home. I don't even want to fall out with him.


I think about turning the car around at least four times on the road to town, and again outside the leisure centre. I feel humongous in my leggings, and sports T-shirt – even though it's mansize and loose on me.

Just fucking try it, Natalie.

It'd be worse of a beating I'd give myself if I go home now without doing it. I don't want to have to explain why I'm back so soon to Fionn if he'd be bothered asking.

I suck some air.

Pat's at the front desk and waives my fee. 'Staff are free, Natalie. Go on ahead. Andrea's up there.'

The studio is fairly packed. The bikes are set in a wide semi-circle and Andrea adjusts the seat on one for someone.

I recognize a few of the others attending from when I cover reception, and nod at them. I stand beside the bike in the corner.

Andrea grins when she spots me. 'Nat, you came. God, he must really be driving you mad.'

'Please don't hurt me at this.'

'I won't. Here, the seat goes to hip height. Are the handlebars okay for you?'

I mount and get the feel of the bike. 'Yeah, sound.'

Andrea flicks a switch to dim the main lights and turns on disco lights. She plays loud mainstream pop remixed to a gym beat. She shouts and has us dip, push up, climb hills, sprint. I sweat profusely and think I'm going to vomit. I'm not completely unfit from the swimming but I amn't flying it in the class like the others. They all must think I'm a fat idiot coming to a HIIT class.

I look around and realize nobody in the room is looking at me. They're all huffing and puffing their own way through the class.

When it's done, I wipe my head – the sweat is pouring off me.

'Jesus, Andrea, my legs are like a newborn calf's.'

'Good.'

'That was horrible.'

'It wasn't horrible, come on. Select the right words for things.'

'It was tough on my legs and stomach. I enjoyed sweating a bit, my head is clearer.'

'That's more like it. See you tomorrow, yeah?'

I'm lively from the exercise and get on great with Fionn. I ask him about his writing, how it works and I'm interested in how he's putting his poems together.

He speaks about visualization. 'The poem comes to me unformed. It's a static-like entity in my mind. I have to tune it into itself.'

'How do you know it's a poem?'

'I know my process at this point. I recognize the creative entities from the other white noise of my thoughts. I'm lucky, I guess.'

'Sometimes I wonder why the bad things I think come true. That maybe I've been born with an unlucky streak,' I say. 'Am I inviting them in from the white noise?'

'Maybe. Why use your imagination as a weapon against yourself?'

'I don't know, Fionn, it's the way I am.' I take a big mouthful of water.

He says, 'Sorry, Natalie. It's only easy for me to say this now I'm writing. Now I've reined it in again.'

I offer him a lift in the morning when I'm going to work but he says morning is when he works too.

The thought of him writing out his entities gives me a tiny bit of relief; at least something fruitful is coming from this.

★

I sleep without interruption for the whole night, but in the morning my legs and arm muscles throb. To sit in my office chair, I have to inch down; each movement highlights pain in my body.

Andrea laughs at me, but when I try to join in, my stomach hurts.

'This is all your fault,' I say.

'Again, pick your words carefully, Natalie, pick the right ones.'

'I didn't think much about Fionn, my new housemate, so that's good, I suppose. Even now, he's not bothering me. He's here a week today. What if I showed him where the bus and train station are this evening? Would that work?'

Andrea drinks something green and slimy.

'I won't even ask what that concoction is.'

'Wheatgrass, spirulina, spinach, apple, banana.'

'Fucking yuck,' I say.

'Don't knock it till you try it.'


After work, I bring Fionn on an outing to town, 'one last drive before you go.'

I show him the stations and also let him know there's a private coach to the city too from the square – he can catch that. He seems to be taking it all in.

At the house, I ask him if he has all his things packed.

'I've got so little with me, it'd only take me a few minutes to pack up.'

I go to bed again, confused. Has he taken the hint or not?

On Saturday my body's not as sore from the spin class and Fionn's still perched at Gran's, like she's his own grand-mother. I try putting him off when he comes out for lunch.

'Let's go fill the big turf bucket!' I say to him.

'Let's powerhose the gable!'

He comes with me.

'Let's clean the floors!'

'Let's give the stray sheepdog a bath!'

'I'm really enjoying country living,' he says as he suds up the dog in the yard. 'Maybe it's something I should consider doing full time.'

I press my temples with my index fingers.

He says it's amazing how enthusiastic I am about every-thing too. Even shitty chores. That I have some sort of Zen Buddhist attitude.

Despite it being Saturday, my day off, I can't bear the thought of the long afternoon ahead with him so I go to the leisure centre to a different spin class, run by Mikolaj, the Lithuanian instructor.

It's equally as torturous as Andrea's. Probably worse.

When I come home I fake that me and Gran have to go into town for the evening to visit family. Maybe we can drop Fionn in when we're going?

'Are we visiting, Natalie? I don't remember that?' Gran asks.

'Yes. We'll call into my folks, they'll be expecting us.'

'I must be getting forgetful.'

We all have a laugh but I feel bad – there hasn't been an appointment. And now I'm gaslighting my grandmother.

Still he doesn't take the hint. I'll have to let my parents know we're coming.

Fionn says he'll take it easy for the evening and waves us off.


On Sunday morning, I go on a cleaning frenzy.

'Fionn.' I knock, disrupting his routine. 'I want to change the sheets and sort this room out. I'm putting a wash on and Gran's hips aren't able to do the beds.'

'Okay,' he says. 'I'll go for a stroll.'

I tidy the room to look like it did before he came. I half-pack up for him. When he comes home, he thanks me.

'Will we do one last thing before you go?'

Fionn yawns. 'I'm a bit shattered. Writing into the early hours last night. I might have a nap,' he says.

I'm furious. I tell him a lie about an awful guest called Keano my aunt had in Australia who wouldn't leave.

He's shocked. 'Wow, what a dick.'

I invite Andrea over in the afternoon, to see if she can scoot him.

'There's a hotel in town,' Andrea says. 'It has social dancing and gigs a lot of the nights. You'd probably get ideas for your writing there.'

Fionn smiles at her.

I say, 'I could pay for you if you wanted to check it out?'

Why have I offered to pay for a hotel for him?

'That's so kind of you, Nat.'

Andrea tries to bring him to town with her when she's leaving but he declines.

On Monday morning, I ask him if he wants to have breakfast before he departs. He can even bring it with him on the bus. He eats the breakfast but doesn't go with me.

On Monday evening, I go to a spin class Pat's instructing. It's still tough but I know what to expect a bit more. I vent by pedalling hard.

That night, when I get home, I ask Fionn to do the dishes and to sort the fire out. He does so without complaint. Then I ignore him.

Same again Tuesday evening. We all watch TV in silence. Gran's still cooking for him.

On Wednesday morning I go to work early to catch the morning spin.

'Is he still there?' Andrea asks.

'Yep. Almost two weeks now.'

'Jesus. Do you want me to try move him again?'

'I don't think he will be moved. It's some sort of rebellion. He's squatting in my gran's.'

'I'll call round though, I don't care if he doesn't like me.'

'I don't care either, Andrea,' I say and fold my arms.

'You must do, otherwise you'd tell him to leave.'

When she visits, we talk about the intricacies of the most boring girly stuff we can think of. The differences between acrylic nail and gel nail treatments, wedding decor ideas, then

I start talking about my menstrual cycle. Andrea discusses hers. Fionn doesn't seem bothered or like he's intruding on an intimate conversation. He's completely at ease.

On Friday, I go to spin class again when I finish my shift, to stay away from the house. I buy a bottle of wine after.

I have to tell him. I have to say, just fucking leave. I'm not asking. I have to tell him directly.

I drink half the bottle myself. When he comes to watch the news at 9 p.m., I offer him a glass.

He accepts.

'Look, Fionn, this isn't a free hotel, you can't stay indefinitely. If you want to remain you're going to have to pay rent. It's not courteous to be here all the time and eat our food and use our stuff and then make no shapes for going. It's time to leave.'

On Saturday morning, I wake with a thumping headache. I go to the bathroom and notice Fionn's bedroom door is open. The curtains are drawn, sunlight spills in. His bed is made.

I step in. There's a note on the bed.

His handwriting is beautiful, curled and joined, calligraphic:

*Natalie, I wish you'd have said something to me earlier. I didn't know you felt like I was overstaying. You had not made me aware about how long I could wait for. I often have difficulty picking up on social cues, and though I wish you had been direct with me, I am grateful for my time here. The unpolluted air has cleared my head. My*

*words have come home. I have written over twenty new*
*pieces about the unsophisticated green fields, the burning*
*turf, the harrowing and uncertain sky. Thanking you and*
*your incredible grandmother for the best fortnight ever.*

I groan. Did I send him mixed messages? I re-read his note
many times and decide that it implies no hard feelings. I go
back to bed to nurse my hangover.

That afternoon, I feel lighter, relieved.

I open the lids of the pots in the kitchen. Gran is preparing
carrot soup for lunch and potatoes and gammon for dinner.
The smell of the boiling food makes my stomach lurch. I
consider driving to town for a big feed of greasy chipper food.

Gran adds some turf to the fire.

I fill up the kettle and switch it on. 'Just the two of us again,
Gran. At last,' I say. 'Glad he's finally fecked off.'

'Who?' Gran asks.

'Fionn.'

She looks at me blankly. The kettle begins to rumble.

'Fionn,' I say, 'the poet.'

'Who?'

# Guided Spin Tours

On a mild evening in early May, I come home from work to a smoked-out kitchen.

Gran flaps a dishtowel to banish the smoke towards the door. The cooker's fan whirs noisily.

I rush past her and open the windows. 'What happened?'

She flails. 'I don't know, Natalie. I was down in the room. Looking at notes, or cards, or at something and I forgot. I forgot dinner was on.'

'Why isn't the smoke alarm going off?'

The room is fogged with a putrid burnt food smell. I drive to town to buy batteries and some take-out Italian for dinner. When I return, the overhead fan of the cooker still mills around and Gran has a plate on her lap. She greets me as if I'm just home.

Fresh potatoes and frozen vegetables boil in pots on the hob. In the oven, cod bakes on the tray. Gran eats the burnt meat and spuds from earlier. The meat is a crunchy black and clacks off her dentures.

'Gran, I got us something to eat from town.'

She glances around her. 'But I have dinner on for you, Natalie.'

'Well, I'm going to eat this food, Gran. Not as tasty re-heated and I'm starving.'

I wonder if I should tell my mother what's happening, how Gran's memory is fading, but there's no need. She knows. We all do. Even Gran does during the times she's fully with it.

It's upsetting to watch Gran confused. It's upsetting to react to her dithering with frustration. I try not to comfort eat and instead I swim every evening or go to one of the spin classes. The exercise helps me let go of the fear. I now understand what sweating away stress is.


During spin class, I daydream while pedalling. After a couple of months of frequently attending classes to release, I realize I actually enjoy them. They don't hurt anymore. My muscles are used to it. I don't get so red in the face. I've figured out how to breathe as I move. I'm not sure when this happened exactly, thinking back to my spluttering first few sessions.

Andrea encourages me daily. She encourages everyone. I suppose that's why she's a fitness instructor.

The gym is noticeably quiet as the days grow longer and brighter. People have kids to entertain, GAA matches to go to, holidays to take. Summer activities are prioritized over being inside.

I change for Andrea's lunchtime spin session. Only four participants and me attend class.

It's the usual format. I know when we'll be climbing and seated and going hard or going fast. We're being cued by the music like Pavlov's cycling dogs, ready to pump or change gears alongside the song's beats.

The class is nearly over when Andrea looks at her phone and then at the clock.

She hops off the bike and comes over to me. Her phone vibrates in her hand.

'Nat, I've to take this call – go up to the top and cover.'

'What? No. I can't.'

'Well, do it from here so. I'll let them know. I really have to take this call. I'll be back in five.'

'Andrea, I won't be able—'

'Plan is to keep going with this for another two minutes, then do a three minute endurance ride. Take a drink break. Go for a minute and a half sprint low resistance. Okay? Thanks,' she says.

'No, wait,' I say but she's already at the door.

She turns to the studio and shouts, 'Natalie is going to take over for five minutes, guys. Back shortly.'

I mutter 'fuck' under my breath.

The other four in the class fix their gaze on me and wait; they're slowing down their legs. I have to act before they lose momentum. I compose myself and shout Andrea's instructions to the group.

They indifferently press on. I seem to know naturally what to do but five minutes pass and Andrea's not back.

I try to remember the cool down moves. Spin for a minute or so with all resistance off. One pedal to the floor to stretch your calf muscle. Swap sides. Off the bike. Quads. Stretch by holding the back of your leg to your bum. What's the glutes one? Groin stretch by holding the seat and leaning to each side. Touch your toes. Arms. I can't remember. Neck, turn to each side gently. Chest. Fuck.

Where is she? I look at the clock. The end of the sprint is near and there's still seven minutes to pass until the cool down. How will I fill that time in?

Andrea winks at me when she returns. I feel light-headed with relief.

She mounts her bike and takes control again.

At the end of class, she asks, 'How did that go?'

'You dropped me in it.'

'That wasn't my question, Nat.'

'It could have been terrible. A complete disaster.'

'I asked how did that go?'

I grudgingly smile. 'It was fine. It was kind of fun.'

'You're very capable, Natalie, if only you'd let yourself get on board with that idea.'


The sky is cloudless blue. People are in their summer clothes and the pubs and restaurants have set their tables and chairs outside. I drive through the town with the car windows open; the warm air blows onto my damp hair. The bypass is quiet and I play *Motown's Greatest Hits* CD at top volume. I take the right onto the winding country road towards Gran's house.

Calm envelops me passing the hilly green fields of cows, sheep and horses.

I turn down the music and pull into the driveway, drive around to the back of the house.

Gran is at the turf shed, a filled bucket either side of her. I wave and switch the ignition off.

'Isn't it a shame on me to go swimming on an evening like this?' I say to her as I shut the car door. 'It's promised sunny till the weekend though.'

Gran's not moving.

'Do you want me to carry them inside? Mind your back.'

She's not looking at me.

'Why are you standing there?'

She turns to me, stares as if she's trying to figure out who I am.

'It's me, Gran, Natalie.'

I am motionless now, I don't want to startle her. The headlights on my car turn off automatically. Flies hover around in the fading blueish light.

My heart rate picks up. 'Gran, are you okay? Has something happened?'

No response.

'I'm going to take a step over to you. Don't be afraid.'

I show her my hands and move slowly. She remains still. I put my arm around her waist. 'Come and walk inside with me. We'll get the kettle on. You're freezing.'

How can she be so cold on an evening like this?

'How long have you been out here?'

I usher her gently. She says nothing. Inside, I turn on the kitchen light and sit her down in her chair by the dwindled fire. It's cooler inside than out. I fill the kettle and press it on. 'I'll bring the turf in and we can have some tea, okay?'

She doesn't move.

I go outside and stall for a moment to breathe deeply, try and find my centre of gravity. The sheep in the field behind the shed bleat sporadically. The moon is out, a currach of a waning crescent.

I leave one turf bucket at the back door and carry the other inside.

The TV is on, the curtains are closed and Gran beams at me as she stands at the table. 'Aren't you a mighty girleen bringing in the turf? Do you fancy a cuppa, the kettle's just boiled?'

I add some sods to the fire.

Gran smiles as she opens the cupboard. 'Have we eaten?'

'No. I'm only in from work. I'll go back to town and pick something up for us.'

'That'd be perfect,' she says and puts a teabag into her mug.

I swipe at the corners of my eyes, open the breadbox and bring the chocolate digestives with me as I leave the house.


In the office, I ask Andrea for the format of the spin session. I ask her a few questions about how she structures and adapts the class musically.

'Because it's so quiet, do you want to shadow me at lunch?' she asks. 'But maybe it's such a nice day, you'd prefer to sit outside?'

'No, I'll shadow,' I say quickly in case she changes her mind.

I grin as she gives me a handwritten list of the instructions she'll be calling through the lesson. It's not too hard. Warm up, increased resistance seated, increased resistance standing, repeat, seated sprints, hill climbing adding resistance every twenty seconds, up to standing and max gear resistance, decreasing resistance standing sprints, cool down, stretches.

I follow the session, already familiar with it except now I have the words for what's happening physically. I like being able to label the motions, matching the experience in my body with a description.


I worry, in the evening, about what I'll be walking into today after work. I distract myself by thinking about the class, the plan of it, all the details of muscular movements and beats per minute.

Gran sits in her chair, looking at the crackling fire.

'Are you okay?'

She doesn't seem to hear.

'Gran, I'm worried about you. It might be time to give the doctor a call. Or Mam, at least. I'm not really sure what to do.'

Her eyes bulge. 'Don't do that to me, Natalie.'

'But I feel stressed and like I'm doing something wrong.'

'You're not doing anything wrong, Natalie. This is not about you. You're a grand young one.' She looks at the fire again.

'I don't know what's happening though, how to help.'

'You can't help,' she says and sighs. 'My memory is leaving me. I try to think back on the day, on yesterday, and there's nothing. Nothing comes.'

'The doctor might be able to prescribe something?'

'No. I don't want any of that.'

I bite on my bottom lip.

'Will I forget myself?' she asks. The fire glows on the side of her face.

I have a sudden image of a snake eating its own tail.

In a harsher tone, she adds, 'Or is this even me? Or everyone else? Is it some sort of trick?'

We don't speak for a while. The central heating's timer ticks loudly.

'It's so bloody confusing,' she finally says, in a small voice.

'Gran, you know some people practise mindfulness, to be aware of everything that happens in the now. In this moment.'

Her face still has the same expression but she peers over her glasses to look at me.

'Because now is all that's real, apparently. There's no past or future, those things only exist in thinking. So these people choose to stay present. To be here now.'

'Isn't it nice for these people?' she says and stokes the fire hard with the wrought iron poker. 'Having a choice in the matter.'


I file away membership cards. Andrea drops into the office for a chat.

'You seem a bit off, Nat. Are things okay at home?' she asks.

'I don't know if they are.'

I put the cards down, press my fist against my chest and massage it.

Andrea says gently, 'My father has Alzheimer's. I understand what you may be going through. I really do.'

I touch under my eyelids.

'Nat, would you fancy taking a class for the craic? Leading it? You might enjoy it.'

My blood pulses faster than if we were doing sprints on the bike. 'But I've no qualifications.'

'It'll be fine. You go to so many classes and I know you used to teach.'

'Andrea, maybe not, I don't think that I'd be—'

'They basically know what to do themselves. It'll be a cinch. I'll give you the lesson plan. All you've to do is shout instructions. Simple.'

'Andrea, I couldn't—'

'One of the early morning sessions? Twenty minutes with a five minute cool down. How about Wednesday? Only three regulars go to that class, Djetska, Colin and Lorna. You've been once or twice, sure. You know them already. You can definitely do this.'

My head says no but my body feels sparked with excitement. 'But they'll be going look-at-the-state-of-this-one when they see me coming. I'm not going to pass as a fitness instructor.'

'Nonsense. The majority of people will not know someone's

insecurity until the person tells them. Flags it themselves. Be confident, Natalie, and they will not notice. That's the truth.'

'How can I be confident?'

'Pretend you're confident doing it until you are. Fake it till you make it.'

I want to turn her down. Tell her no. But I can't. I'm smiling and exhilarated, warmed, on fire even, at the prospect of it. 'Andrea, this would be nuts.'

'Not really. It's summer. We've barely any members. Besides, I see potential in you.'

My neck bends forward. 'You do?'

'Of course.'

'What about Pat?'

'Pat won't mind. He'd be delighted I'm training you up.'

'Mikolaj?'

She hums. 'Okay, yes, we won't tell Mikolaj about it. He's too by the book. And he's been edging his way into all the classes timetabled.'

'When will I do it?'

'This day week. The 6.35 a.m. class.'

'This is crazy but I'd love to.'

She squeezes me, nearly strangling me with her bicep.


I practise the class in the evenings when the studio is empty. I imagine myself teaching the group, giving the plan a run through. Andrea said I shouldn't sweat it at all. She'd probably be there during the session, in case I need her. The nerves I feel all week make me regret agreeing to it.

The evening before the session, Gran checks my temperature by feeling my forehead with the back of her hand.

'You haven't eaten all day?'

I perk up. It's true. Maybe her memory's returning. 'Just nerves, Gran.'

She cracks three eggs into a pan. 'Do you want some of these, love?'

'No, I'm not hungry. I'm nervous.'

'Too nervous to eat?'

I nod.

'What's come over you? I haven't seen you eat at all today.'

'I'm teaching in the morning.'

'Did you go back to your job in school? Oh good, your mother will be delighted.'

'Not in school. I've a class to instruct in the gym. The one I told you about earlier. I have to teach it.'

Gran laughs. 'Teaching in the gym? You'll be fine. Worrying won't change a thing, you know?'

'But Gran, what if something bad happens? Like what if one of them goes into cardiac arrest? Or what if I fall off the bike and split my head open while I'm showing them something? Or asbestos or something leaks into the room and we're all poisoned?'

I stop myself before going full-terrorist attack.

'What if any of those things happen?' Gran asks.

I think about it for a moment. 'I suppose an ambulance would be called.'

'Do you want some of these, love?' She points her spatula at the pan, flips the eggs. 'I don't think I've seen you eat today.'

'No thanks, Gran. I'm not hungry.

'Not hungry? What's come over you?'

'I'm teaching tomorrow, like I said. I feel nervous.'

'Do you want to practise? You'll never plough a field by turning it over in your mind.'

'Can you pretend you're cycling?'

'I can pretend anything, can't we all?' She turns the heat off on the hob. 'I'll do it from my chair.' She slides the eggs onto a plate and pinches some salt to sprinkle on them.

I run through the outline while she eats. At the end, I put on the storytelling voice I used to do when I was a teacher, and ask her to close her eyes, imagine she's cycling into a field. There's a patch of ground where a garden hoe lies.

'Pick it up and loosen the fertile soil with it. Now, I'm passing you a bag of seeds where you can plant wishes in the ground. The land is so rich, these seeds will immediately germinate and sprout.'

She opens her eyes and smiles. 'I planted seeds praying that all my family would be happy.'

'You also ploughed a field in your mind,' I say.

She scratches her cheek and then offers me a cup of tea.

*

I sleep roughly until 5 a.m. Daylight lifts the room from darkness and the birds serenade each other with their morning song. Groaning, I turn around in the bed and fall into a deep sleep. It feels like a second has passed when my alarm sounds at 6 a.m.

I huff, willing it to not be time to get up. I stumble out of bed and dress in my gym clothes. I wear a long grey hoodie over them to hide my shape.

The road is quiet as I drive to town on an empty stomach. I try to figure out a decent excuse to tell Andrea for not teaching. I could get hurt somehow, fall down the stairs maybe, or I could have an issue with the car, drive it off the bridge into the river.

I continue on to the leisure centre.

The place has been opened by the cleaners. I check around reception, the office and the pool's deck for Andrea but there's no sign of her.

I go to the studio upstairs and set up the bikes, dragging one to the top and five others into a semi-circle around it. I connect the centre's iPod to the speakers and check the volume.

I want to go to the bathroom and vomit but instead I sit on the instructor's bike and act as if I'm Andrea, cycling and warming up my body for the session.

Colin's first in. He keeps his gaze averted, says hi and hops on a bike. He lays a big white towel across the handlebars.

Two minutes later, Djetska comes in. I say hello.

'Where is Andrea?' she asks.

'She'll be here shortly but I'm leading today.'

Djetska smiles and adjusts her bike. I wait for something, anything, some sort of interrogation but there's none. She pedals away.

Lorna enters and quickly waves, pushes down the seat on her bike and doesn't even seem to notice that I'm not Andrea.

There's no sign of Andrea.

I wait for another two minutes after the class is supposed to begin, in case latecomers arrive. I hit play on Andrea's playlist; the same music as usual blasts out over the speakers.

I clear my throat and increase the level on my bike.

Colin is sleepy looking but the two women are set.

'Sorry, hi, I'm Natalie, your instructor today. We've met before, if you remember me? I know you might be looking for Andrea and wondering what I'm doing here, and sorry about that, she's asked me to cover and...' They pedal and wait for instruction. I need to shut up apologizing and start, so I shout the plan for the session and they turn the level up on their bikes.

I blurt, 'We'll be doing approximately sixteen kilometres today. Or cycling to Milltown.'

It makes them laugh, which makes me laugh and that calms me down.

In keeping with this idea, at the midway point of the session, I say where we'd be geographically and joke about passing the villages en route and going off the track to climb a big hill on the way, with a good view of the Mayo–Galway border countryside from the top.

The class flies by.

We stretch during the cool down, and afterwards Colin says, 'I liked that Milltown thing.'

Lorna smiles tepidly and puts her bike away.

Djetska scratches the tip of her nose.

I say, 'We could go somewhere different next week, if you'd like?'

None of them reply, but they smile, or, aren't grimacing at least, and so it begins.

I shower and find Andrea downstairs.

'Where were you?' I ask.

'I was going to come in but thought it might put you off. It can be intimidating to be observed. Especially on your first try. Did it go okay?'

'I loved it, Andrea. Do you think I could try it again next week?'

'Why not? I wouldn't mind a sleep-in before Aqua Aerobics.'

'Thank you,' I say and squeal with excitement.

Andrea smiles.

In the café next door, I order breakfast to eat and pass the time before my office work begins at 9. While I'm waiting on my food, I click around the internet, see what Ireland's most interesting tourist attractions are. I copy and paste some things into my notepad app.

★

During the week, I try to select the right music to go with the session. It's still Andrea's instructions, with different tunes and a little script in between.

I practise the outline on Gran in her armchair, the evening before. This time I get her to close her eyes and imagine the whole thing. I play the music to check for consistency.

In the morning, the same trio rock in.

'Ye might recognize this one,' I say and hit play for *Riverdance*. During the slow bits, I begin my script. 'Today, we'll go for a cycle alongside the beautiful west coast. Looking inwards, see the flora and the fauna of the Burren, utterly unique in Europe and mystifying geologists since its discovery. Look at the craggy limestone landscape that has hundreds of plant and animal species, look at the deep blue and baby pink petals of the wildflowers. The yellow headed cowslips. Bats, badgers, feral goats, who knows what we'll find on the track. Maybe we'll see the slow-worm, the legless lizard who looks like a snake, one of our only Irish reptiles. Let's cycle through, on this specially created cycling trail for today.'

The trad music turns trance-like as it speeds up. 'Increase resistance. Keep increasing resistance.'

'There, look, the Aillwee Caves, let's take a dip in through them. The underground chill of them. Hear how echoey it is. Stalactites drip drops onto our heads as we cycle underneath. The cave is damp and black but there are lamps on our helmets. I want your resistance kept high for this for twenty seconds on, ten seconds off.'

They pedal away.

'Almost there,' I say towards the end of the climb. 'Now we're skidding a little on the rock underneath but see that big light outside, that's where we're going. Towards it. It's growing bigger and bigger. We can see the sunlight and the earth, the pale blue sky. Okay, everybody, we're back outside again, take a deep breath, let's visit the Cliffs of Moher. 'Formed by erosion from the mighty Atlantic. Let's cycle around the edges. Can you feel the sea breeze, can you smell the salt in the air, feel it tingle on your face as we cycle? Look out there at the sea over the cliffs, see the waves breaking on the shore, the white foam, and across the water, the Aran Islands. Let's sprint on this landscape. Go.'

And on I go.

The class flows until the end.

'Well, that was…' Colin says, and searches for a word. 'Different.'

I flinch. 'Yes. Sorry. I won't try it again?'

'Doesn't make any odds to me,' he says and wipes his red face with a towel.

Lorna asks, 'Will you be doing this class next week?'

I nod. 'I hope so.'

'Where are we going then?'

I hesitate for a moment. The three of them stare. 'New Orleans?' I say. I've always wanted to go there.

*

'Andrea, do you think I could try it again?' I ask. 'It went well earlier.'

She touches her cheek.

'It's so much fun,' I say.

'Well,' she says and ponders.

'I don't feel as heavy about things at home when I can think about the class.'

She pouts. 'I mean, it's still kind of dead around here, it should be no big deal until the autumn back to school boost. But if Mikolaj asks, say I've been in there with you.'


For the whole week, I refine things, correct the mistakes I made where I talked too little or too much.

Whenever I get a break through someone not being in the office or at reception, I research how to make the experience of being in New Orleans seem real. I decide we'll take a spin on the St Charles Avenue Streetcar line, and follow that route on what we'll see in the city. I look up what the place would smell like: mossy trees, fried chicken, marijuana, daiquiris, old mahogany, jasmine.

Maybe I can run it for the whole session this time, see how that goes.

I check out the menus of local restaurants, with their chargrilled oysters, fried fritter beignets, red beans and rice. I get details on the subtropical humid weather, the fragrance of the white flower magnolia and the brown pelican's flight pattern. I watch YouTube videos and read travel reviews to make everything seem more authentic. I make notes on New Orleans's history, art and politics and I find out exactly what local musicians play, try to match the BPM of their music to the exercises. Jazz, marching band, rhythm and blues.

I pay more attention in Mikolaj, Pat and Andrea's spin classes to familiarize myself with different techniques to try out on the bikes.

New Orleans is a success, and I smile the whole day after class. The evening is sunny as I drive to Gran's. I pull in the driveway and notice the back door open. The fire alarm sounds. I race inside. The fire has no guard on but there's only two sods burning in it. Potatoes turn black in a pot and acrid smoke from them is what has set the alarm shrieking. The water must have bubbled over, and is now dried onto the hob. I turn the hob off, move the pot onto the back ring. I open the oven door. It's cold and a big slab of raw beef sits in a tray with uncooked onions and green peppers. On the middle shelf, a piece of salmon is in a tinfoil pocket, for me.

'Gran,' I shout. 'Where are you?'

I run down the hall to her bedroom. The light's on but she's not there. I check the bathroom. It's empty and dark.

I rush around my room, the guest bedroom, the good

sitting room. I run to the front door and open it, checking out in the front garden, the back garden, by the shed, behind the shed, in the trees.

'Gran, are you here?'

I sprint down the potholed boreen, to see if she's gone off wandering. The blackberry brambles are dense on the verge. The strip in the middle of the road is overgrown with grass and dandelions.

Should I call someone, Mam, or the police, or the neighbours? I don't have my phone. It's in my handbag, on the passenger seat. Fuck.

I see a figure moving in the distance, near the bog. I run towards it. My lungs are burning. It's her. She's wearing a big red winter coat.

I bend over, hold my side, try to catch my breath. 'Gran, where the hell have you been?'

Sweat beads on her forehead. 'I needed to get something, what was it again?' She looks down at her hand, turns it and opens it. 'Yes. That was it. Matches. I needed matches.'

'Why? What did you need matches for?'

'For the oven, love. To make dinner.'

'But it's electric. Where did you get the matches from?'

'The old tractor down the bog.'

I don't know what tractor she's on about. I escort her back to the house. 'Are you not roasting in that coat?'

'I thought it might make rain.'

I help her out of it. Her skin is clammy.

There's a knot in my stomach but I have to say it. I've let this go on too long. 'Gran, I need to make the call. You're not safe here anymore. I can't do this on my own.'

'Natalie, please, calm down. You're a very highly stressed young woman, did you know that?'

'Of course I know that,' I say in a highly stressed way. 'But that's not the point. I need to ring Mam. I'm not able to look after you properly. I need support. I'm sorry. We have to figure something out.'

There's a big intervention. I'm riddled with guilt. I am useless and have nothing to do, except worry. And eat. I'm eating loads again, for breakfast, on first break, lunch.

Mam and her family have a meeting to figure out how to manage things. I feel like I've betrayed Gran, especially if what they decide is to put her in a nursing home. She'd hate that.

I'm not included in the decision making process, neither is Gran.

Andrea asks me if I'm okay, that I seem off. I nod half-heartedly and tell her a censored version of what's happening at home.

'Do you want to do another session? Would that cheer you up?'

'Yes, it would.'

After our next class, Andrea says I can continue doing the Wednesday mornings until the autumn schedule is drawn up.

\*

My mam and aunts and uncles who live locally devise a roster. They check Gran throughout the day.

Mam says that I've done a good job but they need to be more vigilant now. 'We hope she can die at home.'

'Jesus, don't say that.'

'Her heart isn't great, Natalie.'

'It's fine,' I say but shake my head.

'She could have a stroke or a heart attack easily. Or a fall. Let us know when you're not around and we'll figure out cover.'

'I'm always around sure.'

'Nat, you're turning thirty soon. You're still young and single. Go do things in the evening. This is our situation. Don't let it interfere with you living life.'

Other than swim or go to spin, there isn't really anything that I can think of doing.

It turns out to be a great pressure off me having the family support Gran. For the next while, I forget about my worry for her, my weight, about food, the future, and focus on making the Wednesday 6.35 a.m. spin classes an experiential session, with culture, education and fun. I even bring in different essential oils and a diffuser, to give the room some atmosphere.

Over the next few sessions, we visit Buenos Aires, the Serengeti, Bangkok. I practise the trips with Gran on the

Tuesday evening to run through everything before the morning sessions. I repeat them if I need to tidy my script because, after twenty minutes or so, Gran forgets we've done it.

'I never went any further than London,' Gran says. 'Your world is very big, Natalie.'

Kim rings me the Friday evening before my birthday and I'm excited to tell her what I've been at.

While I'm on the phone, I absently stand on the scales. I'm surprised to see the number on it, one because I've forgotten to weigh myself in nearly two months and two because it has changed. I'm not consciously eating better but I'm not as hungry all the time. I've gotten stronger, my thighs and shoulders have tightened and if I flex the muscles in them, I can feel muscle, not softness.

Kim says, 'Ah Nat, I was going to offer you the box room we have in our flat. We're going to be renting it soon. It sounds like you're having too much fun in the west to come back to Dublin?'


I lay out the five bikes as usual. This week we're travelling to the remote wilderness of Antarctica. I'll discuss the deathly silence that permeates Antarctica and how sound is the deepest form of touch, it goes inside the body. But I'll mention that in the silence, if we focus, we'll hear the cracking of ice sheets, a research helicopter landing, fur seals fighting, emperor penguin chicks hatching.

I don't bring any oils because the air in the Antarctic is so chilly and clean it's nearly devoid of smell.

I set everything up, say hello to the spinners. 'Wraith Pinned to the Mist and Other Games' is our warm-up song while we cross the ocean.

An older couple enter the room. I'm stunned to see new people in the class.

'Hi,' I say. 'Can I help ye?'

They wave me off and set themselves up on the bikes, adjusting the seat and handlebars.

I know that this pair are fitness fanatics and they'll want a tough no-frills workout. I've seen them at Pat's classes before and admired their energy. They must be in their late sixties, at least.

I dally around but decide to go for it. 'This session may be a bit different to what you're used to,' I say and start.

After we sail to the South Pole, I play the William Orbit Odyssey remix of 'Frozen' by Madonna to cross the terrain. I liven things up for a while with faster paced music. Then I play an Antarctic wind track and run them through the script about its desert terrain, how it's the windiest, driest and coldest place on Earth. I mention the Martian and lunar meteorites found in the ice, Shackleton's *Nimrod* expedition and, as we explore glaciers and icebergs, I talk about global warming's effect. What will the melting of Antarctica mean for Earth's future?

I observe the older couple throughout, to see if they're okay. I'm not worried about Djetska, Colin and Lorna.

At the end of the session, to lighten things up when the script is over, I play Vanilla Ice.

The couple approach me after class.

'How did you do that?' the man asks.

'It was rather trippy,' his wife says.

'I don't know. I used to make stuff up for kids I was teaching.'

'What an adventure. Where are we going next week?' the wife asks.

'We can pay you separately for this?' the man asks.

'Oh no, that's not necessary.'

'Of course it is. Know your worth, girl.'

'I don't think the leisure centre will allow that.'

'Nonsense, they'd never know.'

'I'll check with Andrea.'

'It's best we don't tell her, or anyone, about this. You work your magic and we'll keep all this safe.'

He forces me to take twenty euro, ten euro from him and ten from his wife. He introduces them as Boris and Pamela.

'You work your magic,' he says.


My uncle says, 'Natalie, explain to your grandmother that she needs to stop being stubborn,' as I enter the kitchen from the back door.

Gran is pale, looking away.

'What's wrong?' I ask.

'She's resisting a check-up,' he says. 'Talk some sense into her. I'll collect her in the morning.'

He takes his jacket off the coat-stand and leaves.

'I won't go to the doctor's, Natalie. I know if I go, I'm not coming home.'

'Don't say that. Don't convince yourself with that story.'

Gran throws a sod of turf onto the fire.

'I've seen it too many times. This is what happened with your granddad. With the neighbours. With half the bingo bus. They go to the doctor's and they don't come home.'

Her thick glasses magnify her blue eyes.

I bite the inside of my cheek. 'If that's the case, I can understand why you don't want to go. Look, I'm not going to try to persuade you but I can stick up for you if they're putting pressure on. I'm on your side.'

She smiles sadly, pats my hand. 'Thanks, Natalie. Ignore me, I'm an auld cailleach. I'll go. But it vexes me when they march in here and announce what I'm to do, like I'm their child and not the other way round.'


We're en route to Iguazu Falls in Brazil. I've some wonderful natural sounds and samba too. I open the class with 'Waterfall' by The Stone Roses.

Things kick off with a speedy warm up. A couple in matching blue shiny tracksuits enter the studio. They go to the store room and drag out a bike each, park them in the corner away from the semi-circle. Boris and Pamela tut.

I don't recognize them, not from other spin classes or reception.

They glare at me. I continue even though I'm unnerved.

'So today we're going to go hardcore with the hill-climbing, to get to the top of the falls. Okay, keep pedalling and turn your resistance up two turns. You should feel the resistance but not be stalled by it. Right. Let's start this climb.'

I see my reflection in the back mirror.

'Seated sprint… isolate your core and pedal… race…'

The class pant.

'Okay, we'll reduce our pace. Everybody breathe in deeply through your nose and out through your mouth. Keep your legs moving but we'll slow it down.'

They do what they're asked.

I play soothing waterfall sounds and describe this area of Brazil, the protection of the environment, the folklore and geological history of the falls. I talk about the rainbows that form due to the refraction of light against the mist caused by the formidable flowing of the water.

The blue tracksuit couple make faces to each other.

After class, the blue tracksuit woman stomps over. 'What in the hell was that?'

I feel cornered and step away from her. 'What?'

'Are you some sort of hippie?'

'No,' I say. 'I don't think I am.'

'Or a pagan? What was all that eco-centrism?'

'It was some information on the area we were visiting.'

'Less messing, more exercise,' the blue tracksuit man says.

Boris tips me twenty euro. His usual contribution.

'Why are you giving her money?' the blue tracksuit woman asks. 'Is this madness not covered in our membership? I refuse to pay for this demonic show.'

'It is covered. You don't have to pay. He doesn't have to pay.' I try to hand the money back.

He addresses the woman. 'Claudia, we should all be paying. This young woman is trying to do something different. It is very typical of you and Timothy to come and ruin a club with your conservatism.'

Timothy sniffs. 'Not like the Bolsheviks ye are?'

Djetska, Colin and Lorna slink out of the room. Boris brings up an issue at the golf club with Timothy and Claudia. A shouting match ensues between the old couples. The women seem more likely to get violent than their husbands. I enter into it to mediate but I'm gently shoved away by Pamela. I get the sense this fight has more going on with it than my spin class.

They eventually leave and I tidy the studio.


Gran notices my sadness in the evening. She tries to soothe me. 'Natalie, you have to remember, people like different things. You have to let them be. It takes all sorts to make a world. Wouldn't we be bored senseless if we were all the same?'

'But I don't know how to cope. I'm like a little girl when I get upset.'

'You've a big heart.'

'There's real issues on this planet. People suffer so much, they don't have rights, or votes, or freedom. Some people don't have their health. Some live in warzones. And then there's me. A useless eejit. I don't even have proper reasons to be sad.'

'Natalie, don't break your shin on a stool that's not in your way.'

'But I can't seem to help it. Then I make myself feel bad about feeling bad for not having it bad enough to feel like this. I'm stuck revolving in a guilt circle.' I sigh dramatically. 'It's a bit Irish, isn't it?'

She has an amused look on her face. 'Let everyone else be with their lot, and you yours.'

Timothy and Claudia snigger throughout the next class, a trip to Greece. They correct me during it on details and places they've already been to, from the time they holidayed on a first class cruise to Santorini.

Boris and Pamela defend me, saying that if they don't like it they should piss off.

'Why don't you piss off?' Claudia replies.

'Nobody piss off,' I say.

'Well, maybe we will,' Pamela says. 'It doesn't bode well for a day opening it with your awful attitudes.'

Timothy flicks his wrist. 'Off you go.'

Boris gives a twenty euro tip and says they will not be returning. I make a plea but he acts like he can't hear me. His decision is made. The end.

Lorna is behind him, queuing to speak to me. Boris leaves and she smiles awkwardly.

She rubs her neck and says, 'I'm not sure about these sessions. They've gone a bit unpredictable. I might go to Boxing Bootcamp on Wednesday lunchtimes instead.'

'Sorry, Lorna,' I say. 'I didn't mean for—' but she walks away.

I shower and feel dejected. In the local café, I order pancakes. After pancakes, I have a vegetarian breakfast – the large one.


I prepare a spin class for Russia the following week but the older couple bring Mikolaj with them.

'See?' they say and point angrily.

I flip off my Russian music and switch my phone to a normal playlist. Mikolaj bloody comes from near there. I can't go through with it. I abandon my script plan and panic, trying to conduct a normal spin class, but the first song that comes on my phone is from *Spirit of the Wolf* Native American meditation music I played a month before, when we went to South Dakota.

Mikolaj is dismissive of what's happening.

I get off my bike and apologize, go over to skip the track; a generic pop song rescues me. I revert to Andrea's initial class structure. The same old routine of all the spin classes in the leisure centre. It goes okay until I realize my phone's on shuffle. Sufjan Stevens' lamenting voice comes over the speakers singing a bleak song about his mother's death. The song ends with a loop of him saying we're all going to die. Mikolaj signals for me to leave by glaring at me and then the door, repeatedly. I get off the bike and pull my phone out of the speaker.

I turn at the door, see Mikolaj adjusting the instructor's bike and taking over the class.

In the café, my heart drums and I order a ton of food.

I imagine myself getting bollocked by Pat in the morning when he's in. Andrea's disappointment. Mikolaj's sneer. And I'll be numb, busted out from eating, overfull from everything I've ordered, feeling worthless. Helpless.

Fuck that. There's no need to make everything worse for myself.

I call the waitress back and cancel. Change my order to a coffee and avocado toast.

I know as I walk back, something will happen, but I feel curiosity more than dread.

Pat calls me and Andrea in for a meeting after morning break.

Mikolaj is there too, contemptuous.

'This isn't a magic bike carpet ride. We are not children. Do you know even how to do this job in a correct form?' Mikolaj asks. 'You think because you've attended a few cardio sessions you're a coach? Are you qualified for this work?'

'No,' I say. I keep my head down.

Pat says, 'I have to report it, Natalie. It's irresponsible of Andrea and you to do this. What sort of playlist was that?'

'I had other music lined up, but didn't want to – when I saw Mikolaj—'

'Don't put this on me,' Mikolaj says.

'No, I wasn't going to, I just…' I flounder.

Andrea's head is still but she glances sidelong at us all.

Pat says, 'Okay, explain yourselves, ladies. What the hell was going on? You should already know that people are not interested in anything other than a workout.'

'I wanted it to be more than a spin class. Like a free travel experience, a history lesson, an adventure,' I say.

'I thought it was a regular HIIT workout she was doing. I wish I'd known what you were up to,' Andrea says and turns to me, 'I'd have come along. It sounds like good craic.'

Pat says, 'Natalie, creativity is wonderful in its proper context. But this is a county council job. I was told you were taking money for it? You're not a qualified fitness instructor. What if there'd been an accident? We'd have no cover for it. All our jobs would be on the line.'

Red rises to my cheeks. 'They said it was a tip. I didn't want it. They wouldn't take it back.'

Andrea clears her throat. 'It's my responsibility, Pat. I started this. I should have told you that we'd made this arrangement. I thought it'd be a good opportunity for her to learn to instruct while it was low season.'

'How are we going to limit damage control here? I refuse to put my neck on the line over this,' Pat says.

'I'll go,' I say. 'I'm not qualified. I kept pestering Andrea to give me more sessions. She didn't want to. Tell them that I tricked you into it or something, Pat, if they're asking. I'll write my formal notice up this afternoon.'

Outside the office, I say to Andrea, 'I should have told you I was doing mad stuff in the classes.'

'No, I'm sorry, Nat. I should have been supervising. I'd never seen you so happy. You had some direction. You were luminous. I didn't want to take the classes back off you. Truthfully, I was enjoying the sleep-ins.'

'I got too carried away,' I say.

'You were passionate and, you know what, you were a good coach. Djetska said it to me. You encouraged them. You've got something, Nat, develop it.'

'But it's daft.'

'Why?'

'I don't know. I'm not in good enough shape to be doing this work.'

'Who says?'

I'm silent. Who did say?

Mam's tears trickle down her cheek and tremble on her jaw. 'There's a problem, Natalie. Gran fainted this morning so we brought her to the doctor. He said her heart may not be pumping hard enough for blood to get around her body. Her blood pressure is quite low.'

'Oh right.'

'Yes.' She bows her head. 'He stabilized it but we'll be going back to him again in the morning to see if she's deteriorating. If a bed gets freed up in the hospital, he'll probably send her in. Will you pack a bag with her in a while, just in case we've to go straight? She refused to let me do it. She might be okay with you. I want her to have her own things with her. Beads, a notebook, a picture of Granddad, just in case. I'm going to head home and ring Dolores in Oz and the lads in England. They might want to come back to Ireland now as soon as they can.'

'Just in case,' I say.

Mam's face is pained, she squints. 'Enjoy the evening with her, won't you?'

'I always do.'

Gran sits in her chair. I soak her up.

She asks, smiling, 'How was your day, love?'

'You know what? It was fine.' I stress the fine. 'I learned some things about myself.'

'That's lovely.'

'I quit my job too. Or resigned. Or was forced to resign. Or maybe I was fired. Maybe all those things.'

Gran looks concerned. 'And you have other work found?'

'I'll find something. I had to make sure my friend's job is safe. She has two young kids. Anyway, it's probably time.'

'What will you do now, pet?'

'I don't know, Gran. Kim offered me a room in Dublin. But maybe I should stay with you?'

'You will not.'

'Why not?'

'No, Natalie. You're a young woman and you need to spread your wings.'

'That's okay. I like it here.'

'It's time to go. I love you and I always will but you need to move on, live your life. I said this same thing to your aunt Dolores when she mentioned Australia. Go. I never got to see the world. Your generation can. Go and enjoy it.'

I don't want everything to change again, even though I know it's about to. 'Will you even remember I'm gone?'

'You won't be gone. I won't be gone either. Won't we always be in each other's hearts?'

I hold her hand for a while. Her tiny fragile bones under mine.

'Mam asked me to ask you to pack a bag, Gran. In case you've to go to hospital tomorrow, it might be good to have what you want there with you.'

She agrees.

'But first, do you want to go on a trip?'

'Yes!' she says.

Her delight makes me smile.

'I love these. Where are we going, Natalie?'

'Back to 1930s Ireland. When you were young and ye cycled everywhere and the time you met Granddad. You can tell me all the details again if I forget them. Ye'd go to the dance hall near the mountain on a Saturday night, all perfume and curled hair. The time Granddad picked you out of all the girls but you made him wait before you said yes.'

'Always make them wait for a short whileen, they like that.'

'You'd put the bet on the All Ireland final, and won ten pounds on it. And every Sunday, ye'd make black pudding from the pig you killed yourselves.'

'It was the loveliest black pudding, Natalie. I remember it well. We'd be coming back from mass, through the fields, and Daddy would be there waiting for us, laughing.'

She begins, her memory crystal clear when she returns to her teens. I sit back in the chair and Gran takes me on one of her trips for the last time.

# The Lepidopterist

Kim and Pete decide that it's time I seek a love like theirs.

We're sharing a lazy Saturday meal, sourdough loaf, mackerel curry and a big bowl of mixed Russian salad. Pete pours us a glass of merlot each. February light spills through the open window and after the grief-stricken winter, the succulent plant on the sill shoots new bright green leaves in all directions. Birdsong harmonizes with the city's din; a far-off pneumatic drill cracks the stone of a footpath, lunchtime traffic accumulates at lights, kids laughing and crying and shouting, eighteen moods a minute.

'Go on an app,' Kim says enthusiastically.

Pete adds, 'Don't overthink it.'

Kim asks him to play a song. He plugs his phone into the speaker and puts on a Drake playlist on low volume. He nuzzles her neck and they sway together to the beat.

I take a sip of wine and hold it on my tongue, consider things. It's not that they're smug in their comfortable four-year-strong relationship, in their let's-stay-in ways, their muffling groans lest I hear them through my box room wall – they just want me to be happy. As happy as they are.

'Find yourself some action, Natalie,' Kim says. 'Why not, it's 2016 after all. Can't a woman seek a willing man in the cyber world? Hook ups. Netflix and chill. It's all the rage.'

She says she'd be at it too if she hadn't Pete. He says he'd be at it too if he hadn't Kim.

A chill breeze rolls in through the open window, lifting the net curtain in the kitchen. I rub the goosebumps on my arm. Pull my sleeves down.

'I suppose it would be nice to meet someone,' I cede. It's been a long time since I had any semblance of a romance.

'You can't beat it,' Kim says and kisses Pete's head. He gives her a swift smile.

Before we finish eating, I download an app on my phone and open my laptop on the kitchen table to trawl through my social media account for decent pictures. Kim gathers the dishes and scrapes the leftover curry into Tupperware. Pete doles out two scoops of mint chocolate ice-cream into bowls for each of us.

'I suppose I've to make it look like I've a wonderful and varied lifestyle,' I say and scratch my head.

'Use that one as your main picture,' Kim says, pointing at a portrait of me laughing. 'It's beautiful.'

'I look like a loose heifer in it.'

'Do you know how insulting it is when you won't take a compliment?'

'Sorry.'

I add a group picture from my cousin's wedding, one where I wore a navy jumpsuit and hair piece and stood in the back row.

'Delete that, Nat,' Pete says.

'Why?'

'It's too hard to tell which one you are. Your family looks alike. And you need to put in a full body one.'

'What? Why?'

'So there's no surprises. Trust me. A bit of cleavage would go a long way too.'

Kim slaps his hand playfully. He loads the dishwasher and Kim wipes down the counter and the table.

I scan through the app. It's pretty shallow. There's lots of headless, topless men who are 'looking for fun', 'here for fun', 'just trying to find some fun'. The bare-torsoed fun police.

Pete takes his phone out of the speakers and the room is silent except for the slosh and pump of the dishwasher. I look up to see the kitchen sparkling.

'We're off to town, Natalie. Gonna have a browse in the shops before Pete starts work. Catch you later.'

I nod at them and flick through profiles again, trying to guess what a man could be like from the handful of photos and one-sentence tag line he chose to present himself.

The room grows dimmer and dimmer until it's hard to see. I check the time. Two hours since Kim and Pete left. My thumb aches from the repetitive swiping motion. My vision is blurred and squaring. This is exhausting. I decide to put my phone away on the next fella that I click Yes to.

Vincent is his name. He's a bearded, sandalled type. He smiles broadly and drinks a bottle of root beer as he sits leaning against a tree. His profile says he likes times past, open-minded people and that he's much too old-fashioned for this type of gallivant; however, if I like perusing his profile, to merry up his day and give him a right swipe.

There's something about him, maybe it's the shoulders, the muscle tone through his blazer. He probably likes Vietnamese coffee, craft beers and all things decreed cool by edgy podcasters and indie magazines.

Still, his profile's more intriguing than a dick pic. I swipe right, put my phone on charge and go for a walk around the block to touch base with the real world again.


A couple of hours later, Kim and I channel surf and graze on popcorn when my phone vibrates. Notification.

It's a match.

Vincent likes me back. I feel flushed with excitement.

'What do I do now?' I ask Kim.

'Message him.'

'Should I wait, he says he's old-fashioned?'

'How is he old-fashioned if he's on Tinder? Seriously.'

I compose and delete a few messages. I don't know how to initiate.

'How do I do it?'

'You type out "hi". That's all, Natalie.'

I take some deep breaths and type 'hi'. It looks so awkward and needy, two little letters, boring and plain, nothing to go with them, nowhere to go after them except for another 'hi'.

Then what? Then would I have to come up with something else? I delete it and sigh.

Kim flicks the station to a Saturday night chat show. A bunch of movie stars sit on a couch. The excitable audience cheers anytime any of the stars speak about anything.

I jump when my phone buzzes.

A message from Vincent.

How now, fair lady?

I clamp my hands to my chest.

Kim laughs at me, and at him.

'Stop, Kim, I'll get too embarrassed.'

'Okay, okay, I won't say anything except don't reply too quickly.'

I watch the rest of the show with her, not paying attention to any of its mumble-whoop.

When it ends, I wait for the weather forecast then say goodnight and go upstairs. I lie on the single bed in my tiny bedroom and reply to Vincent.

We have a nice flow in our conversation. We over and back until midnight.

In the coming days, I find myself looking forward to his messages and enjoy thinking of responses to them. I am filled with anticipation and nerves at the prospect of meeting him when he finally asks me out.

He's nearly five years older than me and very, very quirky. I haven't had sex in thirty-seven months.

We arrange to meet at the Unitarian Church, to go for a nice picnic.

I alight the tram and spot him across the road, in front of the neo-gothic church. My stomach sinks a little.

He wears tweed trousers and smokes a vape pipe. He's like someone out of a Dickens novel, except for the SuperValu bag-for-life he's holding.

I take a deep breath and walk across the road. The sun creeps out from behind the clouds and it's warm on my skin.

Vincent kisses me jovially on each cheek. He smells of lavender and wood.

'Are you coming from some sort of historical re-enactment?' I ask and he blushes, thanking me profusely.

Despite all this, the date goes quite well as we sit on a woollen blanket in the Green. He pours a turnip and leek soup from a flask into a cup, hands it to me.

'I made it myself,' he says.

He lays out some homemade bread, smoked herring and cold meats. For sweets, a fruit salad with yogurt, and treacle cake with ginger jam. He has another flask with mint leaf tea and a glass bottle of iced water with lemon.

I'm moved by the effort he's put into it.

He says things are 'spiffing' and 'marvellous'. When he curses he says 'blazes to this'.

I ask him, 'Where are you from?' unable to place his accent. I wonder has he fallen from the sky like Mary

Poppins, if he's some sort of commitment-phobe time traveller too?

'Oh, out yonder,' he says, waves his hand behind him. He takes out a gold pocket watch and checks the time. 'A small village in Meath.'

He walks me back to the Luas stop and unlocks his Remington bike. 'Can I get your number for WhatsApp, maybe?'

'Sure,' I say. The interest is nice.

Kim fries onions and peppers when I get home. 'How was the date?'

The kitchen sizzles.

'He was kind of like someone from Victorian times.'

'Natalie, hipsters are cute.'

'They sure try hard.'

'You're judging again.'

'Kim, you don't know what it's like being single these days. And you're judging me if you're saying I'm judgemental.'

She considers this. 'Maybe I am.'

'Anyway, we had a good time. He made a picnic, mostly from scratch. It tasted great. Then he put on a shadow puppet show for me.'

'He did what?'

'I know.'

'What was that?'

'With his hands. In Stephen's Green. It was mad. But maybe a bit beautiful too.' I face my palms towards me and cross my wrists and thumbs, flexing my fingers and raising my arms as I show Kim a flying bird shadow puppet.

'Jesus Christ,' Kim says, her eyes open wide. 'Arty farty, eh?'

I go to the sink and fill the kettle. 'He thought I was being racy with my ankles exposed.'

'Oooh.'

'His moustache was in a debonair style, like a young Sean Connery. He was kind of strange, maybe in a deliberate way, maybe not. It was like he thought it was 1900. But he works for a tech start-up, so, yeah, it's all a bit bizarre.'

'Give him a chance. You're too quick to dismiss men. There was nothing wrong with Benjy.'

'He couldn't remember my name.'

'Yeah and you had a problem with his clothes too.'

'Aw, Kim, he was dressing like a teenager, but I didn't care about the skater dude thing. It was the being stoned all the time that put me off. I had to keep re-introducing myself.'

'He was handsome.'

'He wasn't even lucid.'

'Well, what about John?'

'He shouted at the waitress. Called her thick. To her face. For mixing up a sauce on his burger. It was awful, so embarrassing to be associated with him. What a bollocks. You know the phrase, watch how someone treats staff and then you'll know the real them. John was a top class bastard in sheep's clothing.'

'Back to the clothes again. Always clothes with you.'

'It's not. I meant John seemed normal but he was a prick.'

'More reason to give Vincent a chance.'

'True.'

'The clothes do not make the man. What about Dave, actually?'

'Yeah, there was nothing wrong with him but I didn't fancy him.'

'Do you fancy Vincent?' Kim shakes soy sauce over her veg.

I think about it. 'Yeah, I do, I suppose. His chest is broad and his shoulders are all squared.' I make the shape of them with my hands. 'He's quite hot.'

'Be open. I mean, to all aspects of him and his personality. You must have cobwebs at this point.'

The kettle trembles in its cradle, giddy, as the water in it boils.

'I reckon I'd have muscle memory when it comes down to it.'

'Of course. Hey, Natalie, don't be looking at what's wrong with people, look at what's right with them. It'll make life a shitload easier.'

I meet him for a second date. We watch a hypnotist's show near O'Connell Street. Bit offbeat but I enjoy it. I wonder if the hypnotized people are planted actors.

'It's fake?'

Two women play air guitar and drums like they're in a world famous rock band headlining the biggest concert of their life. Another person thinks his belt is a snake coiled around his waist. His panic is palpable. He's frozen, but tries to signal for help with his eyes.

Vincent disagrees. 'People are suggestible and most of us don't question our own thoughts or belief systems. It's why marketing works its magic on us so easily.'

Next person on stage believes he's an alien and speaks in an extra-terrestrial language. The language is comprised of coughs and squeaks along with K-sounding words. When the hypnotist looks for a new volunteer, I shrink into my seat and look down at my red ankle boots.

Vincent takes my hand in his, gives it a squeeze, to indicate that it's safe, someone else has been chosen. We hold hands for the remainder of the show.

He walks me back to my Luas stop. The moon is yellowish and huge. He kisses my cheek. I turn my face, look directly at him and he dips to kiss my lips.

There's a heat in the moment that I didn't expect.

On the tram, I look out the window over Harcourt, Ranelagh, Beechwood, wondering if the Victorian style is him going through a phase like when I was in university and wore thongs, or drank Smirnoff Ice, or overplayed Damian Rice's O. I'm confused. I enjoyed the kiss. Really enjoyed it. Maybe I should meet him again. I will. If he asks. But for the third date, I decide that drinking is going to have to be done.

Vincent is less outrageous with the pints. He becomes a bit more Meath. He's funny, his guard is down. In The Stag's

Head, we bump into some people who belong to him and they seem quite normal and to like him a lot.

When he invites me to his, I accept. He unlocks the front door to his ground floor apartment and flicks on the lights. He has a home gym in his front room.

'It's styled after Eugen Sandow,' he says as I check it out.

'Who's that?'

'The Father of Bodybuilding.'

The barbell's weights are iron balls. There's a pull-up bar on the wall and a rickety-looking seated leg press machine near the window. In the corner, a red Everlast punch bag is hung, and it's jarringly modern against everything else.

I follow him through to the kitchen. Empty iron pots and pans sit on top of a woodburning stove. Assorted china plates and cups fill a wooden dresser against the wall. Vincent offers me a sloe gin that he brewed himself.

I read a poem framed on the wall:


'The Shortest and Sweetest of Songs'
by George MacDonald


Come
Home.


I drink some of the red-coloured gin and it's harsh on my throat. Vincent comes closer to me. I swallow another mouthful and he takes my glass and puts it down, then leans in. He kisses me with passion and it's not long before we fumble down the hall to his bedroom.

We strip in an ungainly way, and Vincent tears a condom wrapper with his teeth. I lie on the bed and he scuttles in beside me. He leans on one arm and tries to smooth the condom on with his free hand.

He grumbles and lies down, using both his hands. I wait.

'I think this contraption is inside out,' he says with a sigh. He throws it onto the floor.

I slow my breathing. 'These things happen. Do you have any others?'

'I do, yeah, but…' he says and pauses, looks down.

I follow his eyes.

'Blazes to this.'

His body is rigid with disappointment. I move closer, cuddle into him. I fall asleep with my head on his chest.


We try again in the morning and the sex is decent. I feel so relieved that my body is okay and it's happened mostly without awkwardness.

He pets my hair. His eyes are green but have brown on the outer circle, his eyelashes are lengthy. His bed has the same lavender scent as his skin.

'I read a book on hysterical paroxysm. Would you like to try?'

'Sounds painful,' I say. 'What is it?'

'It was an orgasm that women achieved by doctors trying to calm them down.'

'Yeah?'

'I saw some illustrations. You can tell me to stop at any time.'

'Okay, give it a go so.'

He hits somewhere inside that makes me involuntarily shudder, my voice is faraway from the point I'm aware of, where he touches me. Is this my g-spot? My breath is hard and short and loud. I'm not sure I've ever felt anything as pleasurable.

I lie unmoving for about ten minutes after, except for trying to settle my breathing. I suddenly remember something, bolt out of the bed in one swift motion. 'I better go to the bathroom.'

Though it's unsexy to break the moment, a UTI for the following days is even more unappealing.

'Second door on the right,' he says.

I almost limp there. The bathroom's checked black and white tiles are cool on my bare feet. My breathing echoes. I feel love-hormoned up.

I check my face in the mirror, clean the black make-up that's bled under my eyes and swallow some of the minty paste in a container on the sink.

I take the first door on the left but it's a wrong turn. This is not his bedroom.

It's like walking into the Natural History Museum with

the smell of cosmoline and framed butterfly displays. I gasp in horror at them. Every wall is covered. The butterflies have a little marker underneath saying their species' common and Latin name and where they come from. The Sooty Cooper from Germany. The White Barred Charaxes from Mozambique.

In the centre of the room is a big mahogany desk with files and instruments. I wander around naked, looking at everything.

There's a guidebook and a jar with a trapped yellow winged butterfly bumping into the glass as it tries to fly, to escape. A moment from a creepy old film drops into my mind, something I saw years ago. I can't quite visualize it, it's at the edge of my memory but has a disturbing feel to it. It was about a butterfly collector who murders the girl he caught when butterflies weren't enough for him.

Is Vincent going to try to kill me? Ugh. I slept with him. This is why. This is why they say not to have sex with strangers. And *Silence of the Lambs*, doesn't that have some butterfly psychopath too?

How am I going to make a quick getaway?

I go back to his bedroom and gather my clothes from the floor. I dress hastily. Vincent looks childlike as he naps. I feel a pang of connection towards him.

'Something's wrong?' he asks, sleepy-mouthed.

'No.'

'Nat, was it me? Did I put pressure on you?'

'No. No. I wanted it too.'

'I can make you some breakfast? I have these delicious lychees from the Temple Bar markets.'

'Vincent, I feel a bit funny.'

'Why?'

'I saw all the butterflies.'

'And?'

'Do you collect them or something?'

'Is it a problem?'

'Isn't it murder?'

'No. Not really.' He sits up. 'If the collection is created from a species that isn't endangered, there's no problem.'

'It's kind of murder.'

'Natalie, insects are dynamic. I'm sustaining them. I wouldn't harm them. I've been growing some alder buckthorn in my back garden to cultivate them.'

'Why?'

'Because I could sell them to collectors on the internet. And then I could opt out of things and survive financially. The appreciation of lepidoptera is my passion.'

Full-time butterfly murdering.

'It's all ethical. I swear.'

I slip on my ballerina pump shoes.

'When you were younger, Nat, did you not go into the woods with a net, collecting?' Vincent asks.

'No. I watched MTV or went to the playground or visited friends.'

'Town life. When I was a boy, and I've realized that I probably knew more about myself and the world when I was eight than now, twenty-seven years later, I'd go outside and sometimes I could see butterflies flying and glimmering in the sunshine like gold coins in the sky. We'd all these wildflowers and bushes growing abundantly around our farmhouse. Nature gifting us with beauty, ceaselessly.'

'But you grow butterflies to kill them?'

'Nowadays, where can we find this pure environmental awe amidst the concrete, the noise? Kids are hard-pressed to know much about nature outside of their classrooms. They can't even climb trees without their parents filling in forms. And even then, they can't be fucked.'

'It makes me worried to think you kill things.'

'Natalie, the thing you should be worried about is apathy. People don't care about the destruction of our countryside. Of all our green areas being sold for property and roads. That's the actual killing that's going on. The killing of our environment. And these children now being raised hooked on screens and not knowing or giving a fuck about the natural world. What will happen when they become adults?'

He's nearly crying. I sit beside him and stroke his arm.

'I never knew someone to care so much about something,' I say.

'It's dreadfully unfashionable these days to care. Look. I really want to see you again. I want to bring you out collecting. Experience it with me. Be open-minded.'

I think about us, running around a meadow, the sun shining as we wear white and frolic. It seems quite a nice fantasy. 'Okay.'

He kisses me zealously. I'm not sure whether to get back into bed.

I leave his place and go, light-headed, into the white-skied day.


Kim is crying in the kitchen.

'What's wrong?'

'We've ended it, Nat,' she bawls.

'What?' I feel like I'm going to fall over.

'Yeah. We had a chat. I never knew. Pete doesn't want to have kids, now, in the future, ever. I didn't know. There's no point us staying together. How did we not talk about this?'

'Oh fuck.'

'Yeah. I'm not saying I want kids but I'm open to it. I'm open to what might happen. He's not. No way. Not with me. Not ever.'

I think about Vincent. How is it that overnight, I'm more advanced in a relationship than Kim?

We spend the day watching full series of comedy shows. She sporadically bursts into loud sobs. She leaves the room to clean her face and apologizes when she comes back. Her skin is blotchy and her eyelids are swollen.

'It's okay, Kim, let it out. Will I order some takeaway?'

'I'm not hungry. Don't want food.' She sniffles and rubs her eyes. 'So how was the third meeting? I'm sorry, I never asked you. I forgot.'

'It was good. Or weird. I'm not sure.'

'What do you mean?'

'I don't think he's a hipster anymore. I don't think this is about image. It's lifestyle. He's into the olden ways. I don't know if I am.'

'You're not seeing him again?'

'No. I didn't say that. We had sex. It was good, Kim. Really good.'

'Yeah?'

I nod. 'Kind of amazing in the end.'

'You are seeing him again?'

'I dunno, Kim. He's a bit strange but the power of the O compels me.'

'The power of the O would do that indeed,' she says and cries again.


Vincent wears a cyclist's uniform – black T-shirt and black pedal pusher-style pants for our collecting date. I discover he gets his clothes bespoke sewn for him.

We take a public bus out to a field close to a river, somewhere on the outskirts of Dublin near Meath.

We walk to where the sun and shade meet and stalk an area for butterflies. It could be very romantic in the setting, with the long grass and flowers beginning to bloom, but Vincent is intensely focused on the activity and everything feels formal.

He creeps up on a butterfly resting on a leaf. He positions his net under it then swings it up and turns the handle. The butterfly is caught. He folds the net over so the butterfly can't escape.

He has a box to persuade the butterfly into and, when it goes in, he slides the lid across it.

'Do you want to try to identify it?' He hands me the box and an Audubon guidebook.

'Do you not know what it is?' I ask.

'I do,' he says. 'But it's fun for you.' He investigates the underside of the leaves for eggs.

I identify it as a holly blue. I feel slightly nauseous as it struggles to spread its wings. It's trapped, batting the glass, dying.

I open the lid and the butterfly whooshes upwards at me, nearly brushing against my face and flies away.

'Vincent, I don't want to do this,' I say. I back away, holding the guidebook out for him to take.

Kim springs on me when I return to the flat. She has a full face of make-up on but is in her pyjamas.

'We should go somewhere. I've been thinking about getting the hell away from Dublin for a couple of weeks until these disturbing feelings have passed. You know that saying, "Don't sleep around in your hometown."'

'No?'

'Well, it's a saying. Look at what travel's done for you. It's made you a much more together person. You even joined a gym. You even instructed lessons. In fitness.'

'Travel forced me to be my own friend because it was too fucking lonely not to be.'

'Yes. That. I need that. An enormous part of me has been ripped away. The Pete part of me. It's gaping and bloody and I don't want to be a mess in Dublin. I have to live here.'

'Aren't we so privileged.'

'Maybe but let's go. You're not committed to those temp jobs you do here. You like travel.'

'Where?'

'Peru?'

'I don't know, Kim.'

She pulls a baby voice on me. 'All I've done for you over the years. Can you not return me some kindness? Remember when you were this way? How can you forget that?'

'I don't forget it, Kim, I'm grateful to you, you know that.'

'I know but please, please, I don't want to go alone. I'm too scared. Do you not want to go because you've a boyfriend now? Is that the story?'

'I don't have a boyfriend.'

'You want to stay here with your boyfriend and chase butterflies around the Phoenix Park with not a care in the world?'

'No. He's not my boyfriend. I doubt we'll even meet again.'

'Well, let's go, the two of us.'

'I promise I'll consider it but let me sleep on it.'

'How did it go with Vincent today?'

I sigh. 'I don't think he's right for me. I don't get him. I'd only try to change him and that's not fair.'

'Will you have a go on your Tinder, let me see who's out there?'

'Okay,' I say. She nestles in beside me on the couch. I click into the app and left swipe a few profiles.

And there he is.

I try to turn the phone away but she's seen it.

'My fucking god, show me that, Natalie,' Kim says and goes for my hand.

'No, Kim. Don't.' I throw the phone away from me, the other side of her, onto a cushion. 'It was nothing.'

'Show me the fucking phone right fucking now,' Kim screeches.

My heart pounds. I don't move.

She pounces and takes the phone from the cushion. She opens her mouth. A high decibel banshee shriek comes from her.

'That absolute bastard.' She makes the piercing noise

again. 'He's using pictures I took of him. He doesn't even have hair anymore.'

'Kim, I'm so sorry,' I say.

'That picture is from our anniversary, when we went to Porto, three years ago.' She holds the phone up to me. 'The bald catfish lying mother—' and then she breaks down. She falls onto the floor, crying hard, her whole body heaving.

I left swipe Pete and turn my phone off. I go down onto the floor beside her and rub her back.

Peru it is.

# Rub

'We rise at 3 a.m., have breakfast, and pack. Then we go to the permit controls, wait to enter and get to the Sun Gate for dawn. It is the famous viewpoint for Machu Picchu, the one you see in pictures.

There's a murmur around the table. We're excited, and sad, that this experience is drawing to a close.

The porters serve a watery vegetable soup and a tough brown bread for starters. I slurp the liquid from the metal bowl and lube up bread with oil instead of butter.

Our tour guide, Eduardo, eats with us and continues, 'I want you to know that we need to be awake and out on time. If the porters miss their trains, they will have to pay over a hundred dollars to get the next train. This is paltry money to people like you, but to them, it would leave them in debt and their families would starve for the coming year.'

Someone groans. I want to as well.

The porters clear our dishes and then serve dinner. A tray with an array of peppers is passed around. I take a bite of one and it's so hot it makes inside my ears swell. I spoon a portion of rice, baked trout and two types of potato onto my plate.

The food is simple, delicious.

I eat mindfully, savour each morsel.

Eduardo notes this. 'You eat slowly for a Westerner. You give thanks to the food. This rice, for example, contains the bones of your ancestors. It was grown in the earth where your ancestors turned to soil. We thank them for the sustenance.'

Kim spits her rice onto her plate and wipes her tongue.

I look at my forkful, try to see the rice as the bones of my grandfather, a man who cycled to Dublin and back for the weekend, a man who climbed Croagh Patrick barefoot, praying. Those times in Ireland, everyone guilty for existing. For their human urges. For being Irish.

The bones of Gran too, maybe her as a young woman before she lost her memory, my age, the age she was when she had my mother. Her terrific auburn hair, her sense of adventure even though she had so many kids young. I get a sudden flashback of when we were small, when she'd create treasure hunts for us. She sent us collecting leaves and flowers outside, tracing them into our copybooks and then pressing them. She told us of ringfort fairies and the changelings. My grandmother's imagination was wild. Maybe I was more like her than I ever realized when she was alive.

'Thanks, Gran,' I say, and eat the mouthful of rice.

Halfway through dinner, Eduardo stands and begins his nightly speech, about the poverty that the porters live in. He's totally cockblocking Federico, the Amazonian who Kim flirts with.

I notice when Eduardo makes his plea, his eyes glaze over and the words flow. It's rehearsed, a performance.

He discusses the tips that we're expected to give the porters considering we're people who go back to lands of clean water, political stability, economic growth.

'These men, as you have seen, work so hard. They carry twenty-five kilos of your things in order to make this experience easy for you. They carry all the food you are eating right now. The cooking utensils. Your tents. Your sleeping bags. This tent. The seats you sit on. This table. This cutlery. These men clap you into camp and have refreshments ready. They do not complain and yet they are paid twenty dollars per day for their ox-like work. You have seen what they wear, some of them carry loads in sandals, in ragged jeans and T-shirts. Twenty dollars per day. You probably spend twenty dollars on your lipstick, on your parking spot when you go to your malls to buy your new TVs and new watches. The men work hard. Remember that, when you decide what your tip will be. Compare your tip to what work you do to earn money. Remember this, there are less fortunate people in the world than you.'

He wipes his face of imaginary tears and goes to the flap of the tent, turns around dramatically and pleads, 'Remember,' before exiting.

I stop eating. My hands shake. Everyone is silent around the dinner table except for Konrad, who asks, with a full mouth, 'Is anyone else for those potatoes?'

He grabs the serving dish and checks for a reply; when he hears none, he scrapes all the food onto his plate.

'I'm not going to be guilted by that guy,' he says and puts a potato to his mouth. 'I refuse to be. He knows nothing of my circumstances and he is assuming things of me because of my skin colour. That is racism in my book and I am not a Western European.'

Nobody speaks. Kim grimaces.

'They work hard,' I say. 'One of those guys is in his seventies.'

'I am not saying they don't work hard,' Konrad replies and puts his knife and fork down. 'Those men are incredible. But what would they be doing if they weren't doing this? Carrying cattle up the mountains? Boulders? They get fed and sheltered. This might be a sweet ass number for them.'

'I have kept a hundred bucks spare for my tip,' I say. 'I checked online before I left. That's a slightly above average tip. But I do feel like it might be too little now.'

'That's because of Eduardo. He's manipulated you. He's been manipulating us since we got here. Each of us signed up for this tour because they have marketed themselves as ethical. As a company who treats their workers fairly. Am I right? Why the hell would we have paid an extra two hundred and fifty bucks for the tour otherwise?'

A few people nod.

'So the guide knows we've considered these workers, considered their circumstances. That's why we paid extra. I've calculated it. If those twenty porters are being paid twenty dollars a day, multiply that by three, is twelve hundred bucks. Say the chef gets a bit more. Maybe one of the guys carries more than others. Loose things like that. Bring it up to fifteen hundred. We've two tour guides. They're for sure on more money. These guys speak fluent English, know history, have people skills. They may be on a hundred bucks a day. Another six hundred. That's two thousand one hundred. There's probably insurance, our permits, bribes, could be a grand or so – three thousand one hundred. The food's organic, locally sourced. The fish they're catching up here. They may have brought the paltry chicken meat with them. It's hardly been steak dinners each night. It's mostly plant based. Gonna give them a gratuitous four hundred dollars for food though it may be free. To bring it up to a round number of three and a half thousand dollars. That is the maximum possible cost of this tour. Each of us paid eight hundred dollars to go on this "ethical" tour. So, eight hundred by fifteen is twelve thousand. Minus the three and a half thousand. That is an eight and a half thousand dollar profit for this three-day tour. In a country where the GNP per capita is twelve thousand bucks. And they couldn't pay these men more than twenty bucks a day? The workers are being screwed but so are we. I'm not being guilted into this. I'm not giving a tip. He knows we paid for an ethical company. He knows we already feel fucking bad. That's why he's finding it very easy to squeeze more from us. If you want to tip a porter, give the tip to that porter. I don't trust that motherfucker Eduardo not to pocket the lot.'

The vibe in the tent changes. Kim's head is bowed. I finish my dinner.

'I'm giving a hundred. I have it saved for this. I might be a fool but that's what I'm putting in. You don't have to give anything, Konrad. You've made a good case. We understand.'

I put my money into the box Eduardo left on the table.

Konrad gives a slight nod. He reaches across the table and heaps the leftover veg onto his plate.

The rest of the group add their tips in secrecy to the box.

Federico enters with a tray of dessert bowls. Kim perks up. He wears a purple bandana on his head and his T-shirt is black. His loose cotton pants are black with thin red and white lines. They are newish looking and unripped. He's the most fashionable of the men, the most handsome, and always offered Kim seconds of the hot blackcurrant tea or the lemon squash when we reached camp each day.

Kim flirts with him in her basic Spanish. She giggles and he smiles at her while he serves everyone else.

Eduardo re-enters, scoops up the money box, claps his hands and gives us the outline for the night again. 'Sleep well.'


The water makes me and a lot of the other hikers ill. I know, drinking it, that my body is reacting to it. Gag reflex, throat warming up, stomach closing in. But I have no choice. The altitude is too intense to not stay hydrated.

Kim has her headtorch on when I wake with a stomach

ache. She checks her face with a compact mirror and puts the Vaseline for her feet on her lips, smooths her eyebrows with it. She brushes her hair.

'What are you at?' I ask and search for my flip-flops.

'I'm meeting Federico.'

I laugh. 'Okay, Kim. Where?'

'At the outhouse.'

'Romantic. I have to go there myself. That water is full of stuff my Irish stomach can't handle. Can you see a future with him?' I ask. 'Living in the mountains or even returning to a tree hut in the jungle. Amazonian life in the rainforest. Hunting anacondas.'

'Natalie, fuck off. I'm not going on this leap with you. I think he's cute. I'm going to enjoy it for what it is right now, not for my future as a junglewoman.'

'So you don't see it.'

'I don't know.'

'Your kids would be really cute.'

'He's sexy. I need the attention. That's all.'

'I'd offer to wait for you but I really need to go. Be careful.'

Kim sprays some deodorant under her arms as I leave the tent.

I hate the squatting toilets. The stench of them is an assault. It's too much for my nose to take. I can almost taste it. I can almost see and hear it.

'Bleughhh' is something like the noise I make on entering, as my head recoils. I'm going to vomit. My mouth salivates and my stomach heaves but it passes.

My legs are too shaky and cramped from the hiking. I fear I'll seize in the squat position, or worse, my legs will give way and I'll fall into the black hole of faecal liquid, unable to pull myself out of it.

On leaving the squalid cubicle, I notice a guy hanging around outside. When he spots me, he bolts away. Has he been listening?

'Fucking hell,' I say out loud.

Kim has left the tent but the chemicals off the deodorant linger inside. I leave the flap open to let air in but it's too wet out so I zip up.

I massage my legs and fall asleep. The rain patters on the tarpaulin.

Kim comes home some time later, trying to sneak in. But it's difficult, unzipping all the tent covers, blasting back the shushy material. I wake.

'Hola, Juliet. Did you have a nice time?'

'It was real romantic, Natalie, we went to an Incan hut and Federico had a candle. We tried to talk to each other but after a while it got too tedious. It took him ages to hold my hand. At one point, the cloud cleared and the rain stopped so we stepped out of the hut and looked at the night sky. I swear, Nat, I could see the Milky Way. It was breathtaking. We stared upwards till our necks hurt and then I leaned forward and kissed him. I got the feeling he would try to keep talking to me all night otherwise. It was magical.'

'Are you in love?'

'What is love?'

I chuckle. 'Oh, I don't fucking know the answer to this. I always get it wrong.'

'Well, I don't know.'

'Kim, can you please go to sleep now, we've to get up in two hours.'

'I don't know how I'm going to sleep. I feel like I'm floating.'

I smile, try to imagine floating in this tent, floating off the uneven wet ground, floating out of the sore legs and blistered feet, up to the Milky Way. I relax immensely picturing this. Being weightless in space. Being free. Being love.


It feels like as soon as I drop my eyelids, floating there amongst the stars, there's the knock on the tent.

'Up, up,' and the shuffle of other campers tidying. 'Desayuno, people. Vamos.'

I'm swollen-faced with tiredness.

'Wakey wakey,' comes the voice outside again and there's a thud on the tent. I sit upright; my sleeping bag slides down from my chest.

Kim is asleep. Zips and footsteps and whispers sound from outside. It's still raining. I shake Kim.

'We've to get up. It's Machu Picchu time.'

Kim sighs, opens an eye. 'I'm not going for breakfast.'

'But won't you be starving?'

'No, I want the extra few minutes' sleep. I still have an apple and a Mars bar in my rucksack. I'll be grand.'

I venture outside with my headtorch on. The sky is inky black. The rain mists. I stretch and walk barefoot through the wet grass to the food tent.

Eduardo shouts, 'Breakfast, guys, then we go. Let's move.'

I drink a coca tea and eat porridge. They offer us a tiny bowl of scrambled egg which has been whisked with basil.

'Kim?' Federico says, when he sees me alone.

I put my hands together and rest my head on them. 'She sleeps.'

He nods and gives his dishes to another porter, then leaves the tent.

'I can't wait to have a shower,' I say, looking at my grubby hands.

This sets the hikers off. People can't wait for Western toilets, a beer, the internet, a mattressed bed.

Federico and Kim embrace outside where our tent was. It's been packed away.

I walk over slowly, hoping they'll be finished when I get there.

Kim has tears in her eyes. 'Bye, Federico.'

He lets go and straightens his neck. 'Adios, mi corazón.'

I pick up my bag from the ground.

Kim blows out air, lugs her bag onto her back. She waves at Federico as we pass the porters on our way out of camp. He winks.

'I can't even keep in touch with him,' she says.
'Why not?'
'No email. No Facebook. No phone.'
'No English,' I joke, but Kim scowls.

We wait for ages at the permit control. Kim sleeps on my shoulder. Konrad tells me a story of how he took cocaine in Chile and nearly killed himself.

'What happened?'

'I'd never touched drugs before,' he says. 'Well, except for weed but that doesn't count, does it?'

I shrug.

'I was in this club in Santiago, with locals. Great guys and girls. Wanted me to have a good time. It was maybe 2 or 3 a.m. and I was fading somewhat. Too late for me. One of my buddies goes, Hey chico, you want some coca? It's coca pura, and he whips out a bag with white powder. Clean stuff, chico. Not cut with anything. Pura. I never done anything before, like I told you, but I liked these guys and I wanted to stay. And why not do coke in its native continent? I follow him to the bathroom, past the strobe lights, into the cavernous feeling of the nightclub toilets. He went into a cubicle. Came out, rubbing his nose. Sniffing hard. Good, chico. Beautiful, he said and clapped my arm, gave me the bag. I went in and snorted it. Back in the club, the music was clobbering me. It was beating me up with its rhythms. My heart was trying to jump out of my body. I thought it was going to be like that scene from *Alien*. I was sweating profusely and my mouth and tongue and face had gone numb. My hands were ice cold. I felt like shit. I felt like I was going to explode. My friend said, Hey chico, are you okay? You're looking blanco, super blanco, you're the whitest man I ever seen! And I said, I don't feel good, I'm dying. He said, How many lines did you do? I said, I don't know exactly. Where's the bag? he asked. The rest of the coca? The bag, dónde está? he asked. I said, What do you mean the rest of it? He said, There's two grams in that bag, where is the rest? I said, I took it all, was I not supposed to? and my heart was ticking loudly now, a ticking time bomb. Oh shit, chico, he said and called his friend, spoke rapidly in Spanish, waving at me, the friend's eyes went gigantic and he called one of the girls over. She came over and touched my head. She said something to the first guy. He rushed off. He came back with water. At this point my stomach was wringing itself dry. I wanted to die. She helped me drink the water, my hands or mouth not working so well, she tipped the bottle into my mouth. I was aware of the wet sensation as it went down. The guys sat nervously beside me. She kept rubbing my back. I guess they'd be in lots of trouble if a tourist died on them. The clubbers kept clubbing around us. It passed. It took a long time. They brought me back to their apartment. It finally passed but my stomach is still not right. This was two months ago. I damaged my stomach somehow. I damaged my stomach and I have tasted hell.'

'That's pretty intense.'

'Intense doesn't come close to what it was.'

'You had an overdose,' I say.

'Yes.' He clicks his fingers. 'That's the word in English. That's what I had. An overdose.'

Eduardo returns to the queue at 5.20 a.m. and orders us to follow. We've been waiting an hour and twenty minutes at this point.

We bypass envious hikers from other tour groups. The pace quickens dangerously as we rush to the Sun Gate.

'Why are we going so fast?' I ask Kim.

'So we can beat everyone?'

The flagstones are slick and an older British tourist from our group slips and slices the skin on his knee. 'Carry on without me,' he says, fallen soldier style, and waits for Eduardo and band aids.

We finally reach the Sun Gate and it's completely covered. All we can see is the white wetness of cloud over the view while it drizzles on us. If there was a bit of black and grey it would look like the fuzz of an untuned TV. Maybe a creative entity would emerge from the haze?

Me and Kim take a silly picture together in front of the cloud.

'Well, that was an anti-climax,' I say after all the panic to get there.

It's been a long day already and it's not even 9 a.m.

We continue on downhill towards Machu Picchu. I slow my pace. The sky clears and the sun is hot. Kim is lovesick for Federico. I try to distract her by telling her Konrad's coke story.

She puckers her face. 'What sort of a fucking eejit is he?'

The crowds at Machu Picchu are overwhelming. Not used to seeing people, it's disorienting to suddenly be surrounded by hordes of them everywhere.

One of the hikers complains about the 'bloody tourists'.

'Who, us?' I say.

'No, these guys,' he says and points at the crowds. But still, he moseys over to a llama and tries to get a selfie with it.

Eduardo gives information and recounts stories about Machu Picchu, why it looks as it does, what the Incas used it for, and the seismic activity underneath it. He tells us about the American explorer Hiram Bingham who discovered the place in 1911.

'Did nobody know about it till then?' I ask.

Eduardo laughs bitterly. 'Yes. Nobody with a Yale degree.'

I climb the top of a hill with Kim and some others. We take a picture with the famous view of the terraces and ruins in the background.

'Kim,' I say, 'I'm done.'

'What do you mean?'

'I'm done. I've had my Inca Trail. Over it now. I'm ready to go back.'

Kim hankers around in hopes Federico will carry her off to the mountains. But he doesn't. She unsubtly asks Eduardo where the porters are.

'Gone home to their wives,' Eduardo says, matter of factly.

I link arms with Kim and encourage her to follow me to the bus.

Some of the group are waiting. A local sells chicken

sandwiches in burger buns. I buy one. It's made of cheap bread, cheap chicken. No love went into putting it together, but still it tastes great. I use the bathroom facilities close to the coach stop and nearly cry on seeing the Western toilet, the flushing throne.

In Aguas Calientes we find the restaurant meeting point, order a beer and chill out with the group. I order chaufa and yuca fries. Someone orders hamster and offers it around. I can't try it, with its deep fried little head on the plate, its mouth petrified in a silent scream.

We're all very self-congratulatory. Eduardo hands out our certificates for completing the trail. They're tacky-looking with a drawn graphic of the route and a babyish font. Some other Inca Trail groups got T-shirts. All we get are these lousy certs.

Eduardo tells us once again about how rich we are, how poor Peruvians are.

'I almost feel hate,' Konrad says, clenching his jaw. 'He's making me hate them.'

'Ignore him.'

'But his manipulation is putting me off them all, not making me have sympathy. And how the hell does he know that they aren't as happy as me? He doesn't know where I've come from.'

Two musicians enter and start the familiar 'El Condor Pasa' tune, on a guitar and panpipes.

'I haven't heard this one in a while,' Konrad says.

The musicians walk around to each of us, while we're eating, with their hands out. They linger at the table until someone passes them some soles or tells them no.

Some of the group exchange email addresses and Facebook usernames. Eduardo makes a big deal of leaving.

'Let him go,' Konrad says but there's a chorus for him to stay.

He comes back, all dramatic. Kim gathers our tip to offer to him. He counts it out in front of us and says goodbye, in a slightly edgy way. He says something in Quechua to the restaurant owner, then leaves.


Kim speaks to the owner and comes back to the table with a leaflet. 'We should get massages to cheer us up. Yer man said this place is upstairs.'

'Do they have showers? I'd pay twenty dollars for a shower.'

'Yep. Let's go.'

The parlour is dimly lit and smells of essential oils and scented candles. Kim haggles a shower and an Inca massage for each of us for fifty soles total.

The shower is magnificent. I thank it. I thank the water. I thank my legs and belly and arms and chest as I rub the soap on them, for holding me up through the trek, for feeling so good being lathered, under the water. I stay under it and wash and condition my hair. It's the best shower of my life. It's the first shower of my life. I'm completely present for it. The heat of the water on my sore body. Everything so very sensual. All the dirt washing away. The water, the cleansing. How fortunate I am. I switch the dial to the cold water side, start with my feet and work the showerhead up my body to free the energy in it.

The shower is the highlight of my trek.

I am invigorated, drying myself. I put on my knickers and the robe they've given us. I wonder if I should wear my bra but decide against it.


Kim and I wait in the lobby in our robes for the massage. Kim's masseuse is a small older lady, mine is a Peruvian man who's my height. He wears loose green cotton trousers and a black vest.

I follow him behind a curtain.

'Hard, medium, easy?' he asks.

'Medium?'

I undress and lie on my belly. The rosewood massage oil is warm as he drips it onto my skin. I want to moan in pleasure at his touch. It feels tremendous. I receive it. He dips low under my arms with his oily hands, he's kind of catching my side boob but I let him. Then he goes down to the back of my legs and feet. Up to my ass and around. He's dangerously close to holes. I wonder but thinking takes me out of the moment so I let it go. It feels too good. Eventually he turns me around to my front. I am blissed out.

He starts at the top again, my head and neck and shoulders, then my breasts. He spends ages there. I notice his erection. I can feel it in my open hand as he leans over me. He leaves it there. I don't want to think but thoughts fly in. Is it deliberate?

Is it automatic? I don't know how men's bodies work. If my body turns him on, so what, I'm a little turned on too. Has he left it there to see if I'll respond?

Is this what an Inca massage involves?

Would he touch a male customer the same way?

My inner commentary momentarily pauses as he works down to my lower parts and is so close to my outer lips that I think he might dip a finger in. I am close to climaxing from his touch.

Will I resist? Will I stop him if he gets on top of me?

I don't honestly know the answer to that. I don't feel assaulted in any way, I feel worshipped.

His face is inscrutable as he focuses on the massage.

I let go of all thinking and sink into pleasure.


Leaving the room, I grin even though there wasn't a happy ending. Kim waits for me.

'Why are you smiling like that?'

'Like what?'

'Like the way you're smiling right now, Natalie. You look kind of creepy.'

'Do I?' I laugh nervously. 'Why?'

'Nat, you're acting really weird.'

'Was your massage good?'

'Yeah, lovely.'

'Was it sexy?'

'What?'

'Was it sexy?'

'I had that old Peruvian woman down there. It was lovely. Not sexy. Jesus. No. It was relaxing.'

I say nothing.

'Did you?' Kim opens her mouth wide. 'Oh my god, did you shag your masseur?'

'No, no. I did not, god, no way. It was a bit – a bit full on though.'

I take eight dollars from my purse.

'Are you tipping him much?' Kim asks.

'He tipped me.'

'What?'

The masseur stands beside a window, and it's the first time I clearly see his face. 'You have knots in your back. I recommend you come back to me. I will release them. Come back tomorrow, the next day, the next day? It could take a week to rub them out.'

I giggle. 'Maybe. Thank you.'

Outside I tell Kim everything.

She laughs. 'Should we go for another beer before the train home?'

I nod, still reeling from the pleasure of being touched.


In the restaurant, some of the Dutch guys and Germans are there with the British guy. We all drink slowly and relax, wait for the time to pass.

'What did you learn from the hike?' I ask.

The British guy says, 'You can only take one step at a time. Life seems insurmountable until you break it down. One step. Next step. Next step. How the hell did I make it for those eleven hours uphill with these knees? One step. Next step. Next step. It's all you can take. You?'

'How amazing toilets and water and electricity and a choice of food are. How people live different lives but it doesn't mean they're not happy lives. Mostly I learned my body is more powerful and capable than I thought.'

We get pretty merry and go to the train station. The next train to Cusco is at 6.20 p.m.

We sit on the station's floor, or lie on it, and use our bags as pillows.

A man in full Inca head dress and costume dances into the centre of the tiles and whips out a panpipe. I fall asleep. Kim wakes me to board. We find our seats and settle. I'm surrounded by Japanese tourists.

The air of 'El Condor Paso' loops in my mind and I rest my head against the train window; the iridescent sun bows behind gnarly trees.

# Laundry

My legs still twinge from the trek. I stay in bed on Saturday morning when Kim goes for breakfast. She returns and glumly hands me a roll with boiled egg and tomato squashed in it.

'Here, take this. I can't swallow.'

'You need to eat, Kim.'

'I'm too sad.'

We round up our clothes for washing. We're putting it all together to save money on the laundry load. They charge by the five kilo. Kim has socks and a top she's going to bin and isn't too fussy about her stuff. I need my clothes cleaned though – the Peruvian women's sizes are minuscule.

Kim says, 'So what do we do next? What do you reckon about the ayahuasca?'

'I don't know. That tourist killed another tourist on it a few months ago. I don't want to die high in the Amazon. Actually, maybe that would be a good end.'

'We're not going to die, Natalie. Why do you always have to jump headfirst into the worst possible outcome?'

'Overactive imagination and shaky sense of self, Kim. We've been friends for over a decade. Have you not noticed these things about me before now?'

'What about the cactus juice? I want to detox Pete from my emotional energy field. I want him gone.'

'You want eternal sunshine in a spotless mind?'

'Yes. Let's research it. We have tomorrow to do something before the flight.'

'Okay. But now, let's get these clothes washed.'

Less than fifty metres from the hostel, there's a laundry sign. The prices listed are competitive. We walk through an alley and another sandwich board says 'LAUNDRY' with an arrow towards a doorway in the courtyard. We step inside and press a bell. A little kid, around four or five, looks up at us from the desk. She is drawing in a colouring book.

'Hola,' I say gently. I lift my bag. 'Laundry?'

'Mama!' she shouts into the hall. Another little kid ambles in, wearing a dirty red T-shirt and a cloth nappy. His face is crusty with dried food. He sucks a dummy and tugs at Kim's dress. She ignores him.

'Well hello there, Mr.' I kneel down and rub his hair.

The mother rushes in, a baby on her boob. 'Sí?'

'Can we get laundry, señora?' Kim asks.

We put our bags on the table. She gets out a scales and a receipt book. The bags weigh twelve kilos.

She punches it into a calculator and shows us the price for fifteen kilos.

'A las cuatro,' she says, her thumb hidden as she splays her fingers. 'Hoy. A las cuatro. Sí? Claro?'

'Four,' Kim says. 'Four p.m.?'

I tap at an imaginary watch on my wrist. 'Four? Cuatro?'

'Sí. Collect. Four. A las cuatro.'

She tears out the receipt. We try to pay but she waves us off. 'No. A las cuatro.'

The little boy cries. She sighs and one handedly loads herself with the bags, still holding her suckling baby in the other arm.


'Should we have a look for a shaman?' Kim asks. 'Spiritual tourism place? There's loads of them. Eduardo told me on the hike.'

'You've thought about this a lot?'

'Yep. I want to purge. I'm bored of being heartbroken.'

We wander down the cobbled streets. Music booms from boutiques. Women and children in colourful knits beg for money. Some have decorated llamas with them and offer pictures with the animals.

A smell of incense leaks onto the street and we follow it to a shop called Soul Whisperers. It sells crystals, books on psychedelics, and a selection of drums, feathers and rattles.

'Excuse me,' Kim says. 'Ayahuasca?'

A hippie-looking tourist admires some bongos beside her.

'Ayahuasca ceremony? You know anything about it?' the clerk asks.

'You get sick? You release demons?'

He bites the side of his mouth. 'It's not that simple, ladies. It's plant medicine. It's not to be taken lightly. We run groups from here. You don't eat. There's preparation. I'll give you a brochure.'

'Have you done it yourself?' I ask.

'Many years ago. Just once.'

'Good fun?' I chance.

'It's not fun. It is hell. You will face and purge your ego. You will rise with the serpents and ride the waves of the primordial universe. You will be plunged into the unconscious world of imagery and nothing will be the same again. You will also vomit violently and probably shit yourself.'

'And we pay a hundred and fifty dollars for this honour?' I wince at Kim.

'Does it get you past a break-up?'

'It doesn't do anything for you. You have to surrender to its power. You have to do that for it.'

Kim smiles. 'We'll think about it.'


In the hostel's computer room, I check out other ceremonies.

'What about the San Pedro, Kim? Wachuma. It doesn't seem as brutal on the body. I'm scared of doing ayahuasca with randoms.'

Kim is stalking Facebook.

'These plant medicines cure people of addictions. Jesus. Not illegal either,' I say.

She's too distracted to listen.

'Kim, you're not going to get over him by looking at his shit. You're in Peru. Is that not enough? Don't torture yourself.'

A guy walks in and shyly says hello. He's tall and wears beaded bracelets and a thin leather neck chain. His T-shirt is faded blue.

I detect his accent. 'Are you Irish?'

'Sí.'

'Inca Trail?'

'No. Well, I did it a long time ago. I've been working over here.'

'Doing what?' Kim asks.

'Different NGOs. Volunteering in the mountains for a while, teaching kids and helping build things.'

'I was a teacher once,' I say.

He smiles at me. 'What are you now?'

'I dunno. Myself?'

'Nice.'

Kim loses interest in him but he and I chat.

'We're researching the ayahuasca or the cactus juice. Have you tried them?'

'Yep. Different experiences for sure.'

'Did you enjoy them?'

'Enjoy isn't the right word. Ayahuasca is living in your worst nightmare but once you let it happen, and come out the other side, you know you can survive or do anything. Cactus is more grounded. You see how connected we all are.'

'What do you mean?'

'Well, we're all connected. By life or energy or whatever made us. With the cactus, you'll be able to observe these connections. It'll unlock a state of consciousness, or perception. You'll see fields and things that are usually invisible.'

'Sounds amazing.'

'Sounds whack.' Kim rolls her eyes. 'Does it help you move on from your past?'

'I guess it does different things for different people. Trust what you're shown would be my tip.'

'Oh shit, Kim, it's five,' I say and jump off the swivel chair. 'We've to get our laundry. Everything will be shut tomorrow.'


'Ronan's cool,' I say as we walk up the street.

'If you like hippie-geeks, yes, he is. Hey Nat, where's the place?'

We look for the sign but it's not there.

'There was definitely a place here. An alleyway? We went through it.'

We wander up and down.

Kim lingers around a spot and says, 'I think it was here. I remember that flag?'

But there's no alleyway.

We stand in disbelief, eventually figure out that it's gated up and locked.

'Fuck. What do we do, Kim, all my clothes are there?'

Kim knocks on the steel gate. Nobody comes. She rubs her raw knuckles.

'I won't have any clothes for the rest of the trip. I don't want to buy more. It takes me a while to find stuff that fits my shape right.'

'You won't have to, Natalie, our clothes are ours.'

I knock for a while.

Nobody opens the gate. Twilight skulks.

'Is there anything on the receipt? A number we could call?'

I scan the paper; a line on the bottom in tiny print has some numbers.

Kim says, 'Okay, let's get the hostel woman to ring and speak Spanish to them. We'll get the clothes back.'

We march to the hostel and the girl at the desk dials the number. It rings out for ages. She hangs up.

'Will I try again?'

'Yeah.'

Ronan walks by. 'All okay?'

'No, our laundry went missing.'

'What?'

'Yeah, it vanished. Our clothes are gone.'

'Good luck with that.'

The receptionist watches YouTube videos of people playing video games. Military men crawl around Afghani bomb-strewn streets, shooting and throwing grenades.

The number rings out again. We begin to lose hope.

'You'll fit into my clothes, Nat.'

I frown. 'I'll buy something new, Kim. I don't need to put myself through that humiliation and you don't need your clothes stretched.'

Finally, someone answers. The receptionist drums out her conversation, pauses, makes notes. 'Ahh, sí,' she says every so often.

She flicks a look at us with her large brown eyes. Her eyeliner is thick and winged at the edge of her eyelids.

'Sí, sí,' she says and scribbles again. Then she glances at the screen, to see what's being bombed by the gamers. The conversation lasts for ages. 'Okay, gracias.' She hangs up.

'Your clothes were returned to the warehouse when you did not collect. That is where they are washed. The warehouse is on this street.' She circles some writing on the receipt and uses her pen to indicate directions on the street map of Cusco laminated on her desk. 'Is here,' she points, 'and we are here.'

'Okay,' Kim says. 'And can we get our clothes back?'

'The warehouse is open until 21.00, but maybe is best to go right now.'

'Okay,' Kim says. 'Muchas gracias.'

We take a paper street map, the receipt and set off. People are getting ready to go out; a Saturday night murmur of anticipation fills the dusk. We walk quickly on the cracked footpaths. Drunks argue in a park. At the city's centre, we take a left, down a side street for two kilometres.

We find the dishevelled street where the warehouse is supposed to be. It's wide, unlit and unpaved.

'Welcome to real Cusco,' Kim says.

'This is pretty sketchy.'

It's getting dark. The hair on my arms bristles. The air is shadowy.

The houses have no numbers. To call it a poor area would be an understatement.

'There,' Kim says and points at a big rough building. 'That must be it?'

There are no lights on. It looks abandoned. I press a bell but nothing happens. We glance around. I press the bell again. There's no sound going on within.

Kim pushes the door and it opens. It's dark inside.

'Aw, Kim, let's go. I'll burst myself into your clothes. This is too scary.'

But Kim has already stepped in. The corridor is murky and cool. The floors and walls are tiled.

'Kim,' I hiss. 'Come back.'

She goes in further.

I sigh and grumble and follow her, shutting the door gently behind me.

I can barely see the outline of Kim ahead of me.

'Noises,' Kim whispers. 'Can you hear?'

I hear my heart whipping my chest. Behind that, yeah, I can hear muffled industrial sound.

'Kim, wait for me. Please,' I say.

She puts her hand back and takes mine. My hand is sweating. Hers is cold.

The noise grows louder as we continue on the corridor. Our shoes clop against the tiles. There's a door ahead.

We creep towards it. Then Kim tries it, and it opens with a creak. She pulls it wide and the light blinds us.

I shield my eyes. 'Oh my god,' I say slowly and put my hand to my mouth.

The washers and driers are deafening. The smell of laundry detergent is overpowering. The workers ignore us as we stand there with our mouths gaping.

'I can't believe it,' I say. I've never seen anything like it before.

The workers are children.

I assess them in terms of my primary school classes, a handful of young teenagers, maybe thirteen or fourteen years old, the rest are younger, eleven, ten, nine, eight. One kid can't be more than six. He folds a towel.

'This is a sweatshop,' I say.

'No, a sweatshop is where clothes are made. This is a laundry. A child labour laundry.'

I feel sick. I wonder are these children being educated?

'Natalic,' Kim says. 'Look at them. Look at what they're doing.'

One's on a phone. Another does an impression of someone to a crew who laugh their heads off. Two of them jump between machines.

'Nat, they couldn't give a fuck!'

They're being kids.

We walk to a desk at the front and stand there but we're ignored. We observe them for a while. They're dwarfed by the machines. They chatter and laugh and sing, barely audible, over the noise of the tumble driers.

'How are we going to find out where our clothes are?'

Kim grows bored. 'Hey, hey, hey.'

They pay us no attention.

'Hello,' Kim roars, 'Hello,' and one or two kids stop and look. 'Here, aquí, ahora. I want to talk to you.'

They eye her and each other and return to what they were doing.

We stand there for another two minutes or so.

'What do we do?' I ask.

'These little shits are ignoring us. HELLO,' Kim shouts again. Then she stomps over to the nearest kid and says, 'I want to speak to a manager.'

The kid gives a face like she doesn't understand.

Kim tries again, politely.

The kid is blank.

Kim loses her patience and bends down. 'Su jefe, AHORA.'

The kid cries and toddles over to an older kid. The older kid hits a different older kid, and the struck kid is the one who comes over to us.

'Que?' he says, hand on hip.

'Su jefe, ahora,' Kim says and copies the hand on hip.

The kid sighs and pushes her back behind the desk. He picks up a phone and calls someone.

'Espera!'

He swivels on his heel and goes to his buddies.

'They're not getting much work done,' Kim says. 'Do you reckon our stuff's been washed.'

'Kim, they're children.'

We wait around. Kim's about to go into the factory floor again when a slim, well-dressed man comes in and claps. The kids spot him and tell each other quickly. All of them stop their messing and pretend to be busy.

The man goes behind the desk. 'I am very sorry,' he says and tugs the receipt from Kim's fingers.

He inspects it and flicks a switch which turns off all the machines. He wanders around the floor, smiling at us.

Then he proceeds to scream at the children, first in Spanish, then half-facing us, in English.

'You are disrespectful. You are stupid. You behave. You do your work. Very disrespectful. You work hard. You respect the tourists. They put food on our tables. You work hard. You respect.'

Kim tilts her head from side to side.

He flips the switch on again and returns to the desk holding three neatly pressed clear plastic bags. The kids are silent and give us looks as in, you stupid bitches. You're going to get us punished.

The manager says, 'Many apologies, señoras. I have your clothes here. They have no respect for me,' he says and wipes spittle off his chin. 'Idiotas.'

He checks the receipt again. 'Fifty soles.'

Kim says, 'I'm not sure about this service. It's disturbing and we've been inconvenienced.'

'Forty?'

'Twenty.'

'Thirty?'

'Okay.' She fishes out the notes.

I hold the bags close to my chest.

Before we leave, I take another look; the kids fold clothes and handle the machines solemnly.

In the cool corridor, I ask, 'Should we ring the cops? Or do something?'

'What could we do?' Kim says. The noise fades behind us.


Back at the hostel, Kim is still rude towards Ronan and I try to buffer it.

I tell him the story of what we've seen.

'Yeah, though children's rights are improving in Peru, still around thirty-four per cent of them are in the workforce.'

Kim says, 'Oh god, I need air. My skin is crawling since that warehouse.'

She leaves. Me and Ronan drink some coca tea.

'What are you doing next?' I ask.

'I'm going north to a coffee plantation.'

'To teach English?'

'Yes, and other things. I'll probably also farm. They may not want their employees getting too much information.'

'Are the plantations corrupt?'

'What do you think?'

'Why don't the workers revolt?'

'Well, like an oppressed group, they keep each other down. They're pitted against each other. Divide and conquer. Individual power over the collective.'

'I'm going to go out and maybe have a walk around, see if Kim's okay. I'm worried about her. She's acting erratically all the time.'

'Break-ups are hard.'

'They sure are. Will you walk with me? It's been such an odd few days.'

'Yeah,' he says and goes to his room to get his baseball cap and jacket.

We roam the streets and he explains different things about Peru. He also tells me about landing in a village in the middle of nowhere on a bus and, at the station, this man was waiting for him.

'He was acting like my friend. I didn't get a sex energy off him, he wasn't a pervert. He invited me back to his house for dinner. I was hungry. I went. There he introduced me to his wife and children, his neighbours. He showed me around his garden. I ate, and afterwards, he came in with a big photo album and a white glove. He put the glove on to turn the pages and showed me pictures of him with other white people. The penny dropped. He asked if I'd do the honour of being in a photo with him. I said okay.'

'That's kind of sweet,' I say.

'Kind of.'

Kim is on a bench in the main square chatting with a man. She waves us over.

'This is Heraldo, he's a musician.'

Heraldo tosses his long hair behind his back. It reminds me of a horse's silken mane. 'Mucho gusto,' he says and shakes our hands.

Ronan leaves us to it, says he wants to get some food.

'Heraldo is going to find us wachuma in the market tomorrow,' Kim says. 'I've told him everything.'

Heraldo has exceptionally long fingernails and wears his guitar case on his back. 'No problem, I will be your guide.'

'We'll go to Sacsaywaman, do it there.'

The mosquitoes are out. A golden statue of an Incan king dominates the centre of the square, brandishing a weapon in one hand, outstretching the other.

A beggar woman with a baby on her back tries to sell us painting prints, keyrings and imitation alpaca wool scarves.

'I play tonight, in that bar.' Heraldo gesticulates to somewhere across the square. 'Come listen, Kim, bring your friends.'

Kim nods. 'Heraldo, we'll meet you at the market in the morning.'

He kisses both her cheeks.

'I don't want to be in a bar,' Kim says, when we're out of earshot. 'Plus we have to purge now, in preparation.'


I sleep fitfully, struggling with images of little children's hands reaching for me in the dark, touching me.

In the morning, Kim says she had a rough night too.

We walk to the market smelling of newly washed clothes. Kim finds Heraldo at a juice bar.

'Hey chicas,' he says.

Kim immediately flirts with him, dipping her head to the side and putting on a girly voice.

'I can get you some good stuff. You need a guide though, someone who's not high. I am from the Amazon. I can show you the way.'

'Cool.'

He selects the powder. The manner in which he's testing it is showmannish and my gut has an unpleasant tingling sensation. We pay for it, five dollars.

I'm not sure about Heraldo.

He says he has a gig near Aguas after, so how about we join him. 'Muy tranquilo,' he says. We'll be in the Andes, it'll be very spiritual, and he can play for us.

Kim smiles. She turns to me. 'Will we go? Would be an adventure.'

'Can we talk about this for a minute, ourselves?' I say and drag her outside to the hot street. 'Kim, he seems like an okay guy but this is how people get killed. Who's going to be with him?'

She mutters, 'Dunno.'

'What if we get to some fucking field in the mountains and his five friends are there and we're high? I don't know about this. And I'm trying to not jump to the worst possible scenario for once – this is an actual potential scenario. This man is a stranger. We are in a foreign country. I want to be cool but I have to fucking say this. He's putting on a show in there. What he was doing with the powder was an act. I can spot these things from when I used to perform my scripts in the gym. I don't trust him.'

Kim speaks hastily. 'I don't want to go, Natalie. I don't want to tell him no either. I brought him in.'

'Oh for god's sake.'

Inside, I thank Heraldo for the history lesson and for picking a nice bag of stuff but we have to decline.

He appeals to Kim, which makes me even more suspicious of him.

'Heraldo, we said no. We'll pay for your smoothie. Thank you for your time. Maybe we'll catch one of your gigs here? Más tarde?'

He puts his hands together in prayer position. 'Kim, come with me. I can free you of your heartbreak.'

'Only Kim can do that,' I say, trying to nudge her away. I grab her arm and turn her to face me. 'Do you want to stay with this guy? Everything might be fine, despite my fears. This is your life and your journey and I'll respect your decision but I am going back to the hostel.'

'No, I'll go with you.'

'Okay. Be firm, he's trying you. Can't you see that?'

'I dunno anything anymore.'

'Okay. It's grand. I'll do the talking. We can go home and go for breakfast and get packed for the flight.'

'Okay.'

I turn back to Heraldo. 'My stomach is too bad. Necesito un baño todo el dia.'

'Kim,' he says, jerking his head slightly, attempting to catch her eye.

I put my hands on my hips. 'Look, buddy,' I say firmly. 'We're not going with you. Entiendes?'

'Sí. Claro.'

On the crowded streets, in the morning sunshine, I take a big breath and say, 'Kim, try to be a bit more aware of the men you're attracting. You can't fill the pain of Pete's absence with another man.'

'Like you couldn't fill your emptiness with food?'

The sting of her words blinds me for a moment.

'Don't act like you've it all together, Natalie. I can see through it. Let me have my comforts. I don't want your advice, I know that I'm being unhealthy. Can't you understand?'

I nod. And in that moment, I know exactly what I feel, her rejection swiftly followed by a desire to eat.


After a while of us browsing in intense silence on the hostel's computers, Kim says, 'I like how you've found your voice, Natalie. It suits you.'

'Thanks.'

I take it as an apology and forgive the morning.

A Colombian backpacker logs into the third computer and Kim smooths down her T-shirt. She begins a conversation with him and giggles as he speaks.

I log out and go to the room to organize my rucksack for the flight in the morning. Laying everything on the bed, I note the bag of wachuma powder, wrap it in a scarf and put it in the side pocket. My clothes have a sharp freshly laundered smell.

# Father and Son

It's not yet dawn when Kim and I get off the overnight bus from Lima to a dusty bus stop in Máncora. I fish out the paper with the information Ronan gave me about a guesthouse. Passengers hop into the mototaxis but Kim wants to negotiate a better price. The stream of mototaxis dwindles. I'm too tired for this and get irritated.

'I'll pay for the bloody thing. Let's get a lift before it's too late.'

The noisy mototaxi drives down the main street then takes a left, onto a sandy road. I can smell the ocean. We feel every bump under the wheels.

There's no way we can buzz the guesthouse.

'We have no booking,' I say. 'The owners will be in bed.'

'It's a guesthouse, they'd be used to this craic,' Kim says.

'No. It's rude.'

Other mototaxis pass and people check into guesthouses nearby. We sit outside. The sky is pink as the sun rises; it promises a hot day. Kim sleeps on her bag. I walk around to stretch my legs from the cramped bus. A white bird shimmers across the roof and cries. What the hell is that? A goose? A feather floats and falls down in front of me for a moment before it drifts upward in the air and away. I nearly buckle at the sight of a giant cactus in the area behind the house. It's well over twenty feet tall, intimidating and powerful.

I meander back to Kim. 'Should we walk to the beach?'

'Not carrying our bags there, fuck that,' she says.

The morning light is so bright, I wear sunglasses to read *Women Who Love Too Much*, which I picked up in Cusco in the book exchange. I underline passages and read some out to an unenthusiastic Kim.

At 8 a.m., after an hour and a half's wait, the top of a surfboard is visible over the gate. A key jiggles in a lock.

A deeply bronzed white man wearing a purple trucker cap appears. 'Hey chicas,' he says. He holds his board. 'Have you a reservation? What are you doing out here?'

'We're looking for a room,' Kim says, and fixes herself.

He has a surfer dude ripped chest and strapping arm muscles.

'What kind of room?' His accent almost sounds North American but it has that Spanish intonation.

'Two beds, or two rooms. Whatever. For the two of us.'

'Okay, momento,' he says and puts his board onto a rack. 'Follow me, ladies.'

The courtyard is charmingly shabby. There are small potted coconut palms by a three-seater outdoor swing. Paddles, snorkels, wetsuits and other ocean accessories are in the corner near the rack. A shaggy dog is snoring in front of a bookcase. The tiles are sandy underfoot. Kim smiles at me, and I nod, but we stay quiet as we walk through it and up the stairs. The vibe is sleepy in the whole guesthouse.

He shows us a room on the second floor with two single beds and a bathroom. The thin indigo gingham blankets folded at the end of the bed match the curtains.

'Is this okay?'

'Sí, cuantos?'

'Ten dollars per night.'

'Each?'

'No. Total. Okay?'

'Sí, sí.' Kim gives him a dazzler of a smile.

'Okay, ladies, make yourselves at home. Rest. Settle. If it's okay with you guys, I want to go catch some waves. I will show you around in two hours, at 10 a.m. Check-in is then. Cool?'

'Cool.'

He gives a shaka sign with his hand and departs.

'What a fine thing,' Kim says. 'He's gorgeous.'

'Oh here we fucking go.'

'I'm think I'll shower and then check the beach.'

'Well, I'm going to sleep, Kim. See you later.'


Nico shows us around the building. His partner Carla is a rock surf chick hybrid. She's all eyeliner and ocean talk and plays Guns N' Roses on the speakers. She gives us directions to the nearest supermercado, and we go to buy some supplies.

In the guesthouse's kitchen cum dining room, we prepare a large pot of vegan stew and fruit smoothies for lunch. A beautiful little boy rushes in and turns on the TV, pressing up channels to cartoons. We sit beside him. I chat to him but even Kim seems interested in listening to his kid-speak. She asks where he works.

'Work?'

'Yes, what do you do for work?'

'No entiendo, señora.'

Kim scratches the side of her eye. 'Do you work or go to school?'

'I go to school,' he says, looking totally confused. 'We have holidays at the moment. Papi!' He jumps off the couch to greet an arrestingly handsome man who has walked in.

'Ride,' Kim slowly mouths in silence to me.

The father kisses the child. He speaks no English. Both me and Kim are all smiles for him. Next to enter is another son, we guess. He's maybe seventeen or so. He has scruffy blond hair and is well built. His English is pretty good but the child's is the best. We find out they're on holidays from Lima, here to surf.

Kim offers them lunch. They accept it gratefully.

The father says something and the older son laughs.

'What did he say?' Kim asks.

The kid replies, 'He said it is great to have the touch of a woman.'

I give Kim a face.

The father says something again to the kid to say to us.

Kim is staring at the father.

The kid says, 'My papi says you are an excellent cook.'

'Gracias.' Kim touches her face coyly.

'De nada,' the father says.

'What are you all doing for the day?' Kim asks, in feigned nonchalance.

'We're surfing,' the kid says and jumps up and down.

'What time?'

'Soon, now?' The kid speaks to his dad and brother. 'Yes, next, we go.'

'I'm going to the beach too for a run. I'll walk with you guys,' Kim says and smiles.

The kid translates.

The father says, 'Sí,' excitedly.

Then Kim remembers me. 'Nat, are you joining?'

I decline.


I explore the town alone. I check out the tourist spots, walk around the markets and I'm drawn to a crystal.

'You don't choose the stone, the stone chooses you,' the woman at the stall says. 'Blue lapis lazuli. For inner truth and acceptance.'

I can't put it down so I purchase it.

She wraps it in a cream crochet pouch. 'La bolsa es una yapa.'

I buy watermelon slices from a street merchant and stroll back to the guesthouse.

I sit in the hammock outside the room and take bites out of the slices; juice explodes from them. I wipe my chin, take smaller bites but there doesn't seem to be any way of doing this without pink mess. The fruit is too ripe.

Kim returns sweating profusely.

'Have you been running till now?' I ask.

'Yep. Well, I hung out with the family for a while then I ran. Ten k maybe.'

'Jesus, Kim, you haven't been running in months and you've gone straight to ten k, will that not hurt?'

'No pain no gain. Hey, Nat, I saw a dead thing. A whale I think, on the beach. It's way up, you go around a corner, after the last of the beach houses. I didn't inspect it though. Pretty cool, eh?'

She asks what I did for the day but when I answer she interrupts me to ask what age I think the kids are.

'The small one is probably seven or eight. The other one? A teenager, maybe sixteen or seventeen? Because the dad can't be much more than forty. I'd say he's late thirties even. So maybe he was a young dad, when he was twenty, twenty-one?'

'Yeah, I thought something like that. He's attractive, isn't he?'

'Who, the dad?'

'Yeah. Well, both. The son is so hot. The little kid is gorgeous cute too.'

'The sons are good-looking, yeah, good-looking family. I wonder where the wife is.'

'He wasn't wearing a ring. Do you think he maybe has brought his boys on a mid-term holiday before they go back to their mother?' She taps above her eyebrow. 'Do you think the mother died tragically or ran off with a Brazilian and left this poor lovely father solo?'

'I thought I was the one with the overactive imagination. I dunno, Kim, why don't you ask him?'

'No. Jesus. You don't ask men these things, Nat. No wonder you're single.'

'Hey, you're single too.'


We hunt for a restaurant for dinner. We find a newly opened place with an English and Spanish sign promising the best desserts in Máncora. We eat dinner lazily but it's still too early to go back to the guesthouse for the night.

'Will we try one of these best desserts in Máncora?' Kim asks.

We share the mousse and then Kim orders a caramel walnut slice. She looks at me.

'Am I terrible?'

'Kim, come on, who you talking to? If you're going to order seconds, you may as well enjoy them.'

'Say, Nat, you know those stationary bike classes you ran in the sticks and that crazy Catholic woman complained?'

'Yep.' I sigh. It's still raw.

'You should give them a go in Dublin. It wasn't the idea, it was the small population and demand that was your problem with them.'

'I wasn't qualified, Kim, that was the problem.'

'Get qualified. I was thinking about this when I was running. You have a talent.'

'No I don't,' I say, feeling really prickled by her comment.

'What, Nat? That's a fucking compliment.'

'It was a silly idea. Adults don't want to play. They want straight up serious shit when they spend their money.'

'Bull. I'd love to go to your kooky class. It sounds fun. You hit on something you were excited to do with your time. Don't squander it like the rest of us. Break out. You are brave, you know. Despite how chickenshit you are about pretty much everything, you're brave too.'

I pretend to look at the menu. 'No, I'm not.'

'You're a ball of anxiety and ridiculous worry at the best of times but you do stuff anyway. That's pretty brave, kid.'

'Don't kid me, you who fancies a teenager.'

'He's sexy, Nat, and if you don't agree, you're lying to yourself.'

'He's too young though.'

'Is he? What if it was the other way around? It'd be normal if it was a man perving on a young one. Loads of men are much older than who they're hitting on.'

'But some of them would be on the same page, maturity wise.'

'Are you implying I'm as mature as a seventeen year old?'

'No. But maybe, sure you and Pete got together when you were younger. And you went out with that Sligo fella for a few years before that. The last time you were single, you weren't an awful lot older than the hot son.'

Kim wrings a napkin. 'Fucking Pete, the wanker.' Her eyes fill with tears. 'What do you think he's doing now?'

The waitress lays Kim's dessert on the table.

'Not having a delicious piece of cake in a Latin American surf town. That's what he's not doing.'

'Will I ever feel normal again, Natalie? I'm really scared.'

I rest my hand on her shoulder. 'You'll make a new normal.'

'Do you want some of this?' she asks, flecks of it spraying from her mouth.

'No,' I say and mean it. 'I'm full.'

Kim is getting up for a run when I wake.

'See you later, yeah?' she says and jogs out the door.

I'm not really sure how to pass the day. It's nice to do little after the Inca Trail but I have a feeling me and Kim are drifting, that I'll have to let her go.

I walk through the town, taking each step slowly. Lots of tourist buses pass on the road. I stroll by new hotels and guesthouses and eventually I'm at the outskirts and start passing shack houses, ones made of patches of tin and wood. I turn back.

What if I became a fitness instructor, what would that mean? I look down at my figure. They'll laugh at me if I go in with this body.

Would they laugh at me? Do people laugh at each other?

Only gobshites do – do I care what they think?

I walk to the beach. There's a dead turtle in the sand, its head meat is all gone. I turn him to look at his shell. Its scutes are shiny olive and radiate black lines.


Kim is dolled up in the kitchen, cooking. She throws her head back with laughter. The father sings.

'Hi Mom,' I say.

'Do you want lunch, Nat? I'm making paella.'

'I've just eaten. Thanks.'

'We're thinking of surfing this afternoon, do you want to come?'

'Who?'

'Me and the guys.'

The teenager picks some chicken out of the pan. Kim jokingly wags a finger at him. He burns his mouth and makes a gasping noise, frantically fills a glass of water.

'Honey, be careful,' Kim says.

It feels like a scene in a weird sitcom. I try to smile at Kim but she has a mask on and I don't know who she is in this moment.

'I'm not able to surf, Kim. I may relax here and read.'

'Okay,' she says and the little boy asks her something. She bends down to his level and is fully attentive.

Is it a show? I wonder in my hammock. Or is it real? Is she experiencing something she's always wanted right now? Who the fuck am I to call her fake for it?

I hear them all having their moment downstairs.

I swing in the hammock and figure out how I'd describe this scene in a spin class. I'd bring in the grey sand beach, the thrum of the mototaxi engines, the sweetness of the local café's mousse and these glorious feathers that keep falling from the sky.

Kim comes bounding upstairs to freshen herself before surfing.

'What will you do for the afternoon?' she asks.

'I've been thinking about the fitness qualification. Maybe it's something I'll look into.'

Kim beams. She puts some light make-up on and sprays grapefruit perfume on her hair, underarms and on her feet. She dashes after the men.

I go to the side pocket of my rucksack to find a pen and notebook. I see the bag of powder, the San Pedro.

I have nothing else to do for the afternoon. I get a spoon of it and put it into a glass of water. It blends terribly. I stir it about but it doesn't dissolve so I take a gulp. It's so plantlike and bitter I have to whine after taking a mouthful. I block my nose and drink the rest of the glass.

Then I sit in the hammock and write goals, listing the actions I'll have to take to achieve them. Small steps.

After about forty minutes, the world feels a bit different. Shimmery. I suddenly know what a flower must sense as it faces the sunshine. The head of the turtle I realize doesn't need protecting, its body does. The body is the temple. I understand it now. The temple is where you go to contact God. So maybe heaven isn't above, it's below?

I feel the pedals of the spinning bikes being pushed in gyms around the world, the ocean surrounding Kim's wetsuit, the hope in her heart to feel better. I lie in the hammock and gaze at the sky. It's infinite petrol blue. I wonder how much space and time exist between me now and the me who knows what she's doing with her life?

Then it dawns on me, how space and time are dependent on observation, and that all potentials exist simultaneously. Therefore, if I can dream it, it's already done.

'What the fuck?' I scratch above my eyebrow, not sure where this quantum theory has come out of.

A bird flies by. The divine white of its plumage glistens. It stops on the plastic roof above me. I see its webbed orange foot. It's a goose. She yangs and honks.

The cleaner woman arrives downstairs and greets Carla. The women speak in Spanish, and though I don't know what words they say, I understand exactly what they're expressing to each other.

Natalie, a voice that's not a voice utters from somewhere in my chest. What you need you already have, it says, but speaking isn't the way we're communicating. It's a knowing. It's a vibration.

I know, I respond.

I amn't even I. I am everything. Everything is me. The fat white goose plodding on the plastic roof. The Rolling Stones tongue on Carla's T-shirt. The grains of sand all over our bathroom floor. The salt in the sand. The father and son. The beach noises, laughs and waves and wind blowing, singing. The bobbing seaweed. The perpetual might of the Pacific. The gripping sun.

I see a flash of the twenty-foot cactus in the yard. I could go downstairs to talk to him but there's no need, I can speak from here.

I'm in the universal mind, amn't I?

He laughs, in a cactus way. He's very distinguished.

Do I need to know anything?

He's smiling but serious. You don't need anything. You have it all. You are it all. We all are.

I know! I say and surge with joy. I'm a bit mental right now, yeah? I'm talking to a cactus from inside and he's talking back.

We don't make the laws, lady. You've opened a new route in your mind. You know this is not forever but you also know it is, because now is forever, if you'll let it be.

I know! I want to squeal. But I don't know what to do about Kim.

What is there to do?

She's going crazy.

You're talking to a cactus.

Okay, good point. I don't know how to help her.

You don't have to help her. She has her journey. You have to accept her.

She's annoying me.

You're seeing in her what you don't want to see in yourself.

Am I?

He doesn't reply. He doesn't have to.

I am.

The goose tramples the plastic until she ends up right over my head. I love her. The noise. Her foot. The plastic.

It's all beautiful, you're a witness.

All? Even me?

He has a prickly, wheezy laugh this time. Why do you doubt it? It's not a question. You're alive. You're beautiful. Don't un-acknowledge the universe.

It's my ego. It's out of control. Isn't it?

The cactus laughs again. It is what it is. You're doing fine.

Do I try out this idea of being a fitness instructor?

You already know.

Yeah, I do. It's so weird, Abuelito, it's so weird to be out of my own way.

It is what it is.

It's lovely is what it is.

I close my eyes and hear far-off drums, rattles, see the life force of trees and plants. I knew they grew but I never really recognized what that meant before now. I never considered the 'being' part of being alive, behind our personalities, how we share that – our existence – with plants, with animals, with everything.

I wake and haven't a clue how much time has passed. A few seconds? Hours?

Whatever it was has faded, and Kim is home to shower.

'We're watching a movie downstairs? Come down for a while for drinks.'

I join them for one rum and cola but I'm not feeling it. Kim grabs a cardigan and leaves for a bar with Nico, Carla, the father and older son.

We're in a small modern café, on the main strip, for breakfast, and I notice Kim is binge eating. She blames it on her hangover and goes for a long run again when we get home.

I am relaxed. I wave hello to Kim's new family and go for a walk on the beach.

I sit for a while and watch the ocean, in and out, each slow wave its own, each wave connected.

In the afternoon, Kim wants to go for a ceviche in a locals' secret place, recommended by Nico. To keep the peace, I join her. We hop into a mototaxi and off we go, way past the tourist side of town, through the tin and patch house neighbourhood, taking a right down a side street.

'Is shantytown an offensive term to use?' I ask.

Kim says, 'Is slum better? Jesus, how do they access water in those shacks?'

My eyes prick with tears trying to imagine. 'I don't know.'

The restaurant is crowded and noisy with many conversations happening at once, cutlery clanging off plates, steam hissing from the kitchen, and a big cloudy bubbling fish tank on the wall packed with lobsters, crabs and other shellfish. A smiling waitress gives us a window seat. We're the only white-skinned people in the building.

Kim orders ceviche and a seafood stirfry. I order chips.

'This is perfect,' Kim says, squeezing the lime onto her dish. She takes a mouthful and offers me some but the raw fish texture freaks me out.

'Hey, Nat, do you want to see the dead thing?' she asks, slurping the last of her food from her plate.

'The whale?'

Kim nods.

We walk along the beach back to the guesthouse.

The sun is raucous and my skin is a bright rose colour as it burns. I wrap my yellow scarf over my head and across my shoulders and back. We amble up the beach until it's quite deserted. I pick interesting-looking shells and rocks off the grey sand. Kim points to a black mass in the distance.

'That's it there.'

We continue on; the tide licks our toes as we walk barefoot on the cool wet part of the sand. The mass grows larger and it looks like driftwood.

'The smell,' I say, when we get closer, and cover my mouth with my scarf.

'I'm too hungover for this,' Kim says.

'Did you drink a lot last night?'

'I'm not telling you.'

'What? Why?'

'Because you'll judge me for it.'

'No, I won't. I like a good drink every so often too.'

'When is every so often now that you're all healthy?'

'What?'

'We've had no sessions in Peru.'

'It wasn't really the craic here though, was it?'

'Since you've been healthy, you've stopped being fun.'

'I've not pushed anything on you about health.'

'Yeah, but look at you, all butterfly coming out of the cocoon, all arrogant, got my shit together, got my plan.'

'Kim, what is this? Why are you lashing at me? I know you're hurting, I get it, but don't do this. I'm still here, we're still friends, even after all your—'

'After all my—?'

'After all this.'

'After all what, Natalie?'

'All your instability.'

'I wish he'd call me or something, I wish he'd tell me he changed his mind. I don't want to be alone, Nat, I can't do this. I don't want to go to weddings alone. I don't want to go out and try to find someone. I want him and that comfort again. I need it.'

'Everything you need is right here.'

'In Peru?'

'No, in you. You're only alone if you're not there for yourself.'

'Is that a line from your woman rescuer self-help book?'

'No. It was a line from a plant.'

'And I'm the unstable one? What plant?'

'A cactus.'

'Did you take the wachuma without me?' She looks disappointed.

I nod.

'Why didn't you wait for me?'

'You're gone all the time.'

'Why didn't you tell me about it?'

'You're never there to listen. All you want to talk about is the father and son. Or Pete.'

'Fuck you, Natalie.'

Someone shouts from behind. A man dressed in a khaki green uniform holds a machine gun and hollers in Spanish. He guards a fancy hotel behind him. We walk back, unsure of what he wants.

'Inglés?'

'Sí, señor?'

'Peligroso, chicas. Muy peligroso.' He uses his gun to point at the strand ahead, which is desolate except for the big dead whale. There's only Pacific to the left and the sand dunes to the right.

'Lo siento, señor. We wanted to see the thing up there,' I say. 'Por favor.'

'Okay, okay, I look. Quick,' he says and waves us off.

Now we're filled with dread as we edge towards it. The man holds the machine gun in his arm and watches us.

'What's up there, d'ya think? Are they lying in wait in the hills for tourists?'

Kim shudders. 'I've been jogging up here.'

The smell is like fish oil gone rogue and all pervasive. Or a week-old open mass grave. Or a billion rotten eggs. It's like the Inca Trail's toilet facilities, but in the sun. The smell permeates our skin.

He's bloated since Kim saw him first, she says. He's rotting and expanding in the equatorial sun. 'Oh shit actually,' she adds and puts her hand to her mouth.

I look around suddenly, wondering if the unseen bandits or rapists are coming for us, wondering if there'll be a shootout.

Kim's face contorts. 'It's going to blow.'

We gawp at the putrid mass, at the hills and at the security guard.

There's a sense of something about to happen. The sun is shaded by some clouds, which gives immediate relief. Then it puts its glaring spotlight on us again.

'I'm going surfing with the guys again tomorrow, Nat.'

'But what about our bus to Lima?'

'I'll get it the day after that or the day after that.'

'But I really wanted to spend our last weekend in Lima and explore it properly.'

'I know, Nat.'

'I don't want to stay on here, Kim.'

She nods. 'But I do.'

My eyes hurt. I close them. There's nothing I can do but accept this.

'Claro,' I say.

We walk in silence until we reach sunbathers and hotels again, until people peddle their helados and pineapple chunks.

The next day, I board the bus alone. There's a sudden bang. I clasp my chest.

The end of a friendship – a gunshot – a whale exploding – a backfiring engine – the start of something new.

# Bridge

Bobby walks over to a full-looking black bin bag. He takes plastic-wrapped T-shirts out of it, piles them on his desk. 'You'll be wearing these on the gym floor each week. This is our uniform. We want the gym users to know that you're students and it's good to be visible.'

He tears a pack and displays the black T-shirt; on front it says 'APEX FITNESS' in lime green capitals and on the back it says 'STUDENT INSTRUCTOR'.

I'm the oldest in the class. The group are fit-looking, athletic, young. The only thing that's easing my discomfort is that we're in a blaring light, bland beige carpeted, whiteboard on the wall, flipchart in the corner classroom setting. The classroom is on the same floor as the gym and studio, above the squash courts. A squash ball is audibly battered against a court wall and the beat from the gym music is monotonous.

I sit in a black stacking chair at the top desk beside a soccer player called Lucy. She wears a green jersey and her hair is tied loosely with a purple velvet scrunchy.

Bobby passes a sheet to each of us with a column listing different body areas – chest, waist, upper arms and so on – and an answer box beside each.

'Now is the perfect time for you to practise taking measurements. As we're all aware, women are obsessed with the numbers on a scale. But really, a good instructor knows that for weight loss or weight gain, a scale is bullshit. To know how your body is doing, you measure it. If you can do this well, you will immediately be perceived as professional. So take a tape and pair up. I'll give out the T-shirts after.'

Lucy shakes my hand. 'I'll measure you first?'

'Okay,' I say. My body constricts.

We work at the side of the table.

From the top of the room, Bobby says, 'Ideally, when measuring calves or thighs, we would like tape to skin contact but always ask a woman first. Why?'

Nobody responds so I chance, 'You shouldn't touch someone's skin without asking if it's okay with them?'

Bobby says, 'If the woman hasn't shaved her legs, she'd be understandably ashamed of herself.'

Lucy is like a tailor, the tape in one hand, a pencil behind her ear. She works away and chats about her morning drive. She describes the Red Cow Roundabout as 'worse chaos than being near Nowlan Park after the Leinster Final', and the Red Line Luas as a 'fucking Quentin Tarantino movie'.

I laugh at her comments, and relax as she measures my thighs, scribbling down the number in inches.

Bobby stalls in front of us and makes an announcement. 'What's Lucy doing wrong here?'

She is open mouthed looking up at him from the ground. I scratch my hand, the side of my face. Everyone's eyes are on us.

'Think about it. Look at her positioning.'

The room is silent.

'She should do it from the side, maybe?' I say.

'Yes. Don't measure a client with your head in front of their crotch. Always come from the side. Same for the bust and chest.'

Lucy shuffles to the side and continues. Bobby examines her page.

'What have you written for waist?'

Lucy reads it out. With both hands he pinches my stomach and sides.

'You need to try that again. That number is way too low. Inaccurate. Do the measurement again.'

My face glows red.

Lucy tries again, crosses out her original number, and puts the new one over it. Bobby nods in approval.

I measure Lucy. She's about five feet tall and has a petite frame.

'I'm like a wee eleven-year-old boy,' she says as I wrap the tape around her hips. 'But I'm fast as fuck. Lightning Lucy.'

Bobby hands out the T-shirts and tells us to put them on straight away. 'Ladies, you can go to the bathroom if you're too embarrassed to change here.'

In the bathroom, a woman who was sitting at the back of the classroom, called Magdalena, poses and checks her appearance from all angles in the toilet mirrors.

'This is such an ugly shirt, no?' she says.

'Your accent is lovely. I was in Latin America on a trip earlier this year. De dónde eres?'

'Venezuela.'

We chat about travelling. With no English, Magdalena moved to Ireland a year ago, and is a housekeeper in a B&B.

She says, 'I want to work in a gym but I'd like to turn professional as a sports model. I compete in three months, in a bodybuilding bikini contest. Have to get down to twelve per cent body fat. There'll be lots of scouts at the contest.'

Lucy says, 'Sounds like an invisible woman contest.'

Magdalena says, 'Maybe, but a strong invisible woman.'

'Twelve per cent?' is all I can say. I repeat it a few times to get my head around it. I look down and wonder if I carry on my chest all the fat Magdalena has on her body.

'Come on, we better go back in before yer man releases the hounds on us,' Lucy says, holding the door open.

Bobby is explaining the skeletal system, with a slide show. I take notes and draw diagrams.

Lucy exhales noisily and looks out the window. 'This is so boring,' she whispers.

Bobby throws a few questions out about the function and movement of bones.

I innately know a lot of the answers, I don't know how, maybe from childhood or from biology in secondary school. If

I don't know, I still hazard a guess at the answer. Sometimes it's easy because of the way Bobby phrases the questions. I enjoy the recap quiz at the end, and get eighteen out of twenty in it.

'Natalie is slaughtering you all in here,' Bobby says and I rub the back of my neck. 'Your nearest competition scored ten.' He addresses the group. 'You need to study hard. Theory will not only get you past the exams, it'll make you seem professional.'

He outlines our first assignment, due a week later. Then he puts us into pairs and tells us to follow him to the gym. I'm matched with a strong young fella called Christian.

The gym floor is bright, large windows wall the space. It has that paradoxical chemical-clean odour from bleach and sprays, and a natural sweaty smell from the people working out.

We walk by the line of treadmills and elliptical machines to the free-weights area.

'I want you to instruct three exercises. One simple, one compound and one on a machine. Tell me what muscles are being worked, what the plane of motion is, teaching points and how to modify it to make it easier or progress it,' Bobby says. 'I will be back shortly to see them. Go.'

'I don't really know any proper moves,' I say to Christian. 'Will you teach me how to teach you?'

'Let's do a bicep curl first, it's easiest.'

Christian passes a two kilo dumbbell to me.

'Keep your elbows close to your body. Bend them to curl the dumbbell up to your shoulder. Pause. Slowly lower it back to the starting position. Movement is elbow flexion. Muscle is bicep. Progress it with a heavier load. Easier with a lighter load.'

We practise by me parroting him.

'Are you a bodybuilder?'

'Yep.'

'Do you wear tan competing?' I ask as Christian returns the dumbbell to the rack. He nods.

'Why?'

'If you put someone the exact same build but with a tan beside a pale person, the one with the tan will look more muscular. To showcase definition or striation you need shadow.'

I tilt my head to the side and visualize Christian as a green-skinned hulk flexing.

'Which machine will we do?' Christian asks. 'Lat pulldown?'

'The what?'

He sits at a machine, extends his arms overhead to grasp a dangling bar and pulls it down. 'This works the latissimus dorsi.'

Christian shows where the muscle is located on his mid to lower back. He then offers teaching points on the machine. I try it out with no weights attached to the bottom of the cable.

We're about to decide on a third one when Magdalena and Lucy holler at us to come over.

'What does this bad boy do?' Lucy says, pointing at the machine called Vibro-Plate 3000. She switches it on and hops onto it, holding the handle while the plate vibrates at high speed under her feet. 'Jesus, it feels like me brain is moshing against me skull.' Her voice shakes.

We all have a go. My vision blurs as it aggressively sends vibrations through my body. I get off, and my head is wobbly. 'That thing is vicious.'

'Maybe it'd be better craic to sit on it,' Lucy says.

We're loitering around and don't see Bobby return.

'Right, Christian, Natalie, show me what you've done,' he says and claps.

I wipe my hands on my tracksuit bottoms as I follow Christian and go first with the bicep curl. Bobby corrects me on a few parts of it.

Christian shows the lat pulldown.

'And your third move?'

'We didn't have time for a third move,' I say.

'Bicep curl is the simplest one to explain. I want you to show me a deadlift, Natalie.'

'A deadlift?'

'Yes.'

'Okay,' I say and hover over the dumbbells.

'You're doing it with a dumbbell?'

Christian points at a kettlebell.

I pick that up instead.

Christian demonstrates the move behind Bobby.

I try to copy him but haven't a clue.

'Natalie, that's not a deadlift.'

'What is a deadlift?' I ask.

Bobby double-takes me. 'You're serious?'

I say nothing.

'Christian, show her.'

'With a kettlebell or a barbell?'

'What's it called with a kettlebell?'

'A Romanian deadlift.'

'What's the difference?'

'They're the reverse of each other?'

'That'll do. How could you modify it?'

They may as well be speaking Chinese.

'Reduce load. Use the Smith machine?'

'No. That would be dangerous.'

'What's a Smith machine?' I ask.

Bobby turns and says, 'Natalie, one second, look around you. This is what is called a gym. Have you ever seen one before? And that is a barbell. And this here is a rack. Bloody hell, woman.'

'You told me that I'd be learning these things when I signed up?'

I recall the phone call with him, when I rang for information on the course, wondering if there was any point me being on it considering my inexperience. He assured me that they had many students who were new to the gym, who wanted a career change or a second income.

'Pay your deposit, put three hours of study and three hours of gym training in weekly and you will make it through the course,' he said.

'Even if I'm not as toned as the others,' I asked, and he

comforted me, saying musculature wasn't as important for an instructor as the ability to motivate.

I wonder if he meant any of it.

'There are things you should already have an understanding of, Natalie.' Bobby makes notes, scratching his page with angry motions of the pen.

My gut compresses, I feel a shrinking sensation of inadequacy, but a radiating sense of humiliation throughout my body.

I am silent and my hearing seems to have turned itself down.

Bobby takes long strides over to Magdalena and Lucy. Lucy points at the Vibro-Plate and says something; the three of them laugh.


I am mute for lunch. Words don't want to come while I feel like this. I wonder whether I could get a refund if I left the course?

I sit beside the others in the cafeteria. Christian has brought a packed lunch of four chicken breasts and kale salad in a large Tupperware box. He has a tin of tuna, a big tub of Greek yogurt and a bag of trail mix too. He alternates drinks from an energy drink can and a protein shake bottle.

Magdalena orders porridge with water and a glass of water which she adds blue powder to.

'Is that your twelve per cent lunch?' Lucy asks, distorting her mouth.

'Yes. I have a strict food plan to follow.'

Lucy opens a bag of cheese and onion crisps; the strong smell off them wafts.

'They look delicious,' Magdalena says as Lucy scoffs.

'D'ya want one?'

'No. I cannot. Not until the contest ends.'

'Your discipline is intimidating,' Lucy says, licking her fingers.

'It's not discipline, I do not want to work where I work any longer. This is my path to freedom.' She picks up a spoonful of the watery porridge.

I buy a cheese and ham sandwich from the fridge, and take out my flask with my homemade smoothie: wheatgrass, spirulina, spinach, apple, banana. I listen to chats about whey shakes, bodybuilding contests and supersets; stories of alternate universes.

After lunch, we're lined up in the studio for group instruction. It's been recently renovated and has a new hardwood floor and a fresh paint smell. Bobby drills us on an aerobic routine. Tap toes to get warmed up, march forward, step touch, curl our heels to our asses, then take a step knee lift.

It looks simple but I'm breathless as I follow the choreography.

Bobby hits play on his ghettoblaster. 'Now, one of you instruct the class, with those four basic steps. Someone volunteer. Anyone?'

I avoid eye contact.

Bobby tuts. 'No one? I'll pick so. Christian, you're up first.'

Christian walks slowly to the top of the room.

'Count us in,' Bobby says.

'Three, two, one,' Christian says, not in time with the music. He tries to explain what we have to do but mumbles his sentences. We remember the gist of the steps. He can't keep the beat.

Bobby switches the music off. 'Mr Muscles has two left feet. I'm hardly surprised.'

Christian wipes his nose.

'Lifting is not going to help someone like you on this course. I recommend you go to zumba, step, line dancing – anything. Go and learn how to move in time with music instead of kissing your guns in the gym.'

Christian nods and walks to the back of the room.

'Okay, who's next?' he says and I make myself small. He calls on Magdalena. She walks to the top smiling.

'I must apologize for my English,' she says.

Bobby presses play and Magdalena counts us down on her fingers. She goes through the first part of the routine without saying anything.

'Explain the movements to the group,' Bobby says.

'And we go, with this leg, to cross it in front of the other,' she says for the move, stunting us and losing the beat.

'Afterwards, this other leg, it will go to this side,' she says. The whole thing loses its flow. 'Then we will go to the first side again.'

She gets frustrated. 'Next, is this movement, to go this way,' she says, hesitates, trying to mime the movement.

The group try to stay enthusiastic as we wait on her.

'And then we will put this leg to this place,' she says. 'I am sorry. I do not have the words.'

Bobby is checking his phone.

'Do it in Spanish,' Lucy shouts.

'Excuse me?' Magdalena replies.

'En español.'

Magdalena looks over at Bobby. She waits for the beat and snaps her fingers.

'Okay, vamos a bailar,' she says. 'Cuatro, tres, dos, uno.'

She shouts confidently and for a while we dance, and understand Spanish.


'Day one is done,' Lucy says. We exit the turnstile and walk across the reception foyer.

'I think I'm in the wrong place,' I say, the first words I've spoken in hours.

'Why?' she asks. 'You chose to be here?'

I nod.

'And you paid for it?'

'Well, yeah.'

'Then you have your reasons for wanting this. Remember them.'

'I wish I had more confidence.'

'Fuck off, Natalie. You've loads of confidence. In class, you're the only one who guesses.'

'Yeah, but it's no big deal.'

'How about when you guessed and got it wrong earlier? How did that feel?'

'I dunno. I never thought about it.'

'When you got it wrong?'

'I can learn from getting it wrong. I'll know the next time.'

'And what's that, d'ya reckon?'

'Yeah, okay, the theory is easy for me. But I don't know if I'll get good at the practical stuff quick enough. I don't know how to even do the basic exercises properly.'

'So what, Natalie? You don't have to be perfect.' She pulls the door open, lets me go out ahead of her into the weak early evening sunshine.


On the second week, my classmates are friendly and happy to see me as I enter.

Bobby gives us a lecture on the respiratory system.

Any time he asks a question, the class automatically turn to see what I'll answer. I stay silent for someone else to guess, but when no one does, I say something.

Bobby says, 'I want to talk to you today about proofreading your work. Christian, I had a read of your assignment. It's polluted with errors. Did you even spellcheck it before you printed it?'

Christian scratches his stubble. 'No.'

Bobby reads out a line. 'The gym floor has place for weights, keep the floor clean, off the weights.' What the hell does that mean? Is that even English?'

Christian blushes. 'I meant about the obstructions, when people leave the weights on the floor, it's a health and safety risk.'

'That is not what I'm reading here. Look, none of you have been to college so you wouldn't know that you can't hand in any old rubbish when answering questions. You need to proofread. Hear me?'

I gasp as Bobby tears the paper in half.

'Proofread your assignment and bring it in next week. You all have weaknesses, work on them before I point them out to everyone. Some of you, it's rhythm, or the gym floor exercises, or voice projection. For a lot of you, it's simple grammar.'

Christian bows his head. I feel a small fire in the pit of my stomach.

'I went to college,' I say belatedly and then clear my throat.

'What?'

'I went to college, I've a degree and a postgraduate diploma. And Christian, I'll proofread your work,' I say.

Bobby sneers. 'Okay, college girl, let's show these guys some moves. Come up here, up to the top. Teach us how to do a squat. A squat is one of the Big Three exercises. Basic. Teach us that, Natalie, university queen.'

Shit.

I stumble to the top of the room. The last time I squatted was on a South American mountain.

As we break for lunch, I stay back to speak to Bobby. My mouth is dry and my tongue feels thick. I say, 'You're making me feel inadequate.'

His eyes are alight. 'I'm not making you feel anything.'

'You are.'

'I'm not inside you making you feel things. I've my own feelings to deal with.'

'But I feel—'

'Exactly. You feel. You're responsible for how you feel. Natalie, you're not training, and for all your knowledge of theory, you're not going to pass the practicals if you don't train.'

'I am training.'

'You're not.'

'I am training.'

'If you're training, why can't you do any of this?'

'I am fucking training. Call to the gym I'm in and have a look at my admission history. I'm in there every evening.'

Bobby chuckles and put his hands up. 'Okay okay, calm down, woman. No need to be oversensitive.'

★

The table talk is about steroids, competitions and cheating, as we eat lunch. I'm oblivious to all things doping and how it's poisoning professional sport.

'Winning is more important than being honest?' I ask.

'For a lot of athletes, winning's the only thing,' Lucy says.

'And they cheat to win?'

'They'll do anything to win.'

'But cheating is lying? Is that not an automatic loss of integrity?'

'I dunno, Natalie,' Christian chimes in. 'A win is a win.'

Lucy and Magdalena nod in agreement.


I lie on the bench under the twenty kilo bar. I can't lift it off the hook, never mind press it.

Now as Bobby glares at me from above the bench, I notice the asymmetry of his nostrils, the roof of his mouth, how some of his grey eyebrows stick out rather than fold along with their counterparts.

'Why haven't you done this before?' he asks.

I sit up on the bench. 'Because the rack and bench are over by the men on steroids who are grunting and looking in the mirror. It's intimidating to go in there.'

It's one thing to be in the gym, it's another to strut around it like you know what you're doing.

'Intimidating is an excuse. If you've paid membership, you've every right to use the rack as much as those men. I have a feeling you don't do any resistance training. Zero.'

'I don't, not really,' I say.

'Why not?'

'It's boring.'

'Boring?' His eyes grow wide. 'Do you think fitness is supposed to be entertainment?'

'It wouldn't hurt if it was a bit more exciting.'

'We are not clowns for lazy people. If you can't lift that bar, give me teaching points at least,' Bobby says.

'They're not lazy. They're just not sporty. Sometimes there's a big chasm between athletic people and the rest of us.'

'Big words too like chasm. It's lazy, Natalie Dillon. In plain and simple language. And you're lazy, why aren't you benching daily?'

'I've already told you.'

'How do you expect to make it through this course? Why on earth are you even here?'

'Because I see how to bridge that chasm.'

'You need to go back to an office, woman. This is delusional.'

'You aren't even aware of the market I'm talking about.'

'Oh right, the lazy market?'

'Look, Bobby, who's out of their comfort zone here?' I ask. 'Who's doing something different?'

Bobby taps the bar. 'Get back down and show me where your hands should be. Put your hands equidistant on the bar, judge it by the ring marks.'

'How wide should the grip be?'

'Depends on which muscles you want to target. Bring

down the bar to the midline of your chest, don't pause, push the bar back up.'

'Do the action, since you can't lift the weight.'

I mime bench pressing, exhaling noisily as I raise the imaginary bar.

'How can we regress this for people who are too lazy to be in the gym?'

'Push-up.'

'Okay, you know something at least. Let's see your push-ups.'

I go onto the ground and feel a tremble come to my hands as I kneel.

'No more excuses, Natalie. Everyone gather round, let's watch this.' He waits until the other students, all eight of them, are in a semi-circle around me. He folds his arms and smirks.

'Teaching points, go.'

'Assume plank position,' I say and put my palms under my shoulders.

'More teaching points,' Bobby says.

'Keep your back neutral, you don't want to arch or bend it.'

'More.'

'You can modify by putting your knees on the ground.'

'A lady push-up, okay,' he says. 'What are the muscles involved?'

'Shoulders, chest, core.'

'Muscle names.'

I hesitate. 'Pecs. Triceps. Deltoids. Abs.'

'Now dip,' he says.

I take a breath and go down, trying to get as close to the ground as I can. My arms are shaking. I go low and then push myself back up to the starting point.

'Again. That one doesn't count.'

Fuck.

I bend down low, feel the pressure on my upper arms, push up unsteadily.

'Are you breathing out on exertion? I can't hear you. Go again, that one doesn't count, not low enough. Your elbows are flaring.'

I go low, my arms turn jellylike. On the ground, I notice a hairball with a red string tangled in it.

'Now push,' Bobby says and I push shakily back up. 'Another one. That doesn't count.'

I sit back on my knees and say nothing.

'What's Natalie's problem here?' he asks the class.

They look at their feet.

Christian says, 'She isn't used to doing it.'

'No, well, maybe yes, she hasn't created the neural feedback in her muscles for this move, but what's her big problem? It's pretty obvious. We're all fitness instructors here, there's no need to be mincing our words.'

Here we go.

'We're going to be meeting many clients like Natalie, full of excuses, no responsibility.'

Everybody stays quiet.

Bobby says, 'Natalie's problem is that she's at least ten kilos overweight thereby making a push-up extremely hard on her already weak arms. She is too weak and too heavy.'

Some of the others in the class appraise this statement by staring at my body. Lucy pretends she hasn't heard and is intently watching a man run on a treadmill. Magdalena makes a face at Bobby when he's not looking.

Christian tries again. 'She needs to train her arms. Get more power in them.'

'Yes, Christian, it's true she's no gym rat like you but she also needs to release all that excess subcutaneous fat. You're all aware that your body is your selling point as an instructor? Who's going to go to someone like Natalie and say "yes, I want to be that shape, sign me up"? No one.'

Christian says. 'Chill, man. I don't think it's necessary to—'

Bobby breaks in. 'It's the truth and I'm saying this so you people know, your body is a visual display of your fitness prowess. Natalie will be making minimum wage on the gym floor, if she can't master these basics. Life is tough. Be tougher.'

I wipe my hands on my Lycra leggings. I roll my shoulders back and forward to loosen them.

A kaleidoscope of images and sounds inundate my mind, coaches of my childhood leaving me on the bench, reluctantly being picked for a team by peers at a lunchtime game, people laughing when I ran, the nicknames, my secondary school PE teacher's contempt when I brought a note from Mam saying I wouldn't be able to participate. My kneeling-down tear-stricken pleas to Mam on school mornings to write those notes excusing me from sports.

I chew on the inside of my cheek and think of the girl I was.

Bobby stops me as I walk away. 'You must train more or you won't make it, smart and all as you are. Get over your insecurities.'

My jaw grinds. 'Maybe if you weren't exploiting our insecurities as a teaching strategy, I'd be getting on better.'

'Did you learn that lingo in university?' he says with a fake smile.

'Yes, I did actually,' I say. I stand up taller. 'You're using shame to motivate then modelling that coaching style to us. You're essentially training people to bully. Do you think that's healthy?'

He takes a step back. His face is pink and he shows me his palms. 'I have to get you to a certifiable level. That's all I'm trying to do, Natalie. Stop taking it so personally.'


'How the fuck did I end up here?' I think out loud and shake my head as we walk to the studio.

'Pardon?' Lucy says.

'I'm in the wrong place,' I say. 'I dunno if I can do this to myself anymore.'

'Why?'

'Every time Bobby pulls me up on stuff, it stokes all this self-consciousness in me. I hated myself and my body in the past. I'm not going back to that place again.'

Lucy squeezes my arm gently. 'You're still here.'

'What do you mean?'

'He's stirred all this up and you're still here. You survived,' she says, and winks.

I swallow. She has a point. Has the worst that could happen already happened?

Is this the worst that could happen?

This?

Something inside me freefalls with that thought. Then it clicks, illuminates. Suddenly I realize how lucky I am.

'Natalie, remember we're invincible so there's no need to worry,' Lucy says.

'Who is?'

'We're going to absolutely smash the course. With all our powers combined.'

'Who?'

'Us!' She looks exasperated.

'Me and you?'

'No. Our team. Magdalena's got rhythm. All that studio stuff, she doesn't even have to practise. It's a language her body speaks fluently. Christian is king of the gym. He knows exactly what and how to pump when it comes to muscles. You, Natalie, are our classroom hero. Fearless when it comes to spelling or the exam papers or assignments.'

I laugh and sigh at the same time.

'And me? I am Coach. The one who sees how parts of the team can work for the whole. Not bad for a dyslexic, rhythmless woman from a Kilkenny dairy farm who'd never been inside a working gym before. If I must fucking say so myself.'

She looks at me, waiting. 'Enjoy yourself instead of worrying, it's a much better way to use your time. Am I right?' She has her fist out for a bump. 'Natalie, am I right?'

'Yeah, okay. You're right.' I bump it.

'Good,' she says with vigour. 'Now let's have a motherfucking dance.'

'The little woman is up first,' Bobby says to Lucy in the studio.

'Okay, man with thinning hair.'

Bobby's surprised by her comment.

'Are we saying what we see here?' Lucy asks innocently.

Bobby grins. 'You little shit.'

'You're a massive shit. That won't flush.'

He laughs heartily.

Lucy is uncoordinated but unapologetic about it. She applauds herself when she finishes.

Bobby stares at me, uses his thumb to point at me and to the top of the room. I feel tense walking up.

He blasts the music on.

I overthink the choreography and try to make a poem in my head with the moves to remember them in order but I go blank when I have to shout them. The class look at me and wait for my countdown. I miss the beat and muddle the explanations.

Overwhelmed at making a complete balls of it, my movements are flustered, awry, as I try to catch-up on the routine.

Bobby switches the music off. 'What is Natalie doing wrong?'

'No, Bobby,' I say and put my hand out to stop him. 'Wait. Let me do it again. Put the music on.'

He smirks.

I remain in the central position in front of the group and take a deep breath. Blood thumps in my ears.

'I said press play, Bobby. I'm going again.'

'Finally,' Bobby cheers and punches the air. 'This is the spirit, people. This is what I need to see from you all. Show me how much you want this.'

He hits play and I find the beat in the eight count.

# Skin

I bite a hangnail at the side of my thumb as the plane begins its descent. I chew at the skin until it lifts off in a slab, going deeper and further down my finger than I intended. Gasping, I suck it and put my hand in front of me to inspect. The pink rawness of the wound pools with blood. I clasp the base of my thumb and more blood gushes. I put it in my mouth. It throbs. The man at the window seat looks at me and winces.

I take my thumb from my mouth. 'It's fine. Bad habit.' I wave my free hand.

'Nervous about landing?' he asks.

'No, no, I love flying. Well, not love it. It doesn't bother me. I like the view.'

I dip my head to glimpse out the window. The sky is heavenly white. The clouds below the plane are wavy and carpeting. 'It's like an ocean of cloud.'

'I was thinking the same thing,' he says and smiles. He turns to the window. 'It's beautiful.'

I lick my teeth to clean them, realizing I might resemble a vampire. I crane my neck to see through the gap that his head makes as he looks out.

The air host walks down the aisle waving scratch cards, offering them to passengers in an enthusiastic way.

'Feeling lucky, punk?' I mumble to no one really.

'Excuse me?' The man in the seat beside me turns to face me. 'Were you speaking to me?'

I laugh nervously. 'No. I was joking. I thought I said it in my head but I must have said it out loud. It was about the scratch cards. I've never seen anybody buy them on a flight. Never heard of anyone winning on them either.'

I guess he's near my age, the way he has fine lines starting on his forehead, the crow's feet barely tracing the edge of his eyes, afraid to stamp their mark yet.

We spend a minute like this, sort of looking at each other, expectant for something but not sure what.

'Do you want to swap seats?' he asks, breaking the silence. 'I've been watching the ocean of cloud for quite some time now. I wouldn't mind sharing the view. And you could see Amsterdam as we go down?'

'That's really kind. I'd love to. Thanks.'

As we stand to swap, the woman on the aisle seat groans in her sleep and changes position. I flatten out my denim skirt, smooth the creases in it and rewrap my maroon poncho cardigan over myself. I notice the length of his legs underneath his black baggy jeans. He must be six feet three or four. I smile as he spreads himself upwards, rolling and squirming his body with the stretch.

'You must be uncomfortable flying, being that size?' I ask.

'What?' he says quickly and raises an eyebrow.

'Being so tall, your legs must be squashed?'

He sighs with what may be relief. 'Yeah. It's a cheap flight though. Can't complain when you're not paying for comfort.'

I pick up both my books, covering the self-help one with a literary one, hoping he hasn't seen the former. Now we're both standing, I'm up to his bicep, which is large underneath his forest green hoodie. There's a cinnamon scent off him and a cooking smell, of meat, maybe? There's something clinical too, like those carbolic soaps my grand-mother used.

'So how are we doing this?' he asks, smiling down at me. His teeth are white and porcelained. Veneers. They cost a lot of money. Imagine going around with thousands of quid in your mouth.

The pair of us are just standing there.

'I'll ask the lady to let us out, to let us in?'

The woman on the aisle seat is still asleep. I'm sure I saw her down a pill before take-off.

'Excuse me,' I say to the woman. 'Excuse me, could you move so we could swap?' but the woman doesn't wake. Even when I tap her gently. Even when I tap her slightly harder.

'This lady's out,' I say, turning to him again. 'Should I slide in? Or you slide in?'

I don't mean to be flirtatious but I know what it sounds like. His eyes glitter a little.

The fasten seatbelts sign illuminates overhead with a collective ping. I look up at the sign and blush for no reason. I blush deeper when I realize I'm blushing.

The air host who sold the scratch cards stops on the aisle and flags us. 'Fasten seatbelts,' he says and points at the sign. His fake tan is subtle except near his hairline and ears, which are clearly a much whiter colour.

I say, 'Yeah, sure, we're—'

'Sit down and fasten your seatbelts,' he repeats and rolls his hands in a hurry-up gesture. 'The seatbelt sign is lit.'

'I know, but we're—'

'Now.' He moves his manicured hands to his hips. 'Please, sir and madam. Now.'

My seat mate's face crumples one side, suppressing a smile. He sits, clicks his seatbelt on. I chuckle as I sit.

The air host makes a 'Puh' sound and fumes off.

'Well, there goes that idea,' I say. 'Thanks for the offer.'

I put my books at my feet again.

'We can still swap. Is he gone?' the man says.

I giggle and check. 'But the seatbelt sign is lit!' I mimic the air host.

'I'll climb behind you and you shimmy in, in front of me. We're gonna have to be very quick. Okay? Deal?'

'Let's go.'

He climbs, I shimmy. We vaguely touch but not really. Not any more than when we were standing beside each other. He readjusts his long legs into the seat, squished more because of my travel pillow and books and handbag hogging the space underneath.

We've our seatbelts on when the air host passes again. He

eyes us briefly, moves up the aisle then turns back to look at us, puzzled.

'He knows,' the man says covertly without moving his lips much. He's looking down at his feet.

I snigger. I look out the window to avoid eye contact with the air host. 'I don't think he likes us.'

'He just doesn't know us yet,' the man says. 'I'm Julian by the way.'

He puts his hand out.

'Natalie.'

I ignore the tiny trembling dancing love feeling in the bottom of my stomach. Take it easy, Natalie.

The ocean of cloud is hypnotic. The plane descends through the white mist, slicing it, until the actual sea is below, navy and unassuming. It reminds me of a geography exam. X marks the North Sea, Y is an industrial fishing ship, Z are oil rigs.

'Look, Julian, a windmill,' I say. 'We're in Holland now.'

The spokes of the mill turn.

'That's a wind turbine,' Julian says.

'The windmill?'

'Yeah, the windmill. It's a wind turbine.'

My neck flushes. 'Oh yeah, god, it is a wind turbine. Did you ever make something something else because that's what you were expecting?'

'I don't think I follow.'

'You wanted to see something so you saw it in its likeness.'

'Life can be like that sometimes,' he says.

The neat Dutch fields follow, along with many more wind turbines. There are little hunks of ships in the sea. As we draw closer to land, smaller boats and tiny people are visible on the shore. Are they sunbathing? I tried to predict the weather, it said mid-twenties but looking at this cloud cover, this greyness, I wonder if I've packed properly. I'll be in Amsterdam for three nights and brought only summer clothes in my hand luggage. Will I regret not bringing a rain jacket?

'So, business or pleasure?' I ask Julian, then realize that it's maybe not the sort of question to ask an attractive man on a flight to Amsterdam. He smiles again. Those rich kid teeth.

'Pardon?'

'Your trip? Too risky to answer?'

'Hey,' he laughs. 'Business. And pleasure. Both. Or neither. I'm the keynote speaker at a conference on Friday. Hoping to check out the sights while I'm here though. It's a beautiful city, I hear. You? Business or pleasure?'

'I got a cheap flight. City break.'

We're silent again as the plane increases its descent. I hold onto the arm rests tightly, so tight my hands blanch. I don't mind flying but I hate landing. That awful thud when the wheels touch the ground. The drama of that huge change, being airborne to on land.

The plane whacks the runway like an unexpected kiss and I let a deep breath out as it slows.

An announcement celebrates the safety and punctuality of the flight. It reminds us to book with the same company again. The pilot thanks us; his accent has a silky European inflection.

Phones switch on around the plane and they jangle greetings. Julian turns his on. His screensaver is a group photo. He's studious as he swipes and thumbs at the screen. He pushes his glasses further up the bridge of his nose, and from side-on he's a lot like Jamie Foxx, that smooth angle to his nose, the clear dark skin, intelligent eyes. Stop checking him out, I shake myself. Stop admiring him. If he catches me.

He catches me.

I smile. 'Could I get my bag, at your feet?'

'Yes, of course.' He hands my stuff over carefully. 'Can I have my bag? At your feet?'

I didn't notice the slick flat leather satchel on the ground. 'I nearly stood on that. Never saw it. Sorry.'

'My tablet and books are in there.'

'There's books in this, it's tiny,' I say and pass it to him.

He opens the zip and pulls out two books. One on economics and one on Zen philosophy. I glimpse into the bag and see a hardbound business notebook and a clear plastic bag with tablets and creams.

'God, how did all of those fit into there?' I ask, stunned.

'Sometimes life's like that.'

The woman asleep on the aisle seat is now alert. She leans back and looks at me as Julian concentrates on his phone again.

'I study auras,' she says.

'Oh,' I say.

'When you got on, yours was greenish and his was purple. Your auras have both changed colour. Merged. They're both orange now, orange and what's the word?' She looks off to the left. 'Shuddering.'

I redden again and hope he hasn't heard her. But he gives me a side-glance that shows me he has.

'I took two Valiums when I got on,' the woman says. 'Haven't done a bloody thing for me.'

'You were fast asleep when I asked you to let us out?' I say. 'Were you not?' I feel tricked somehow, and my instinct is to check Julian's left hand. Long lean fingers, no ring.

The woman winks at me.

The passengers stand, shuffle, move off the flight with a stop-start momentum.

It's our turn to get out of our seats and Julian asks if I want him to lift my luggage down.

'I can manage. I don't have much in it. Thanks though.' He moves out of the way to let me into the aisle in front of him. I take my backpack from the stowaway overhead, notice his chrome luggage case, the tag with his name 'JULIAN GRAHAM' and a contact email address.

I join the queue off the flight, listen to the murmur of people planning their adventures, and, to pass the time, wonder which of the passengers are there for the cultural side of Amsterdam and which are there for its underbelly. I turn around. Julian smiles at me, those unnatural teeth again.

I feel self-conscious, aware of being looked at. I take out my headphones and plug them into my phone, put on one of my dance playlists. Maybe I should exchange numbers with him? How do people do this? How do they be single and maintain their dignity? I flick a glance back to where he is, for a second, and he catches me. A flush crashes on my face and neck. I turn away quickly.

Inside the terminal, I join the European passport holders' queue, which moves at a steady pace. The Non-EU one crawls. I wonder what the passport I hold represents. Irish. Christian. Rich. Though I'm not religious or wealthy.

I look around for Julian.

A heavily pregnant Muslim woman is agitated. It's hot, and their queue is stationary. She checks her watch, glares at the security guard, rubbing her engorged belly. I try to imagine what it would feel like to hold another life inside mine, all the extra weight of it pressing down on my body.

The pregnant woman asks the security guard in English why the queue hasn't moved in over forty minutes.

'We must be thorough,' he says, his English sounding so competent and clear, I assume he's Dutch.

'But I will have to pee soon. I don't want to lose my place. Why is that other queue moving so quickly?'

'Well,' he says and raises his shoulders, 'you should know these security checks by now. It's hardly a new phenomenon.'

'Excuse me?'

'We must be thorough. In these times,' he says. 'If you want to go to the bathroom, I'll hold your spot.'

She sighs a thank you and he clicks the security rope for her. She waddles out, her hands on her back; her bump bulks in front of her.

My queue moves ahead. More arguing comes from behind but I don't look to see what's happening this time. I go through to the baggage reclaim area, Julian queues at the luggage belt. He's polite with people. I think about his smile, his grace, and then reprimand myself.

I want to say hi or something but stop myself. I go on to the main airport, pass boutiques, florists, a jeweller's and a seafood restaurant. Two police officers cycle by, my first experience of Dutch cyclists. I wander around and look for a way out but end up in a train station.

Groups of young excited male tourists try to figure out the machines, itch for a smoke. I don't want to get caught up with them so I follow signs to the tourist information office and ask for directions.

I look for the bus stop and pass by stag parties, groups of young men and pairs of older men. I'm a bit jagged from the flight. I'll nap, shower, eat, relax soon. I ask about buses outside and a friendly man in a luminous orange vest explains everything. I buy a ticket and wait. I hear something musical, something familiar and turn around. Julian is laughing and joking with a cab driver as he lugs his large case to the boot. His satchel is strapped crossbody. He has such an easy way about him. I want to wave and call to him as he climbs into the car, but I know he's out of my league. Someone like that.

Proper wealthy. I wonder what colour my aura is now, grey probably. Dutch sky grey. The bus chugs and I board.

The stops are announced in English as the bus travels through the city. I still manage to miss mine.

I ask the driver, 'Excuse me, am I near the Van Gogh museum?'

She has a quizzical expression.

'The Van Go museum? The Van Goff museum?' How the hell did you say it?

'Museumplein, one stop ago.' She gestures with her thumb.

'Great,' I mumble and press the button to get off at the next stop.

I tow my bag and wish I'd stayed at home, the usual lonely, ratty, hangry feeling of being lost and new and fatigued in a foreign place.

I source some free Wi-Fi from the street and check maps, only to discover I've walked past my hostel already.

The receptionist is a handsome Dutch guy, with a neat haircut and designer sideburns. I wonder about my mascara. I check in and ask if there's a café or restaurant nearby.

He gives me my key, tells me where the lift is and then informs me that food is pretty expensive in the surrounding streets but if I don't mind that, there are many places to eat. I wonder if there's a hint of condescension in his tone or if I'm tired and hypersensitive.

The lift has a marble finish and spotlights around the mirror. The hostel is pleasant for the money I'm paying. It's more like a hotel. When I enter the dorm, I realize it must have been a hotel room before but now it's packed with bunk beds. Nobody is around but two beds have bags, books, PJs and other clues. A black patent suitcase dominates the corner. Man or woman?

I have bed and safe number two. I go to the safe and read the instructions on how to work it. When I open it, I find a bottle of Heineken and a quarter bottle of gin inside. A welcome gift from departing backpackers. I smile for the first time since the flight and twist off the screw top on the Heineken.

I peel back the blind and open the window to a tiny balcony outside. 'Cheers, Amsterdam,' I say and raise my bottle.


I lie in the bunk and fall into a much deeper sleep than I expect. After, I shower and change clothes and normalize. I go out for food. The streets are vaguely familiar after being lost on them earlier. I look at restaurant menus but it's not the price that puts me off; I don't want to eat alone.

I keep wandering, hoping I'll come across a supermarket, but it takes a long time. I try to locate where I am on the paper map I got in the hostel.

'Fuck it,' I say and put the map away; instinct can guide me.

After more canals and narrow houses, many cyclists and fashionable people, I find a supermarket. There's an abundance of healthy fast food in the fridge. I stock up on fruit and veg snacks, and a chicken pesto pasta salad for dinner.

As I walk back, I open it and see there's no spoon. I wonder if the hostel has a kitchen. I never investigated. I'm starving, and fish a piece of pasta out. I eat it with my fingers. Then another. It reminds me of years ago, of a different trip to New Zealand when my eating was much more disordered.

I walk by police officers, who are tall and strong. They shout at men on scaffolding. All laugh.

The sky is a vast, hot, grey cloud punctured with blue. In a square, old men play chess with human sized pieces. I don't know if I hate Amsterdam, as I walk, eating my food like a barbarian, all alone.


The patent suitcase is open and a young man unpacks his stuff onto a shelf. He's athletic and has Mediterranean hair and eyes.

'I'm Leon.'

I wonder if he's Dutch.

'German,' he says, 'but my father is a Spaniard.'

Very nice.

He's begun a Masters in Sociology in the University of Amsterdam and is looking for accommodation in the city.

'I'll stay in the hostel for three nights until I find something.'

'I'm here for three nights too,' I say and open my plastic bag, pull out a tub of strawberries. I offer him one. 'It took me hours to find a supermarket.'

He declines. 'Really? There's one behind that building there.' He points at the window. 'Maybe two hundred metres from here.'

I sigh. 'Well, I suppose getting lost is how you figure a city out.'

'Exactly. I am going for a smoke. Do you want to join?'

'A smoke smoke?'

'It could be. If you want,' he says and grins.

'I don't smoke, thanks.'

The room door opens and an Asian man hurls his backpack on the floor.

'So heavy,' he says.

I sympathize.

'Timothy,' he says. 'Where are you from?'

'Ireland,' I say.

'No way, I left there today. Dublin for the past week. Man, I am partied out. I nearly missed my flight.'

I laugh.

'I don't want to seem rude, but I desperately need a shower. I will see you later,' he says and takes the towel from his bunk.

It's like sliding doors; within moments, an American enters. He wears black-framed glasses and has bright blond hair. 'Hey,' he says and goes to the bed nearest mine. 'What you reading?'

'It's a self-help book on being alive while you're alive.'

'Are there other ways to do it?'

'You could be kind of dead inside?'

'True. Well, I gotta dash.' He sprays himself with aftershave. 'Reuniting with some family of mine and I've got to get rid of this hangover. Nice meeting you. We could talk books tomorrow maybe? If you're around? Have a good night.'

Rejuvenated by making friends, I go for another quick walk to see if I can find the Anne Frank House. I booked a ticket for it the same day I booked my flight.

I notice the I AMSTERDAM sign's big red and white letters. Some kids hang out at the M. It's a breezy evening but not cold. I put my phone's camera into selfie mode, take a picture of myself in front of the sign. The light is bad so I move closer to a streetlight, to try again. I check where I am in relation to the sign and notice someone at the big red I. I blink and check again. It's him. The fella from the flight. This night keeps improving. I trot over to him before I know what I'm going to say.

'Julian.' I try to sound confident. My breath increases its pace.

His eyebrows lift and crease his forehead. 'Natalie? Wow. Hello.'

I smile broadly. 'Fancy meeting you here.'

'Fancy that.'

'I was trying to get a selfie with the sign in the background, but I failed.'

'Do you want me to take it?' he offers.

'Okay,' I say and he swaps places with me. I set my phone up for him, show him what to press. I smile and he seems to take a few pics. I ask if he's got a good one.

'Yeah, sure, but I had an idea. Why don't you go before the S, be I AM and you. Would that be cool?'

For the next few minutes, Julian directs me for this photoshoot.

'Be more Dutch. How about point at yourself. Okay, now point at the sky. Be someone who thought they were in Paris but found out they were in Amsterdam.'

The two of us laugh.

'Come in,' I say and beckon him to sit beside me in one of the letters. 'Come in for one with me. My plane friend photographer.'

'I'm a bit camera shy.' He hands me the phone.

'Really? Why? You've no need to be.'

His elegant face is lit by the streetlamps. His striped scarf hangs around his neck. His lips are full, his stubble light.

'Thanks, but I am. I look weird in photos.'

I reach an arm out, lean into him, take a selfie. Then I inspect it. He looks nice but embarrassed.

'You're photogenic, Julian.' I nod to reiterate it.

The two of us stay hunched in the D, unmoving. I'm pressed against his shoulder and arm. I try to ignore the pleasurable sensations swarming my pelvis.

'You staying somewhere nice?' I ask, looking out over Museumplein.

'Yeah, it's okay. Work are paying for it. Twin beds. Four stars. You?'

'I'm in a place that's grand for a hostel. Only problem is sharing the room with three guys.'

'I couldn't stay in a hostel,' he says.

'Why not?'

'Too old, maybe. Need my own space.'

'I dunno. I mean, I should be fussier but I don't care so much about where I sleep. A hotel is lovely but you don't meet as many people as you do in the hostels. What age are you?'

'Nearly thirty-six, next month actually. You?'

'Thirty-one.'

'True about the hotels. I don't meet many people when I'm travelling around. Maybe colleagues or conference participants. Though older couples seem to always want to talk to me. Mostly I do all the tourist shit solo.'

'I do too. Sometimes. Well, I aim to do it solo and if I make a friend to go with, it's a bonus. Though my last trip was with a friend and it nearly broke us up.'

'Yeah?'

'We had conflicted interests. But we swung it back around on the flight home. Resentment isn't worth the pain it brings,' I say, and pause. 'There's probably some friends you'll never shake.'

'True friends. I've a few of them too. And what are you doing tonight, Natalie?'

'Now?'

'Yeah, do you want to go for a walk with me maybe? Go for a beer?'

I hesitate for a second and look in his eyes. 'Yeah, I do. Do you think I'll be okay like this in a bar?' I look at my clothes – a moss green fitted blouse and black skinny jeans, not quite sophisticated night wear. I'm glad I have at least changed since the flight.

'Yeah, I definitely think you will be.'

His eyes are warm and attentive. I feel protected in his company, as we walk the streets I point out the things I remember from earlier.

'There's this really nice bridge up ahead. Look there on the right, look at that penis lamp.'

'Every town needs a good penis lamp,' he says.

'There's an ass candle holder in the window up ahead. The candle fits into it.'

'What will they come up with next?'

'A vagina sensor light?'

For a moment, I think he's going for my hand, as we walk, but it's something in front of me he reaches for. A piece of paper.

DJ AZILE, TRANCE ALL-NIGHTER –
ELEMENTENSTRAAT, 12TH APRIL, DOORS 8 P.M.

'That's tomorrow. Sounds fun.'

'You like to rave?' Julian asks.

His eyes widen in my silence.

'I can't take the days after,' he says. 'I can't do them.'

'I know what you mean but I'm never thinking about that at the time. Are you a businessman or something, Julian? You have smart luggage for someone in their leisure wear.'

'You're quite observant. I could be a businessman, maybe. Or an entrepreneur. Though they don't quite fit. I suppose the way to put it, the modern term is that I'm involved in a start-up.'

'What kind of thing?'

He pauses. 'Health, fitness. Nutrition. Mainly nutrition. That kind of thing.'

'I was once a spin instructor.'

'Yeah?'

'I got fired though.'

'Why?'

'Ah Julian, it's a long story, for another time maybe.'

'What do you do now?'

'I'm almost a fitness instructor. Waiting on the certs.'

'It's good to learn.'

'My final exams and practicals were last week but they went well. Took me a while to find this path. Very new to it. I'm not making any money yet. Hence the room with the three young men. Hey, is this the red light district?'

The next street is teeming. The prostitutes wear lingerie and stand in the windows of the buildings like real life X-rated Barbie dolls displayed in packaging. They take selfies, or dance provocatively for the people ogling.

The canal reflects the red lights.

'Are you going to get a girl? My god, they are beautiful-looking.'

'Nah,' he says, 'not for me.'

'Ever try?'

'Did anyone tell you, Natalie, not to ask questions you don't want to hear the answers to?' He stops on the street.

'I'll take that as a yes-but-I-don't-want-to-discuss-it.'

'Exactly. What's your plan for tomorrow?'

'I've booked in to the Anne Frank House for 9.30 a.m. I might do some other tourist stuff in the afternoon,' I say.

'Solo?'

'I guess.'

We wander through the streets in comfortable silence.

At my hostel's door, he says, 'I've booked a canal cruise at 4 p.m., do you want to join me? I mean, it's not an issue if you don't. I'll be on it anyway. It would be cool to share it with someone. No pressure. You may have other plans.'

'Julian,' I say, amused at his spiralling, 'yes, I'd like to do the canal cruise and I think it would be heaps more fun with someone than on my own.'

'Shall I come by here?' He gestures to the hostel. 'Maybe 3 p.m.? We could walk to it if the weather stays clear?'

'Yeah, that would be lovely.'

'Okay, thanks. I'm glad we met up again.'

'Me too, Julian, me too.'

Inside the dorm room, I feel buoyant.

'What's happening?' Leon asks, smiling at me as he dries his hair with a towel.

'I met this guy on the flight over. He was interesting. Good-looking. Funny.'

'Tall, dark and handsome?'

'Totally. And I bumped into him on the street. We've spent the last couple of hours walking around, chatting. It's been lovely. Romantic even.'

'Ooooh,' Leon says. 'That's amore. You want to come outside? I've got some sweet j rolled.'

'I've had enough highs for one evening.'

I wake early and visit the Anne Frank House. Within seconds, I'm crying. Anne's story, the treatment of the Jews by the Nazis, how she was a normal teenager in the midst of this. It breaks my heart.

Upstairs, I can't believe I'm in her room. The cramped space. Walking around it, I spot a couple on a date, and wonder if that works. Does it bring people closer together to see the horrors that humans can inflict on each other? Does it make them want to keep each other safe?

I get my tissues out again watching a video, grainy black and white, of Jews boarding a train to a concentration camp. They were in good thick winter coats bearing the Star of David. At the end of the clip, a child boards, she seems unbothered that everyone is squashed. The little girl sees the camera filming and waves heartily at it. She has no idea she's off to starve, off to see her family and people destroyed, off to her annihilation. She waves. Her innocence.

*

The BodyWorlds museum salesman offers me a two euro discount. The street is hot and I need a break from walking. I go inside. The exhibits are all about the body. The effect of cigarettes is disgusting, but what's more confronting is the length of the digestive system laid out from mouth to anus and the amount of work necessary to process food and gain nutrients from it. It shows the intense effects of sugar and junk food on the system, of meat, of grease. I'm appalled at how badly I treated myself scoffing on shit food mindlessly. I'm amazed at what a forgiving and powerful ally the body is.

Two older Brits marvel at the heart. They discuss the various heart attacks they've had. One of the men is overweight and discusses veins and arteries in depth. The pair move on to a conversation about stents. One of them asks where they'll go for lunch and the other mentions a pizzeria next door.

I wonder if I can squeeze in another museum before meeting Julian.

I pay and enter the sex museum. This place would have been altogether shocking maybe fifteen, twenty years ago but now, in the age of internet porn, I realize how desensitized I am. Even the girls in the red light zone – for a couple of minutes it felt weird, objectifying them, but the red light district is no creepier than the average hip hop music video.

I overhear some American students discussing the mushroom trip they were on the day before.

'I spoke to God, man,' one of them says. He looks pretty high still.

'Which shop was it?'

'It's on the street across from this one, in the red light district. The white dude in the shop has dreads and cross eyes, he's French maybe, or fuck knows. European but not Dutch. He has info, bro. Ask him what kind of high you want and he'll hook you up.'

'Sweet, bro.'

I leave the museum and walk to where the student mentioned.

Inside, I get a slight thrill. There's information on how to grow plants, how to save the planet, and all sorts of smoking paraphernalia, hemp products, mushrooms and headshop highs.

The shop assistant wears a colourful hoodie. 'Madam,' he says and doffs an imaginary cap to me.

'Which mushrooms would be best for a beginner? I don't want something too heavy, never tried them before.'

'Truffles,' he corrects me. He runs through my options and I choose Mushrocks.

'Now you got somewhere safe to go? I recommend you go to a park or be with nature. Don't eat, don't drink, just have water. Earth don't like chemicals. Here, take these too,' he says and passes a packet of peanuts. 'You'll need these for the taste. Are you doing this with a friend?'

'Sort of.'

'Twenty-four euro please,' he says. 'Namaste.'

*

The day is still warm and sunny when Julian collects me. I thumb the pack in my pocket when he asks me how the morning was.

'Do you want to grab a sandwich or tea or something for the boat? I've got our tickets.'

'Let me pay you for mine, Julian,' I say.

'No. Please don't. My expenses are on the business. I'm glad for your company for an afternoon. Really.'

'Okay, well, let me get the drinks in. Do you want a beer? Some crisps?'

'I'll have a beer and a water. You know the tap water here is the same water in the showers and toilets and sinks. It's one of the best water systems in the world.'

'Really? I was bloody gasping yesterday and went walking for miles to find a shop. I didn't know I could drink from the taps.'

'You could drink from the toilets here. But don't.'

We board the canal cruise. I tell him about the mushroom shop and the man working there. The high it's supposed to give.

'Do you want to do some with me?'

'I can't.' He shakes his head sadly. 'I convulsed twice before when I tried them in uni. Allergic.'

'Really?'

'Yup. I can be the sober person to your trip though, if you'd like.'

Halfway through the canal cruise, after learning about some famous Amsterdam sites and that, I decide fuck it, take the mushrooms out and down a few. They leave a metallic tang on my taste buds.

'Ugh,' I say, tearing the pack of peanuts and pouring them into my mouth, chewing them into a paste to spread around my tongue.

The houses start to bend towards the end of the cruise and I'm anxious to get off the boat. I apologize. 'I only took a quarter of the packet, imagine if I took more.'

'You'll be okay,' Julian says. 'Breathe and relax.'

'I was going to go to that rave.'

'Hey, don't let me tell you your business,' he says, his empty hands up, 'but a rave is not a good place to go right now. You should maybe be somewhere quiet. I'm going to flag a cab and bring you back to your hostel. Is that cool?'

'Yeah. Thank you.'

'It should wear off soon.'

At my hostel, he gets out of the cab to walk me to the door.

'Thanks for joining me.'

'I'm sorry for spoiling the end.'

'You didn't, crazy lady. Maybe buy some sugary things from the vending machine. As much as I detest sugar, it'll bring you back to this reality if you need to get grounded.'

'Thanks, Julian.'

'Maybe we'll catch up again?'

I nod and go inside. All my roommates are in the dorm

room talking loudly and preparing for a night out. I lie on the bunk and try to stay calm. The room is trippy. Colours are coming off everything. I think the guys can hear my paranoid thoughts. One of them plays metal music with heavy guitar, drums and screeching and it scares me. It's like the song is wielding a weapon and threatening me. I can see the violence imbued in each sound.

I compose a message.

Julian, have you left already? Can I ask you a favour? The lads here are being so noisy. I'm kind of freaking out. Can I come and hang out with you again? Your energy is so calming to be around. Tell me to piss off if this is inconvenient. I'm tripping balls a bit. I should have thought about this beforehand.

You know where my hotel is, Nat?

Around the corner from here somewhere?

I'll send you a location pin. Or hey, come downstairs and outside. I'll come back and collect you.

You sure?

Yeah. It's no problem. It'll pass too, don't worry.

I know. I feel a bit wwwaaaaahhhhhh.

296

You are a wwwaaaaahhhhh alright.

Hey. I don't even know what that is.

I'll be there in seven minutes, Nat. Hang tight.

Thanks, Jules.

I re-read the messages. They beat on the screen like a heart.

Seven minutes later, Julian waits for me in the lobby of the hostel. I hold his arm, grateful.

'Do I look fucked?' I ask.

'I'd be slightly lying if I said no. It's only because I know the signs. The pupils and that.'

'I'm tripping so bad, Julian,' I say. 'Everything has a wave of colour coming off it. It's like a bloody cliché with the trippy colours. Fucking hell. When does it wear off? I feel like I'm seeing the mysteries of the universe unravel and rewind and then play again but I'm not quite seeing it. I'm on the edge of seeing it.'

'I don't know, Natalie,' he says.

We walk across the yard and down the fancy street, take a right to his hotel. A porter in fine threads opens the door for us. I feel like a backpacker but Julian's in casual clothes too.

'This place is so swanky,' I say and get distracted by the chandelier in the hall which vibes purple and blue, then green, pink, yellow. 'I'm going to explode with all these colours and waves. People are walking like they're puppets too. Maybe they are puppets? Capitalist ones?'

'Shush till we get up to the room, okay, Natalie, no need to insult the guests.'

'Sorry.'

We take the lift to his bedroom on the eighth floor. He moves his stuff off the other bed and tells me to lie down.

'You're not going to do anything to me?'

'No, Natalie, I'm not. I'll put on some meditation music, but I'll also be working. You relax, okay? This will all pass soon.'

He says to flick the lamp off if I want, he'll have enough light at his desk.

'Do you trust me, Julian? I am under the influence.'

'Yeah, call me crazy but I do. I know you're sweet and open. Honest.'

'I am honest, look at the state of me to be presenting myself like this to you.'

He works in the corner, studying and typing things up. I breathe with the music and watch him. My trip loses its intensity. Form is not to be trusted yet. Matter still swirls colourful energy. In the dark, I wonder about the shape of him at his desk; I haven't seen it this way before, on the plane or even on the boat earlier in the day. Something about his shape is odd. I can't put my finger on what it is, maybe I'm hallucinating still.

'Just going to use the bathroom,' I say.

His toothbrush is charging and his toothpaste, shaving gel and razor are all on the top of the sink basin. He has face oils, body oils, essential oils and other lotions wrapped up in a washbag. I am impressed with his organic range.

I try to pee but it takes ages and is so uncomfortable. Objects aren't colourful or psychedelic anymore but I'm sensing things halfway between my mind's eye and my eyesight, shapes growing in the mosaic tiles, the wall swallowing itself. He has lots of other creams and potions, Vaseline, inflammation tablets, blister plasters. All these products. Is he some sort of American psycho but an English version? British psycho.

'Are you okay in there?' He raps on the door.

I get such a fright that I knock some pills; I'm not sure what they're for.

'Yep.'

'You sure? I'm worried.'

'I can't pee. I've tried for ages. Everything feels weird. Okay, I'll be out in a sec.'

'I'm ordering room service, is there anything you'd eat? When is the last time you ate?'

'Well, I ate some mushrooms about four hours ago.'

He chuckles. 'I'll order fries for you? Will you eat them?'

'Yeah, thanks, Julian.'

After eating, the trip wears off. My face almost feels normal again.

Julian turns the TV on. We watch some news in Dutch, some CNN.

'Any music?' I ask

Julian flicks around and finds a pop station. We sit in silence and watch the music videos.

'Thanks for helping me out,' I say. 'You're a decent man.'

'You're a wild woman.'

'I suppose I'll head off so. Thanks again.'

'Do you want to wait? There's a spare bed and, like, it might not be fully faded, there's still a chance you'll freak again.'

'Is there?'

'Well, maybe not. But the offer stands if you want to stay here for the night. No funny business.'

'Like a sleepover?'

He laughs hard. 'Yes, Natalie, like a sleepover.'

'Okay,' I say and watch him again. He goes into the bathroom, and I can hear his puttering around. He comes out wearing the clothes he went in with and sleeps in them in the bed across from me. I can't say anything, I'm wearing the same clothes too.


In the morning, we laugh about the night and I'm so happy it's over.

'I will never, ever do that shit again,' I say. 'Thanks for looking after me.'

'You got to stop with the thanks. People helped me out before when I needed them, it's okay. Do you want something to eat? I can order up or you can take breakfast downstairs?'

'There's a café around the corner. Would you let me treat you to a coffee before I go, to show my appreciation?'

'But my expenses cover—'

'Please let me get you something, to say thanks. I'm sorry, last night was a bit hairy. I don't know why impulses get the better of me sometimes.'

'Maybe you shouldn't judge yourself so harshly.'

'What?'

'You're too hard on yourself. Things are what they are. It's done. It was an experience. That's it.'

I feel ropey on the street. The small café on the corner stinks of weed.

'I hate the smell of this stuff.'

'Me too,' he says, 'but the oil is good.'

'You love oils, do you? Some collection in your bathroom.'

He gives me a closed mouthed smile and shrugs as in, what-can-I-say. 'Look I don't want to inhale the second-hand weed. I don't want to get the munchies. I can't, in fact, get the munchies.'

'Weed makes me paranoid,' I say.

'Should we go somewhere that doesn't smell of weed since neither of us like it?'

'Yes.'

We order from a hipster coffee van and sit on a bench to drink it. The morning is fresh. I can't stop smiling.

Julian kisses my cheek at the hostel door. My cheek tingles. I am thirteen again.

*

Later Julian texts to ask if I'm okay.

Yes, much better.

He asks,

Do you want to go for dinner later?

I reply,

Date?

with a tongue-out emoji.
He sends back the blushing emoji,

Yes, if you'd like?

I smile re-reading his messages. Desire strokes me.

I meet Julian for dinner, wearing the nicest outfit I can muster
– a long black skirt and a sleeveless black lace top over it. The
restaurant is beside his hotel. We sit outside and are bathed in
orange light while the sun sets.

'Do I need to apologize again for last night?' I ask. 'You'd think I'd know better. I thought taking a tiny handful wouldn't have much effect. Must have ruined your canal cruise.'

'You didn't. It was fun. I'm sorry I couldn't have joined in, but then again, I'm glad to have not.'

'You're a great person, Julian. Really wonderful.'

He moves his chair over. 'I'm going to try and kiss you, is that okay?'

I nod and he goes in for the kiss. The evening is warm. Amsterdam bustles behind us, people talk in a different language, tall blondes and tourists cycle to cafés or clubs or work or home. He kisses me and I get that faint carbolic smell again; it's sour to my nose. Chemical, sanitizing. It's a smell of sickness, it dawns on me. I stop kissing him.

'Julian, are you married?'

He pulls back. 'No. Why?'

Because there's something, something not quite right, I can't say it. 'I dunno.'

'I'm single for a few years. I'm not sure I could even say I've had a girlfriend. A proper roses and chocolates meet-the-family girlfriend. Do you have a partner or something? Is that why you're asking?'

'No, god no. The last relationship I was in was years ago. A dangerous thing with rescuing and destruction and so much lies. Years back. I spent a long time finding myself. I'm not toxic anymore though, promise. No need for a hazmat suit around me.'

I kiss him this time, putting more pressure onto his lips. There's a clout of hormones coursing through me.

And it's an evening of kissing and I like how it's not horny kissing where all we want to do is rip the clothes off each other. It's distinguished movie-style kissing. Not sloppy. Not deep. It's regal and magical. We kiss and kiss. By the canals. By the bridges. In the main square. In front of hotels and churches and narrow houses. Beside the bicycle lane. Even in the red light district.

We kiss and go for a beer and I think it might be the most romantic night of my life. Actually, I know it is.

The kissing has to end, of course, and we walk back to Museumplein when I'm too cold to stay out any longer. The kissing would need to be warmed up by something sexual but Julian isn't giving me the signs. In fact, he hasn't really tried to touch me intimately, skin to skin. He only momentarily brushed my ass with his hand. I'm a bit frustrated that he hasn't tried to take things further.

I lead him back to his hotel.

'Can I come up? I'd invite you to mine but I don't think you'd like to share a bottom bunk with me.'

'Nat.' He's hesitant. He mustn't want me.

'Since we've already technically slept together, last night and all,' I joke but he's unresponsive. Unmoving.

He says nothing.

'Oh shit. Have I upset you? This is being too forward, isn't it? I don't know how to do these things, I'm sorry,' I say. Panic throbs in my temple.

'No. No.' He shakes his head.

'You are married, aren't you? I knew you were too good to be true.'

'I'm not married, I told you. Not even close.'

'Then what's your secret?'

He crosses his arms and looks away. In a quiet voice, he says, 'Come upstairs.'

Julian is frosty in the lobby as the pianoman plays a jazzy instrumental version of 'Let it Be', as the marble floors shine and the rich people saunter. He is silent in the lift. I seek his eyes, but he's still, deep in thought. The lift ascends at a snail's pace. Thankfully, no one else gets in from the other floors. I avoid my reflection.

I'm sorry by the time we get to the room.

He slides the keycard in and opens the door. Turns on the light. The air feels tense as I slink in behind him. The room is more spacious than I remember. We're a world away from each other. He goes to his bed. I slowly rake my bottom lip with my top teeth.

At last, he says, 'You're perceptive, you know.'

'I can go, Julian, I've messed this up. I've ruined the flow of it. I didn't mean to offend you but I've had such a good time with you. It felt like we totally connected.'

'Do you want something to drink?' he says. 'You're a sweetheart, Nat. I don't come across people like you often.'

'Could I have a small glass of water and then I'll go. I think the boys from my dorm are going to a club. I can chaperone them.'

He fills a glass. Then he sits beside me.

'I'm trying to be a gentleman,' Julian says.

'From the man who's used hookers,' I say kidding, but cringe immediately, knowing once the words are out, it's not funny.

He turns his shoulders away from me. 'Don't sling a past at me that you know nothing about.'

'God, I'm sorry. It was supposed to be a joke. I don't know where that came from. Insecurity. Shit. I agree about the past. We start from now only. From here. I didn't mean to be a dick there.'

We're very awkward as we sit beside each other on the twin bed.

I want him to kiss me. I turn to him but he's expressionless. I note his smell again, the slight sweat, vanilla, meat, cinnamon, the carbolic. I trace where his hairline meets the flesh of his neck. He responds and kisses me. I apply a little more pressure. We move our bodies closer, I wrap my legs around him then we push against each other. He stops cold. Jumps up, steps away.

'What is it, Julian? I don't understand. Please be honest with me?'

'What?'

'I had a deceptive boyfriend before. I know the signs when a man is withholding, when he's being secretive. I went along with it in the past. Even though my gut warned me. I ignored my intuition and it devastated me in the long run. I didn't know how to trust myself for years after that. I won't do it again. It's blaring at me now. You're lying to me about something.'

Julian looks stunned.

I stand. 'I'm leaving. I didn't mean for this to turn so intense. I wanted to have fun. I fancied you since I saw you on the flight. You're smart and funny. And kind. It's been such a nice few days. Anyway, I'm sorry and thank you. Bye.'

I gather my stuff.

'Natalie, no wait, I like you, too.' He stares into the middle distance. 'But I don't want to scare you,' he says and gulps.

'What?'

'It's not something you're going to know how to deal with.'

So many things that could be wrong cascade through my mind that I can't even pin one image down.

'Try me,' I say.

'In the past,' he says and his head bows.

I brace myself.

'I was morbidly obese.'

'What?' I say and close an eye.

'I was once morbidly obese. You know, fat?'

I nod.

'I was once so fat, I was deeply ill.'

'Really?' I try to picture it.

'Yep.'

'You? You were fat?'

'I was at death's door fat.'

I scan his body up and down for this fat. But it's just Julian there.

'I lost the weight,' he says, knowing I'm looking for it. 'It took five years. It took determination and an overhaul of my lifestyle but I lost it.'

We are silent.

He stretches his fingers out and clasps them back in, and seems like he's going to speak but doesn't.

'The thing is,' he says eventually and pauses again. 'There's things about my condition they don't tell you. They don't advertise. There's skin. I still have the skin. I lost the fat. Not the skin.'

'What do you mean?' I eye him, looking all over his body. He's so tall I never noticed more than his height.

'I have ten kilos of extra skin. Excess. It covered the fat. The fat is gone. The skin isn't.'

'Oh.'

'Yeah,' he says. He bites his lip. 'I'm trying to get on the list for the NHS removal but my weight needs to be constant for two years before they'll consider me.'

'Why?'

'In case I put it on again.'

'Could you?'

'I have an addiction. It's like being a heroin addict. Or a smoker. You can quit but can you be sure you're never going to relapse? You're never going to be tempted to take that shot of H, smoke that cigarette? I mean, I don't think I will. But there's always that tiny glimmer of danger. That I could blow out. They have to be careful with who they offer the surgery to. It's an extreme operation.'

I nod slowly.

'It's pricey too, if I want to go private. Costs thousands. That's why I'm here. I'm giving a talk at a health conference. Keynote speaker. It's about weight and bingeing.'

'You're trying to help others.'

'Maybe I'll have to go private. If I can get the money saved up, from these talks.'

'Do you have any pictures?'

'Excuse me?'

'Of when you were bigger?' I'm thinking of the typical someone in one leg of their jeans diet photo.

'Yeah.'

'Can I see them?'

'You sure?'

'Yeah.'

He gets his tablet, logs in. I go to the minibar and take out a wee bottle of vodka and a can of 7 Up. 'Will you have a vodka and white?'

'Hold the lemonade for me,' he says.

He shows his camera roll.

'Holy shit,' I say.

'Yeah. The thing that makes me go, whoa, is that when I was that big, I was invisible. I felt like nobody could see me. Maybe people didn't want to see me. I repulsed them. Maybe I was projecting.'

I squirm and admit, 'I look away sometimes. I'm not disgusted – I'm afraid. Not of the person but of my reaction, that my curiosity is going to offend them, upset them.'

'That's empathy, not cruelty. Do you want to go, now you know the truth?'

'No,' I say and shake my head. 'Sure I've poured us a nightcap. We can chat for a bit. No pressure. Do you want me to go?'

'I don't want you to go. Do you not think it's weird, being a normative-bodied person?'

I hand him his straight vodka and take a drink of mine. 'Look, Julian, I've had my own body shit too. Some people carry their baggage on the inside.'

He smiles and holds my gaze.

'Do you have any music in this swanky hotel? Can we listen to that pop channel from last night again?'

He switches on the TV and finds the Classic Hits channel, which is playing disco tunes from the seventies and eighties. We talk about the music and I pull him off the bed to dance with me. We jump around the room and dance like crazy. We get close and look at each other. We kiss again. More passionate this time. I unbutton his shirt. He's wearing a long-sleeved compression vest underneath. I try to lift that off but it's too tight. His breath trembles. He looks like he's about to cry.

'Are you sure, Natalie?'

'Yes.'

In the softly lit room, with disco music in the background, he strips off slowly, morosely. I sit and watch as he undoes his trousers, to reveal black compression shorts. He finds the edges of his vest and lifts it. He takes it off and is wearing a bandage around his stomach. Loose sections of skin under his arm get free, hang low, droop. He looks at me but I keep still. He pulls down his shorts; his extra skin droops down like an empty pouch below his thighs, covering his thighs. His penis is no longer erect. It's flaccid and deserted against his leg. His ass has pouches of loose skin. His eyes are shining. He's only wearing a bandage now, like a corset around his stomach. I stand in front of him. I undo the clasp on the bandage, begin to unwrap him, twirl him around, slowly releasing him from it.

# Forty-one

There's a reluctance to hire me in local gyms. I'm not what they're expecting. Some of them say as much to me, if I get as far as the interview stage. I'm afraid to mention my spin class plans, in case they'll be met with the same judgement and disregard. It's okay to put me down, but I can't let them murder my ideas.

In her office, the manager of a chain near the city centre ushers me to sit but she stays standing. Her slender frame is muscular under her navy suit and her hair is a bush of black. Hairspray scents the air every time she moves.

Policy folders are stacked on the shelves behind her in clip files. The floor has green carpeting. Fast paced music with a clear beat thumps in from the gym.

Her face lacks expression as she says, 'It's just we have enough "inspirational" staff, Natalie. We employ a woman who's older, like old old. Far side of her fifties. And a man with, well, a leg thing.' She does a flickering hand gesture to explain this. 'There's an Asian member of staff too. Sometimes she wears her hijab. Our brand loves diversity as you can see, but you know, there can be such a thing as too much diversity. We'd hate to cross that line into the unknown,' she sucks her teeth, 'and like, intimidate our core audience.'

I get up, thank her for her time. I know I don't have to catch every ball that's thrown anymore. I leave the office and walk across the bouncy gym floor in my dress boots. People run on treadmills, crosstrain, climb steps, jump rope, press dumbbells, crunch, pull-up and row around me. They propel themselves to nowhere.

Outside, the sky curdles with dirty grey clouds. I take a deep breath and check maps on my phone to see if there are other fitness centres about. The wind whistles. It's a wintry summer's day in Dublin. I follow directions to a place on the corner. This is one with an expensive membership fee but a promise to educate clients on fitness and nutrition. The white tiled reception area is air conditioned.

The receptionist orders me to take a seat as I try to hand her my CV. 'Someone will be with you soon.'

She wears a headset and types furiously.

I sit on the white leather-cushioned hard-backed seats. Magazines strewn on the table have covers with strong men and women flexing. Paintings of fruit and vegetables hang on the bleach-white walls. In the corner, a TV shows headlines from around the world. A suicide bomber has killed people in a busy market, a child shot his classmates and teachers at a high school in the US before the police shot him, Kim Kardashian has been pictured in a blue bikini, unbeknownst to her, on a family beach holiday. A series of close-ups of her thighs and behind follow, to zoom in on any spots of suspected cellulite.

A man comes bounding through the reception area and puts his hand out to firmly shake mine. The veins on his arms pop out like tree roots.

'Joel,' he says and looks me up and down. 'What are your whys for being here?'

'I was hoping to drop in my CV but the receptionist said to wait.'

'We have an array of membership packages and I can run through our testimonials. Success is guaranteed.'

I try to pass him the A4 sheets with my work experience details and aspirations, but he refuses to take them. He's hyper and jittery.

'Weight concerns?'

'No, Joel. I'm not trying to join, I'm looking for work.'

'You do have weight concerns, Missus. It's okay. Even I'm concerned about your weight. No secrets here. I had weight concerns too in the past. Look at me now. We're all friends.' His face is pinched with a smile. 'We have a three-day trial membership for only fifty-nine euro. All access. I can calculate your biometrics and create a full fitness and nutrition plan. Want a beach body in six weeks?'

I don't reply.

'Doesn't everyone?' he says and laughs manically.

'I already have a body that can go to the beach.' I look at him but he doesn't meet my eye.

'Or The Incinerator programme. It's new. It's brutal but it is damn efficient.' He slams his fist into his open palm. The slap of it echoes.

His face gurns.

'I'm a newly qualified PT,' I say. 'Looking for a job.'

He cackles a laugh then stops abruptly. 'What about The Transformation? On this eight week programme you will shed some serious pounds. It is brutal,' he says and slams his fist into his palm again. 'But success is guaranteed. Failure is not an option.'

The receptionist clacks on her keyboard.

'I read somewhere that failure is a door not a wall. I like that perspective,' I say.

Joel isn't convinced. 'If winning isn't important, then why does nobody remember losers?'

He waits for me to answer.

'Missus, why does nobody remember losers?' He says it slowly this time, giving a pause after each word.

'How do we know nobody remembers them?' I wrinkle my nose.

'I asked why. You gotta know your whys.'

'How is this being measured, Joel? It sounds a bit unquantifiable to be true. The losers would remember losing probably. Other people would as well, the winners who beat them, anyone who was a spectator?'

He makes eye contact with me for the first time. His pupils are dilated. 'Nobody remembers the losers.'

'Are you high?' I ask, thinking out loud.

He does the fist palm thing again.

I edge away from him to the glass revolving door.

The air is fresh outside and I dash down the street without realizing I'm running until I stop at the traffic lights. A sudden and heavy downpour of rain comes as I wait for the green man to blink and let pedestrians cross.

My CV turns mushy in my hand. I sigh and ball it up. This is turning into a fucking nightmare. I cross over and duck under an awning, wait for the shower to pass. Sheets of water roll down the footpath into the drains. At the end of the street, a waiter struggles to stack metal chairs. Parasols are unfurled over the tables. I turn to the window behind me and check my face, to see if my make-up has washed away.

I run down to the café and say hello to the waiter before stepping inside. I wipe my face and blow my nose. Checking their specials, I order a cauliflower soup and sit at a table by the window. I strip off my coat, put it beside the radiator, and re-tie my hair.

The rain calms to a steady but weaker flow outside. People dart by the window, suit jackets or scarves over their heads. I take my phone out to Google where my nearest bus stop is. I see, from maps, there's another gym across the road. I look over.

There's a small sign on a board that says 'Fitness Classes Inside', but that's it. The building is nondescript.

I don't know if I can face more rejection today. When I finish my lunch, I pay and head towards the bus stop.

The timetable says the bus will be there in eighteen minutes.

Fuck it. I have enough time to check. I go back.

The rain is spluttery now. The sky is brighter. I wipe myself down and pull the heavy fire door. The gym is at the back of the building. It's signposted through the hall. I follow to a large open room.

In the corner, there are two bench press racks, suspension ropes and a three-tier dumbbell rack. Kettlebells line the floor in front of the weights. A man high-kicks an orange dummy in elaborate ways. I stand at the counter. He doesn't notice me.

I should go.

He continues kickboxing. I feel short of breath as I walk towards him.

'Hello,' I say.

He spots me and stops. The rubber dummy retracts to an erect position.

The man smiles. 'Please excuse me, I didn't hear you come in.'

'That's okay,' I say.

He walks towards me and shakes my hand, tells me to follow him back to the front counter. He stands in behind it and picks up an information leaflet and a black book. He's breathing heavily.

'It's all a mess at the moment. Hold on a second.' He plucks a pen out from underneath a card holder. 'We've nobody to run the desk. I have to do it and it's not my thing. So okay, here we go,' he says and smiles up at me. 'How can I help you? Are you looking for membership?' He tears off some blue kitchen towel and wipes his brow.

My stomach flutters. 'What do you mean you've nobody on the desk?'

'We need someone front of house.'

'This is weird timing. I called in because I'm looking for a job. I've been on the desk for a leisure centre already. I've lots of admin experience. Been doing it for years.'

He grows excited. 'You'd like to work here?'

'Yes,' I say.

'You're sure?'

'Yes.'

'But our day is broken. Starts at 6 a.m., but reception begins at 7.30 until 10 a.m. back for 12.30 to 2 p.m., then 5.30 until close. The hours suck, I know, but that's how we can serve our members best. Nobody sticks around too long with these split shifts.'

'That sounds okay with me. I want to be here. I'd love to be.'

'Okay, I'll ring the boss. Could you start soon? Today? I can't do everything, it's bullshit for me to be on this counter and to set up and instruct and then try to be presentable back here again. It looks bad. I want to sweat freely. I'll tell him to come to meet you right now.'

'Are you not the boss?'

His face lights up. 'I wish but no, I'm a trainer. Vitomir is my name. Nice to meet you.' He smiles at me again and presses at his phone screen.

I know I should mention my cert, that I'm a trainer too, but it feels promising. I can't jeopardize this opportunity.

★

James is there twenty minutes later. He lets me know all the perks of the job, mainly that I can go to a bunch of free classes as long as I let them know in advance which I've chosen for the day. He explains that the main ethos of the gym is accessibility for anyone who wants to get healthier.

'You'll be the first person people see, Natalie, when they step through the doors. It's essential that you are friendly. Some of our members are fighting themselves to even come here and work out. We want nobody feeling afraid in this environment.'

'I understand,' I say.

He welcomes me to the team with a pat on the back.


The reception job is from Monday to Friday. I greet members, update the system with names of those who manually sign up for sessions, check that those who register on the app actually turn up, answer the phone, give information, post on social media, book-keep, send group texts, make sure the trainers sign in and out for their sessions.

I meet lots of interesting people from all walks of life, all shapes and sizes.

I enjoy Vitomir's classes the most. I go to his circuit training, his strength and conditioning and spin classes, all of which are great. He's a martial artist and knows his stuff. He likes that I have lots of questions for him.

The more I learn and improve, the more I realize how little I know and how poor my technique is. I'm embarrassed about how shit I am, and how ridiculous it was for me to want to be an instructor.

At first, I spend the time in between the splits going for breakfast or a long lunch but then as I settle in and learn more, I spend that time in the gym, studying.

Vit notices me hanging on. 'Are you waiting?'

'Yes. By the time I get home, I have to turn around to come back for the evening. I could spend three hours here or on a bus.'

'Would you like to kick Martin with me?'

'Martin?'

'Yes,' he says, pointing at the orange dummy at the back.

'No thanks, me and Martin are okay. I'll read instead.'

'What do you read about?'

'Movement. The body. The mind. I didn't realize I had the power to train myself all these years. I let myself be at the whim of everything and everyone else.'

'You know now. Do you want to join me for lunch?'

In the café across the road, Vit tells me stories about his youth in Croatia, living in a tower block apartment. He remembers the war, but only a little. He was obsessed with video games and played them in a dark room.

'Sun would shine for long hours. Clear blue skies. Things were improving in my country. But I was a shy kid. My mother tried to get me out of the apartment. The beach was one kilometre away. The Adriatic on my doorstep but I refused everything until she signed me up for boxing lessons. I had confidence to go because of Ready 2 Rumble.'

'Is that a game?'

He smiles sheepishly. 'Yes. It wasn't the same to fight with a console as to be in a ring but it was the incentive for me to try. There was a Croat character, Boris Knokimov, but I wanted to be Afro Thunder.' He puts on an American accent and says, 'Light as a feather and fast as a locomotive.'

I smile.

'I discovered my talent and that was that.'

After we eat, I ask, 'Vit, if you gave me your lesson plan for spin, could I suggest some music for it? For one class. If you don't like it, that's fine. It'd give me something to do for the rest of the afternoon break.'

'Yeah, sure. But you'll have to match the beats per minute with the—'

'Revolutions per minute, I know,' I say.

He follows me across to the gym, jogs to the spin room and comes back with a page. 'I will run this one in the evening.'

He goes home for the rest of the gap, and I hunt online, picking music to match the plan.

Time flows until he returns.

I give him the tracklist.

'You coming to this session?'

'No, I'll be out front.'

After the class a bunch of drenched spinners walk by the desk to go home. I watch for signs of them being happier or moved by the music. They seem the same as usual.

Vitomir is impressed. 'That entertained me. You can pick my music next week again, if you'd like. It's not really my thing.'

'I'd love to.'

I change the song selection but still suit the exercises. More people sign up to the class, which has twenty-five bikes. There'd be on average sixteen people in for evening spin but after three weeks of different music, word-of-mouth spreads and Vit fills the lessons. For some classes there's a waitlist.

James notices the upsurge in numbers.

'What's he doing differently? It's been static all year and now this?'

Vitomir's amber eyes are bright. 'Natalie puts together music for me.'

James's face creases. 'Do you want to put some playlists together for my class too? I can never be arsed with the music. I'd throw in some free personal training in exchange for them?'

I say, 'Sure.'


A month later, I give Vitomir a new music outline and run through how the songs will match the exercises.

He walks away then stops. Turns back. 'Natalie, you know a lot about this world. You care a lot about these plans. You ask me about muscles and stretches and modifications. Why?'

'I'm interested.'

'This is more than an interest.'

I don't say anything.

He holds eye contact with me, waiting.

I tuck my hair behind my ears. 'I trained as an instructor. Because I ran these spin classes before. In my hometown. They were imaginary trips as opposed to a hard workout. I wanted to take the seriousness out of the whole thing. Make it less daunting for people, but probably mostly for myself.'

He comes closer. 'What were they?'

'I'd bring the participants to different places, have it researched with information and music. Try and make it atmospheric. Educational. It might have been silly but I liked it.'

'Why haven't you said anything here?'

'About what?'

'About this?'

'Because the more I learn, the more I realize how utterly shite I am at this whole thing. I'm so inept physically.'

'I call bullshit.'

This stings. 'It's not.'

'You're afraid.'

'I'm not. I'm just not any good. I don't have a background in it, how could anyone take me seriously?'

'How do you usually overcome your fear?'

'Vit, it's cool,' I stutter. 'I love working here. I'm really content with how things are. I'm learning.'

'Natalie, the person who shadowboxes in the corner will never succeed. You gotta get in the ring. Throw a few punches. Take a few.'

'I will. In the future, I'll know enough and be trained enough to do my plans.'

'Nobody is ever ready, Natalie. Start where you are. Tomorrow morning, you're teaching my first spin session. I'll be there. People can sign themselves in.'

'No, Vit, I appreciate the offer. But no, it's okay.'

'It's not okay. See you in the morning.'


I quickly scan the format and check my playlist. I try to breathe evenly as people come in and adjust their bikes.

'Hi, I'm Natalie and I'm your instructor. Anyone have any injuries or medical conditions I need to know about? No? Okay. We're gonna get refreshed for the day ahead with this session. Let's warm up our muscles now with a jog of a cycle, adding resistance at the chorus…'

After class, a good few of them thank me before scurrying out.

'It didn't even feel like an exercise class,' one woman says. 'Are you doing any other mornings?'

Vit punches my shoulder gently. 'Good work.'

I smile.

The woman turns to him and enquires about his next ab-blaster session.

'Are you the one from the reception?' a man asks.

'Yes,' I say.

He twists his mouth into a funny shape and turns his head to the side. He looks me up and down. 'You did a good job there, considering all this.'

'All what?'

'This,' he says and traces an outline of my body with his hands.

I should let it go but I say, 'Your comments on my body inform me on how you view your body.'

'What?'

'When you judge me, it tells me more about you and how you see yourself and the world, than enlightening me about how I feel in my own skin,' I say.

'Fuck, sorry, wait, I didn't even know I was doing that. I was trying to compliment you. You don't look like the typical instructor but that was a fun class. I'd like to come to your sessions again. It's good to have a new face teaching.'


After first shift, Vit tells James about me leading the class in the morning and James storms up to the front desk.

'This isn't on, Natalie,' he says.

Fuck.

'I know,' I say. I almost begin packing my stuff away in anticipation for another firing. 'I have a cert, so you would be covered at least for insurance. Sorry, James.'

'Why didn't you say anything before now?'

'Because I've been trying to learn more.'

'What more do you have to learn?'

'I have to get stronger and be more assured and create some plans—'

'You're overthinking it.'

'No, I want to be prepared well.'

He tuts. 'Your generation and information bias. I blame the internet. And universities.'

'For what?'

'Overeducation. You think you need to know it all before you can do something. Think think think. Know know know. Speaking to a personal trainer isn't the same as training. Making a plan for a session isn't teaching it.'

'I want to know enough, be good enough.'

'Jesus, Natalie, we all start somewhere. What is the point of learning and having knowledge if you can't express it?'

I blush.

'It's great to spruce things up in here. I wouldn't mind running extra spin classes to get more of the tech office workers in. Will you do another class for me?'

'Yes,' I say resolutely. I want to mention my spin class ideas but I'm smiling gummily at him.

'I'll put you down for an express session? I don't want to spook you too much.'

It's time to say it.

I nod at him.

Now's the chance. Say it, Natalie.

'Good stuff,' he says and makes a note.

I say nothing.


I kick myself all day for chickening out. During the gap until evening shift, I'm aware of my compulsion to go and buy sweets, crisps, sandwiches, chips, noodles, pizza, a fizzy drink, a burrito, chocolate, anything.

But I know the sound of these sirens going off inside and try to stay with my breath.

Then like a car pulling in to let an ambulance that's driving up its rear overtake, I send James a text about having a quick chat when he gets back. I want to ask him something about the sessions.

All is calm.


I almost squint as I speak to him at the desk.

'James, see, the thing is I used to run these creative spin classes. It was a good workout but it had other elements, learning and entertainment. I'd love to give them a go up here in Dublin. Do you think I could try that?'

He looks at me as though he's smelled a particularly toxic fart. 'Oh I dunno, Nat. That sounds a bit alternative.'

'It is a bit alternative, James.'

'Jesus, it took you two months before you even mentioned your cert and now you want to shake up our whole format?'

I press my palms onto the sides of my legs.

'Where would you be going or what would you be doing? I don't understand what you mean. Is it like the virtual reality sessions they're running in the States?'

'Not really, this would be much more economical. An exercise in imagination. See the screen you have behind the instructor in the spin room? Well, I'd project a landscape onto it instead of us watching which cyclist is where and having people race each other.'

'But how would it be competitive then? How could it be motivational?'

'I dunno,' I say. 'Maybe that's not the point. It's more about enjoying it. As an experience.'

'Sounds pretentious. But look, you got good feedback after this morning's spin session and that was your first go. And the novelty factor sounds appealing. I'll give you an interview for these classes you want. Is that fair? I need to see what you mean before I go okaying anything.'

'Yes, that's fair.'

'If it's too weird, I'll be shutting it down.'

'Understood.'

'So if it's a trip, where are you taking us?'

I look outside. 'The moon, maybe.'

I round Kim up who rounds a few others, including Fionn the poet.

James being in the class is scary but I've prepared it well.

I play 'Fly Me to the Moon' as background music and wander around, greet and screen the class for injuries or any medical issues, adjust their seats.

'You've motivated me into coming to a gym,' Fionn says; his legs glow ghostly white under his shorts. 'I was really sorry to hear about your granny too, Nat, she was a lovely woman.'

I move his handlebars so he has a comfortable grip. 'Thanks, Fionn. She sure was. She liked you a lot too.'

My laptop disconnects from the projector. 'Fuck.'

I manage to Bluetooth an image of the moon to the screen behind me. I flip the lights off.

'We'll warm up for five minutes, adding resistance as we go. Ready?'

I play 'My Moon My Man' Boys Noize remix for the beat.

'Today, we're going to the moon. Is everyone set?'

There's a yes chorus. I'm overcome with affection for them all.

'Okay then. We'll take a moment before we begin. This class is going to have a few elements to it. If you want to workout, then do, no problem, but this will be an imaginary trip and if you open yourself to it, you'll enjoy it. So before we take off, I need you to put on your helmets.' I pick up my imaginary helmet and put it on.

Kim and her crew do too. James doesn't participate, he looks at me like I'm crazy.

'And we need to be light, so everyone take a deep breath, one two three four, hold it for four, release. Let's do that again. Once more. This time on the exhale, let all your worries of today go. Okay, we're ready.

'Most of this ride is getting there, we're going to be on these propeller bikes to get to the stratosphere, so sprinting up to there, then a steep incline, even though we'll be weightless, we'll need to put a lot of resistance on the bikes to get them to the moon direction wise. After that we'll land and do some interval training as we explore the moon's surface.'

I play 'Moon Rocks' for our climb out of Earth, through the sweet metallic zing of the ozone layer, and as we break through the stratosphere, we've to stand and go as hard as possible. We prepare to make our way through space to the moon to the theme song from 2001: A Space Odyssey, 'Also sprach Zarathustra'.

'And here we are, orbiting the moon. Drop your resistance to gear five and prepare to land.' Our landing is synced to 'Moonage Daydream'. Kim smiles at me throughout like a proud mother.

During the peaceful time in class, I play 'An Ending' by Brian Eno and discuss how the sulphurous moondust smells of burnt gunpowder and because the moon has no atmosphere the sky always appears black from its surface. I show them Mons Huygens, the tallest lunar mountain, higher than Everest.

I mention how no woman has walked on the moon yet, we can only imagine it, and add an aside about the natural coincidence of the number of days and different phases of the lunar cycle and the menstrual cycle.

James's face maintains a curious expression.

'Now before we go to the other side of the moon, the so-called dark side which doesn't face Earth, let's take a moment to admire our blue planet, how beautiful she is. All the oceans, which make up seventy per cent of her, blue and clear from here. And our land, we can only see green and mountain brown, desert beige. What an extraordinary place to be from. Let's do some interval work and explore the lunar landings. High resistance and low resistance. Pump pump pump.'

Everyone is sweating.

I say, 'Great work, we're here, guys. Let's cycle around, cool down, turn your resistance off, and get your breath back.'

The opening bars of cello from Arthur Russell's 'This is How We Walk on the Moon' fill the room. A man over to the right is wiping his face with his towel repeatedly.

I get off my bike and check on him. 'Are you okay?'

'I always wanted to be an astronaut but I only did ordinary level maths. This feels a bit like a dream.'

'That's good, I think?'

I go to the top. 'Okay, everyone, thanks for your patience and for working so hard. I've enjoyed it. Hope you have too. May see you again soon.'

We cool down to 'Sea of Tranquility' by Kool and the Gang.

James still looks unimpressed.

The participants thank me on the way out.

James says, 'Well, that was fairly bonkers.'

'It was well done, Natalie,' Kim says, staring fiercely at James.

'Did you hate it or something?' I ask.

'No, it was just odd. But my wife isn't a big gym fan, she finds it too tedious. Would you run this again Monday evening and I'll get her in for the look? I'm not sure about it. We can see if there's an uptake. A trial if you like.'

'Yes, of course.'

It's not a dead idea yet.

I post it to the system with a brief description and go back to work.

I'm off on Saturday, and check the class schedule on the app to see if anyone has booked and then check again. When I check again, ten minutes later, I become conscious of the checking and stop, knowing it could easily give way to panicking, to catastrophizing, to the apocalypse.

I give myself permission to have a look in the evening and let it be until then.

In the evening, I check. 0/25 bookings for the class. It won't go ahead without five people being there.

A wave of disappointment crashes into me. I sit on the couch, sit with the disappointment until it passes, and when it passes, I rise again and smile. A thought glints that maybe this is real love, accepting life as it is.

I check Sunday morning. Four names down. I can rope Kim into it again. It'll more than likely be happening. I spend the afternoon refining the lesson from last week, get the music a little tighter, include better details about the moon.

On Monday, I take my coat off and say to James about there being a low uptake.

'No, there's a good uptake. Both me and Vit plugged it to all the ones in our classes Friday and Saturday. People asked could they bring friends to it. My wife is bringing her mates. Everyone wants to see what it's about.'

'There's only four names down.'

'Four registered on the app. But hold on, let me find the sheet. Yes, here, twenty-six names manually signed up to be added to the system now that you're here. I have ten people who messaged on Facebook for it too. We may split it into two sessions, is that okay?'

'What?'

'I've only twenty-five bikes, Natalie. We'll split it? Will you be fit enough to do it back to back? I'll send out a notification to everyone.'

'Yeah, back to back is fine.'

'So there's forty signed up and me. Forty-one.'

'Forty-one?'

'Where will we be going next week, if anyone's enquiring?'

I draw a breath, smile, and wait for the idea to flash in my mind.

# Acknowledgements

For endless support, thank you Joe, Helen, Mark and Jenny Reapy, Darragh and Sarah K. McGale. For endless craic, thank you to all the Mayo heads, especially the women in the group.

For their kindness: Noel Reapy, Hana Doleželová, Rosaleen McDonagh, Dublin UNESCO City of Literature staff, Irish Writers' Centre, Dublin City Libraries and their writing groups, Claremorris Library staff (past and present), Laura McDonald, everyone at The Salmon Bookshop and Literary Centre in Ennistymon, Doolin Writers' Weekend, Joseph O'Connor, Mike McCormack, the Rooney family and the Rooney Prize Committee.

Thank you MMB Creative, my agent Sallyanne Sweeney, my editor Neil Belton, Helen Francis and the team at Head of Zeus.

Much respect and admiration to the trainers and gym instructors who had patience with me over the past few years, especially Rad Rock. Thank you to Sufjan Stevens for creating *The Age of Adz* which kept me inspired through sports college.

Finally, to Kathleen Reapy, I miss you. Thank you for all your encouragement and love.

# About the Author

E. M. Reapy is a writer and tutor from Mayo, Ireland. Her first novel, *Red Dirt*, won an Irish Book Award and the Rooney Prize for Irish Literature.

emreapy.wordpress.com